**Richard Gordon** was born in ......... .......

on to work as an anaesthetist at St Bartholomew's Hospital, and then as a ship's surgeon. As obituary-writer for the *British Medical Journal*, he was inspired to take up writing full time and he left medical practice in 1952 to embark on his 'Doctor' series. This proved incredibly successful and was subsequently adapted into a long-running television series.

Richard Gordon has produced numerous novels and writings all characterised by his comic tone and remarkable powers of observation. His *Great Medical Mysteries* and *Great Medical Discoveries* concern the stranger aspects of the medical profession whilst his *The Private Life of...* series takes a deeper look at individual figures within their specific medical and historical setting. Although an incredibly versatile writer, he will, however, probably always be best known for his creation of the hilarious 'Doctor' series.

BY THE SAME AUTHOR
ALL PUBLISHED BY HOUSE OF STRATUS

# The Private Life of
# Doctor Crippen

*Richard Gordon*

HOUSE OF
STRATUS

This edition published in 2001 by House of Stratus, an imprint of
Stratus Holdings plc, 24c Old Burlington Street, London, W1X 1RL, UK.

www.houseofstratus.com

Typeset, printed and bound by House of Stratus.

A catalogue record for this book is available from the British Library.

ISBN 1-84232-515-9

It is Sunday afternoon, preferably before the war. The wife is already asleep in the armchair, and the children have been sent out for a nice long walk. You put your feet up on the sofa, settle your spectacles on your nose, and open the *News of the World*. Roast beef and Yorkshire, or roast pork and apple sauce, followed up by suet pudding and driven home, as it were, by a cup of mahogany-brown tea, have put you in just the right mood. Your pipe is drawing sweetly, the sofa cushions are soft underneath you, the fire is well alight, the air is warm and stagnant. In these blissful circumstances, what is it that you want to read about?

Naturally, about a murder.

*George Orwell*


"Cor blimey! You ought to see the landlady – what a face – Crippen was innocent!"

*Music-hall joke*

Dr Hawley Harvey Crippen was sentenced to death at the Old Bailey in London on October 22, 1910, for the murder of his wife Belle Elmore, the music-hall artiste. Three days later, Ethel Le Neve was accused in the same court of being an accessory after the fact. The Crippens were Americans who had settled in north London at Hilldrop Crescent. Part of Belle Elmore's remains were dug from the cellar floor. Her head and her bones were never found.

# 1

The meal had the ill-subdued restlessness of a headquarters' mess on the eve of battle. Men came and went with terse apologies. Silences scudded across the room like the shadows of clouds flying in the moonlight over the snow-dusted Norfolk countryside. The voracious fireplace roared with plenteous logs from the estate. The long shiny tablecloth was brightened by mauve and yellow fresias, between two silver stands piled with grapes, peaches and tangerines. The Royal Household was at dinner.

That evening had assembled only a handful of the 322 persons under the Lord Chamberlain's command. These included lords in waiting and gentlemen ushers. Comptrollers, almoners and clerks of the closet. Ladies – and women – of the bedchamber. Gold Stick and Black Rod. The mistress of the robes, the master of the horse. The poet laureate, the bargemaster and the keeper of the swans. Nineteen doctors, and in case of their failure, a royal coroner.

Upstairs, the King lay dying.

Eliot entered at half past eight. It was Monday, January 20, 1936. His eye caught a typed place card – SIR ELIOT BECKETT VC KBE MD FRCP.

Gallantry rightly takes precedence on brains, he thought.

"Isn't your wife having dinner?" asked Lord Dawson of Penn, as Eliot sat beside him.

"Nancy's with the Queen."

"Excellent. I'm sure she'll steady the Queen's nerves better than any dose I could prescribe."

Eliot reached for the menu in its silver clip with the royal arms. Potato soup, turbot and roast mutton. He supposed one man's death was no reason for another going without his dinner.

Eliot Beckett was 53, tall and lean, the strong bones of his face a memorial to youthful good looks. He brilliantined his thick dark hair, and trimmed his moustache like Ronald Colman's. Noticing the grandfather clock, he glanced automatically at his wristwatch. "Why should the time at Sandringham be half an hour faster than the rest of the world?"

"For punctuality at King Edward VII's shooting parties," Dawson told him.

"King Edward the Seventh! But he hasn't shot for twenty-five years, unless over the Elysian fields."

"Ah! From royal whim to unshakable tradition is an easy step in this country."

Eliot was new to Sandringham. The 11,000-acre estate on the marshy north Norfolk coast against the Wash had cost the former King Edward a quarter of a million pounds. The long, low red-brick house could never contain the exuberant generosity of his hospitality. As a young doctor with an empty pocket, a full heart, low prospects and high principles, Eliot had warmed himself agreeably with indignation at the dozen royal balls there a season, the elaborate shooting of ten thousand pheasants, the "King's special" steaming daily from London, loaded with guests in their tweeds and furs, with their guns and dogs, their leather luggage polished like saddles by their packs of servants.

In York cottage beyond the lake, a villa of suburban glumness overwhelmed by shrubbery, the King's son George played bluff naval officer turned blunt squire and waited for the throne. Now King George V, a quarter of a century later, lay comatose over their heads, his quitting the world only another regal formality.

"The King went downhill very rapidly this afternoon." Eliot refused wine from the tail-coated footman.

"That Privy Council meeting this morning severely taxed him," said Dawson. "Yet it was nothing but a tragic pantomime. The King sat in his dressing-gown, leaning on a bed-table across an armchair. He could make only a couple of 'Xs' for his signature."

Dawson was the only medical man among 400-odd politicians sworn as a Privy Councillor. He seems to collect honours as an actress compliments, Eliot thought. Dawson had a taut face, straight eyebrows and a bushy moustache. He was genial, sensitive, ambitious and impatient. As the King's physician, he had penetrated British consciousness like airwoman Amy Johnson or cricketer Jack Hobbs. His name footed the brief handwritten bulletins policemen hung on Buckingham Palace railings when the King was near death before, in 1928. He was the man the newspapers telephoned for a doctor's view on the Modern Girl, the Motor Age or Whither Europe? Eliot heard that the King chose Dawson as his doctor because he never fussed and was good with dogs and horses.

"Why hold the meeting at all?" asked Eliot.

"Ramsay MacDonald insisted. He wanted a Council of State to hold power during the King's incapacity. As in 1928. MacDonald's a terribly nervy fellow, you know."

"Isn't the King's death a favourite moment for revolution? Lord Wigram can tell us."

On Eliot's right was a straight-backed, smooth-faced man with a clipped moustache, a former Bengal Lancer in his mid-sixties. He wore a starched shirt and dinner-jacket. A dying King created difficulties of convention – no gentleman in the 1930s dined in a lounge suit, but doctors could hardly attend the sickbed as though dressed for the play. Eliot and Dawson retained their professional uniform of morning coats, striped trousers and wing collars.

"Yes, indeed," said Wigram, the King's private secretary. He could talk of constitutional subtleties like the King's butler of the wines in his cellar. "On the death of King Edward, a troop of Life Guards was under orders at Albany Street Barracks, ready to be turned out within five minutes of a trumpet call."

"Perhaps I deserved their attentions?" suggested Eliot. "Remember, I was a bolshevik. I'd probably have stood cheering, if we'd cut the hedonistic old gentleman's head off in Whitehall like Charles the First's."

"You cannot make our flesh creep," Dawson chaffed him. "Even Mr Pickwick's Fat Boy had to grow up. Wigram, we shall need to compose a bulletin."

"Yes. I looked out the final one on King Edward in 1910." Wigram efficiently produced a folded sheet from his inside pocket.

"I know what it says. I signed it," Dawson reminded him. " 'His Majesty's condition is now critical' was stark enough for the morning papers. Now we have the wireless. The BBC will want something to put on the air between nine and ten, when people start going to bed. We must send a message which will touch their hearts."

Dawson reached for the menu card in its clip, and wrote quickly on the back –

*The King's life is moving peacefully towards its close.*

Wigram nodded appreciatively. Eliot wondered how early in his patient's illness Dawson had composed the phrase.

"I'll take it to the Queen at once, then have it telephoned to Portland Place." Dawson rose.

"I'll come with you," said Eliot, abandoning his fish. "I'm not hungry."

The remaining men at the table also stood. Lady Beckett had entered the dining-room.

Nancy Beckett was better known than Eliot in Mayfair or Monte Carlo or Manhattan. Her social star had twinkled before cultivating Americans in London society had moved from the freakish to the smart. Her hair was cut square and loose like Greta Garbo's, and had never been a richer shade of auburn. She had large green eyes and a pert nose. Her pale skin, as clear as a silk mask, was submerged regularly under mudpacks in Bond Street. Her figure represented a slim-waisted trophy for self-discipline. She wore a black silk calf-length dress, and in deference to the melancholy evening no jewellery except a diamond the size of a humbug.

She exchanged a smile with her husband. Her place was next to Lady Evesham, a lady-in-waiting with pale grey hair, which Nancy suspected she would have loved to peroxide.

"I was *so* thrilled at Sir Eliot's VC," Lady Evesham began. "I was a VAD nurse during the war, you know, at the base hospital at Wimereux – the medical men were terrible old dug-outs. It was *such* a boost for our morale – a doctor at the front winning the supreme decoration. That terrible March of 1918! Ludendorff taking us completely by surprise on the Somme, poor Hubert Gough sacked for retreating, the Germans expected in the Channel ports any day, and Douglas Haig's wonderful order about 'Our backs to the wall.' "

Nancy was aware that the war had been conducted for Britain largely by members of Lady Evesham's own family.

"You must have always known Sir Eliot a brave man?" Lady Evesham added.

"I'm afraid I'd no chance to tell. You see, he was a conscientious objector until the middle of the war." Lady Evesham looked aghast. "When conscription came in 1916, my husband had the choice of going either into the army or into jail. And Eliot is simply a man who develops wholehearted enthusiasm for anything he happens to find himself doing. Pacifists are the fiercest of people," Nancy confided. "If Bertrand Russell had provided himself with a machine-gun instead of a typewriter, there wouldn't be room on his chest for medals."

Eliot and Dawson were walking upstairs together. The Queen was with the Prince of Wales and the Dukes of York and Kent. Princess Elizabeth and Princess Margaret had been packed back to Windsor, where their mother the Duchess of York was recovering from pneumonia, complicating flu caught in that winter's savage epidemic. The Duke of Gloucester was in Buckingham Palace with a sore throat. The three Privy Councillors – Ramsay MacDonald, Lord Hailsham and Sir John Simon – had the unsought adventure of a flight back to London that chilly, bright afternoon. The Prince of Wales' offer of his private plane from nearby Bircham Newton aerodrome was unrefusable. Archbishop of Canterbury Cosmo Lang, past seventy, gaitered and aproned, bald and sharp-nosed, fonder of Christians if they were kings, had arrived with vulturish timing.

Eliot wondered if Dawson resented Nancy as well being invited to Sandringham, but decided him too seasoned, too secure a courtier. Eliot had been summoned from their home in Kent by telephone at three on the Sunday morning. Dawson recognized that Eliot knew more about the heart than himself, and the King's was starting to fail. He almost killed the old boy in 1928, Eliot reflected, missing a pocket of pus hidden behind the lung until almost too late. Everyone had heard how he failed his exams as a student at the London Hospital. Dawson's skill was stage-manager of the sickbed, the impressario of dramatic illness.

"I read your *Health of Nations* when it was published after the war," Dawson said politely.

"I'd toned it down enormously. A young man can do his future severer damage by publishing a book than indulging his irresponsibility with racehorses and women."

"No man is one person, but a succession," Dawson ruminated. "We're like the portrait-gallery of wicked ancestors in *Ruddigore*, always liable to step from their frames and haunt the latest version. I'd trimmed my own views, when I reported to the Government on our medical services in 1920. But a State health scheme *will* come one day, be sure of it."

"It's unthinkable to the medical profession."

"The unthinkable is often inevitable. The death of kings is more certain than the birth of princes."

Eliot admitted, "I suppose it was unthinkable to kill germs with mouldy bread, when I tried in 1910. Now Professor Fleming at St Mary's has proved me right. He's even purified the penicillin mould, you know. But unlike me, Fleming's a canny Scot, he doesn't claim too much for it."

"Very sensibly. Penicillin will never have any use whatever outside the laboratory."

"I offered it as a panacea because I was a zealous revolutionary." Eliot smiled. "And revolutionaries generally come to grief through their own egotism."

"Thank God for all of us you did, in those particular activities." Eliot was gratified to sense Dawson's feeling as genuine.

They had reached the landing. Behind the door to their right lay the ruler of an Empire on which the sun never set. He received the loyalty of 66 million white subjects, and of 372 million coloured ones, who had no option. King George V had a talent for fatherliness, whether at a Delhi durbar or on the wireless at Christmas, and had presided with equal composure over the House of Lords revolt in 1910, the General Strike of 1926 and the Great War.

"Did you find much change this evening?" asked Dawson.

"No. The cyanosis is worse. There's only slight pulmonary congestion, but the heart is obviously failing."

"His illness of 1928 ran a heavy overdraft on his powers of recuperation."
Dawson paused, menu-card in hand. Seventeen years later, Eliot was to see
it again, at a dinner on the evening of his patient's granddaughter's
Coronation. "I must not delay this message, but I hope for another word
alone with you this evening. About yourself." Dawson hesitated. "If this
Government – or a future Government – decides to take over the medical
profession, the wisest of us will safeguard ourselves, and our fellow doctors,
by becoming sufficiently important in the eyes of the country to dictate the
terms."

They exchanged glances. "Very well," said Eliot.

That night did not end for Eliot until six o'clock. Nancy was asleep,
smeared with cold cream, the bedside lamp burning. She stirred as he
gently opened the door. "He's dead?"

"At five to midnight. I had to stay up. The embalmers got lost." Eliot
tore off his wing-collar. "I could do with a bath, but it's about half a mile
away. What a ridiculous country! Why must snobbishness be equated with
unnecessary discomfort?"

The Becketts lived in a castle, gutted and refurbished with steam
heating, gushing plumbing, hygienic kitchens, efficient drains. Its off-
white reception rooms were designed as a favour by Syrie Maugham, and
hung with Impressionists chosen by Nancy's admirer Lord Duveen.
Nobody gets value for money like an American millionairess.

"When's the funeral?"

"Today week. It's been planned by Lord Wigram and the Lord
Chamberlain down to the last tap of muffled drums. Parliament must
meet, and Stanley Baldwin's going on the wireless." He sat on the silk
coverlet, taking her chin in his hand. His eyes gleamed with the mingled
excitement and exhaustion she seldom saw now. "Why must you lard
yourself like a joint for the oven, old thing?"

"Surely you wouldn't have me wrinkled?"

"Creams and mud baths are useless. Let me send you for a face-lift to
Harold Gillies."

"If you let me send you for monkey-gland treatment to Professor
Voronoff in Monte Carlo."

"We're not going to Monte."

"Oh, Eliot! You know London's absolutely empty after Christmas."

"Don't be cross." He grinned, dropping his hand. "There's something worth staying to enjoy. I'm to be made a lord." She drew in her breath. "And our eldest son shall become a lord. And his eldest son, and so on forever and ever. Dawson told me, while we were waiting for the King to die. Oh, we're two real professionals, Dawson and I. He's to be a viscount. The only medical man to reach it. It's the age we live in, isn't it? Ever since MacDonald's Socialist cabinet appeared in their knee-breeches at Buckingham Palace. Or does it prove again that a doctor's reputation depends on the distinction of those dying in his care?"

Nancy kissed him. "So I'm to be a lady twice over? Well! How do I live it down in the States?"

"You'll be the envy of New York. Americans are crazy on titles. Have you seen the rapture of a bishop from the mid-West called 'My lord' at a London dinner party?"

She was sitting upright. "Everyone will say you did it through my money."

"I'll tell them that first. No doctor hides the truth. Dawson wants me with him and Lloyd George in Germany next September, to meet Herr Hitler."

"Surely he's not for those awful Nazis?" she exclaimed.

"Only on the keep-fit level. He thinks our unemployed should have compulsory physical jerks. Dawson fancies himself as a politician. Well, I did once. We fail, because we imagine everyone's mind as disinfected of emotion as a doctor's. Hitler will make a dreadful fool of him."

Eliot pulled off the heavy silk-lined tailcoat he had been wearing almost twenty-four hours. Nancy asked, "What was the end like?"

"Imperceptible. Lang appeared in his cassock to say some prayers. Does it better a man in Heaven, being seen off by the Archbishop of Canterbury, or by the chaplain of Pentonville jail? As I watched the King die, I found myself thinking quite ridiculously about our old friend Crippen. Though the prison chaplain doesn't say prayers," Eliot recalled, "he reads the burial service. Which is rather kicking a man when he's down, don't you think?"

"The chaplain's farewell would stand a man better in Hell, where presumably Crippen went."

"Thank God the poor little fellow didn't hear the authorities bury him, no more than subsequently feeling them hang him."

"If he swallowed your dose."

"I'm sure of it. I heard from Campion, the prison medical officer." Eliot drew his white shirt over his head. "I'd not be attending His Majesty tonight – nor entering the House of Lords next month – without that nasty little murder twenty-six years ago in Hilldrop Crescent."

"If Charlotte Corday hadn't murdered Marat in his bath, Napoleon would be remembered only as a competent artillery officer. I do wish you'd forget that Crippen episode."

"Who could? When Paul Martinetti died in Algiers a dozen years ago, *The Times* said only, 'Crippen Case Recalled.' Yet he was famous on the halls before you and I knew him. It's as hard as Leigh Hunt being only remembered as Shelley's friend. And I really think Crippen didn't murder her."

"You thought so then because we were terribly romantic."

"We were terrible hypocrites."

"I *certainly* wasn't bogus! I honestly wanted to devote my life to the sick."

"There isn't room for more than one Florence Nightingale in the century, my dear. Anyway, she was a dreadful woman. She saved the lives of the rabble by driving good men to their graves." He unstrapped his wristwatch. "You needn't look twice at the time tomorrow. His new Majesty King Edward VIII has put the clock back at Sandringham. His first act on accession. Is that significant?"

Nancy slipped under the bedclothes. "And no one in England knows about Wallis Simpson?"

"No one. No one common, I mean."

"She'll be the next Queen."

"*Pourquoi pas?* Edward's the first British monarch to fly. Why not the first to wed a twice-divorced American? God, I'm dead beat. Quite suddenly, my inner supply of adrenalin's given out. It'll be getting light in half an hour. Just think of those poor blighters of reporters, shivering the night away inspecting the decorative ironwork of the gates at the end of the drive."

"It wasn't Crippen who led you here, my darling," said Nancy sleepily. "It was accident – the next compartment to mine being empty in the *wagon-lit* from Basle to Calais."

"Accident!" he exclaimed. "I knew perfectly well at the time you'd engineered it."

"Well! You've waited long enough to tell me."

"No woman cares to believe that she contributed to her own seduction, no more than any child cares to stop believing in Father Christmas." He yawned. "This place depresses me. I've ordered the Bugatti at the door by eleven."

# 2

On a May morning in 1909, two young women of surpassing beauty were travelling in a grey-upholstered first-class compartment on the express which followed the littoral from Geneva to Lausanne.

From the fertile meadows in *La Côte*, cows belled like circus animals looked up with tolerant curiosity. The sprouting hayfields were speckled by yellow, mauve and white flowers, the houses with top-heavy roofs clustered at every cross-roads all looked brand new. The only cloud was the belch of the engine, shredded in a breeze which broke the surface of Lake Geneva into glittering ripples decorated with white paddle-steamers and yachts. There is always winter somewhere in Switzerland, but it had lurked to its lair in the mountains.

"I guess I'm a total fraud."

Jane Grange was twenty-one in a week's time, fair, fresh-faced, blue-eyed, everyone called her "Baby". Her sister Nancy was almost two years older. Both wore the "neo-directoire" fashion, which had reached New York from Paris the previous fall. Baby had a grey scarlet-lined travelling-coat over a narrow ankle-length pink merino dress, her wide-brimmed felt hat with a panache of pink-dyed ostrich feathers. Nancy wore a green cape, a navy-blue serge jacket with tight skirt, a hat equally large with crimson muslin roses and big-dotted veil. The sisters had renounced petticoats, and Baby even wore the latest "fish-net" stockings.

"Maybe they'll take one look at you and send you right back home to New York," Nancy agreed.

"Then I should feel an even bigger fraud, shouldn't I? Making all that fuss, coming all this way, for absolutely nothing. How should I *ever* live it down?"

"It wouldn't be embarrassing at all. Everyone would be so glad to see you back."

"Yes, I guess so," said Baby animatedly. "We'd have the most wonderful party in the world. Why, I can still hold my ball, can't I? It wouldn't be too late. We can use the same invitations, I never threw them away." She looked through the window, over the coast road across the lake. Excitement flickered from her face. Both knew there was no chance of being turned away. "Is that Mont Blanc?"

"It's Mont Salève. They call it the cab-drivers' Mont Blanc. Tourists get bilked, taking an afternoon trip. That's so, Maria-Thérèse?"

Mademoiselle Maria-Thérèse Lascalle sat in a long black alpaca coat and black straw bonnet, clutching a large black handbag as though expecting to be robbed. Like many middle-aged Frenchwomen, consecutive mourning for remote relations allowed economy in dress. She had been engaged in Paris through familiarity with English and with Switzerland. Her English had become worse and her taciturnity greater during the journey, but ladies travelling without a maid could neither attract respect nor keep their own. She said she knew nothing about the taxicabs.

"Oh, all mountains look the same to me," Baby dismissed the skyline pettishly.

Across the buttoned-cloth seats lay their rolled tartan rugs spined with a cluster of parasols and umbrellas, a pair of gold-clasped alligator dressing-cases, Nancy's handbag of gold-threaded tapestry, Baby's of mink trimmed with its tails. Baby slowly turned the pages of the *Illustrated London News*, the only magazine available in English. She was perplexed at the ceremonious, punctilious heartland of the world's greatest empire, a country which had previously crossed neither of their thoughts. Nancy looked up from Elinor Glyn's *Three Weeks*, which she had bought in the Boulevard St-Michel, and which was banned in Boston.

"Did you take your temperature this morning?"

Baby gasped, hand to mouth. "I forgot."

"Oh, darling! It's the first thing they'll ask."

"Does it matter?" Baby asked frivolously. "They'll probably want to make a fresh start. And I've been so good at taking it. Well, quite good, I guess. It's not the nicest part of your toilet."

"How do you feel now?"

"Fine! I could swim the lake."

"You sweated last night."

"It was hot last night in Geneva. Don't say it like that, darling. You sound as if you are accusing me of being naughty."

"I'm sorry. I don't want you to do anything foolhardy, that's all."

They changed at Lausanne. Nancy and Baby lunched at the station buffet, which they heard were the best places to eat in Switzerland. Maria-Thérèse arranged transfer of their dozen pieces of baggage, and was given a franc for a *casse-croûte*.

The next train was short, without corridors, the first-class compartments lined with shiny black leather. The stubby engine with a conical smokestack, like American ones, panted out billows of black as they climbed among fields with more cows, stopping at every station, some no more than a white hut and a signboard, the waiting passengers a man or two in blue blouse and beret smoking a long, thin, crooked cigar, a woman in a shawl with a milk churn or a crate of live geese.

Pasture turned to rocky grass, the cows were replaced by goats. Baby complained she was cold and had Maria-Thérèse unwrap the tartan rug. They went through tunnels, quickly pulling the windows tight against the acrid smoke. They looked down the valleys at bright torrents, trickles in summer, now fed by the melting snow and fierce enough to shift the boulders. The train circled the waist of a mountain, its piercing whistle echoing off the rock, and they unexpectedly found themselves in the terminus of Champette.

The station was a sturdily-roofed shed. Across the cobbled square, a four-storey stone building bore in gold letters, *Hôtel Grand Palais de Champette*. Nancy decided the grandeur was relative to the village – half the size of Oyster Bay, the setting of their Long Island house. Nancy sent Maria-Thérèse with the hotel concierge and luggage-cart. She must accompany Baby to her journey's end. A closed carriage with a pair of horses was waiting. A man in gold-braided grey uniform supervised stowing the luggage, settled the sisters on the leather upholstery, and solemnly tucking a rug round them climbed with the driver on the box.

Baby was flushed and tired, but grew livelier as they jogged up a narrow, paved road that twisted through a steep, dark pine forest. "It's like fairyland," she exclaimed. "In fairyland there's always a forest like this, with a turreted castle in the middle containing a beautiful princess."

Their castle was on a broad ledge of the mountain, a long, thin building facing south. Each of its seven storeys had a dozen tall, shutterless windows looking on deep balconies edged with white-painted iron railings. A broad gravel forecourt ran to a wooden fence guarding the drop to the village below. From the flagpole in the middle, the red cross on a white ground snapped loudly in the mountain breeze.

They stopped under a glass canopy, covering a flight of steps. Sweeping off his cap, the man in uniform opened the plate-glass double-doors which protected from draughts a square, white lobby transfixed by four slender pillars. Electric bulbs hung in clusters of curly brass, the floor was covered with coconut matting. A tall, stooping man in a brown suit broke his conversation with a woman in a yellow pullover, both inspecting the newcomers with solemn curiosity. The lobby smelt of carbolic, with eau de Cologne which disguised it no more successfully than it generally succeeded with human sweat.

From a desk to their left, a young man in a frock-coat approached with eager servility.

"Miss Grange?" Nancy noticed a wide, deep scar running from the angle of his jaw and disappearing into his wing-collar. "Welcome to the Clinique Laënnec."

He left them in a white-painted room with an expensive tapestry sofa and so many chairs that they indicated its use for waiting. It was dark, looking north over a small garden at the mountainside. A maid in black bombasine with lace apron and starched cap brought a large silver tray with teapot, kettle on spirit-lamp, buttered toast on a dish warmed with hot water, cream gateaux and the delicate spicy biscuits which Voltaire called pets de nonne, nun's farts.

"They must think we're English," said Nancy.

"What do you suppose this is?" Baby had been looking around inquisitively. She picked from a ledge in the corner a white enamelled metal cup with a lid like a German tankard. She opened it with her thumb, wrinkling her nose. "It's got carbolic slopping about. Do you suppose it's to fumigate the atmosphere?"

She lost interest in it, and stared in silence through the window at the Alps, Europe's last savage land, barely scratched by the roads and houses of the busily civilizing Swiss, and which killed with equal contempt intruders seeking amusement, excitement, health, or life.

The disease had struck Baby like a bullet-wound. She was hurrying from her bedroom in their father's house on Fifth Avenue and 68th Street when something warm and salty gushed in her mouth. She spat into her washbasin a demi-tasse of bright blood, and instantly she knew that she was seriously ill. When the shock and confusion, the family alarm, the urgent traffic of doctors had subsided, Baby treated her sickness with the persevering frivolity which she applied to the world. It was an affectation which she discovered in childhood won her easy attraction, and which she preserved as her defiance against a life which often frightened her. High-spirited friends at her bedside were divided in thinking her extremely brave or extremely stupid.

They left New York in April, in brass and mahogany comfort aboard the French Line's *Bretagne*, for Le Havre. Their father had impatiently wanted them aboard the brand new four-funnelled *Lusitania*, with prototype steam-turbines, which could cross the Atlantic in four and a half days. Even John Grange could not bribe Cunard to divert the liner from her passage to Liverpool – which she continued to ply until torpedoed off Ireland by the U-20 six years later.

The sisters had violent quarrels. Why shouldn't she stay up to dance, play tombola, join in the ship's concert? Baby demanded. When she would spend weeks, perhaps months, in a gloomy Swiss clinic? Baby gave in, but the row sent up her temperature, which crushed Nancy with guilt. They had another quarrel in Paris. They were staying a night at the Crillon, but Baby spat more blood. Nancy summoned the hotel doctor, who called a professor with a Legion d'Honneur rosette in his buttonhole. Baby demanded to return home. "As you wish, mademoiselle." The professor shrugged. "But your family will welcome you as a corpse."

Baby sulked in bed for three weeks, propped with pillows, gazing through the long windows at the *fiacres*, motor taxis, touring cars and limousines, the carts, drays and bicycles, the motorbuses which were ousting the three-horse omnibuses, all swirling round the Obelisk from Luxor in the middle of the Place de la Concorde.

A luxury hotel is a better place to be ill than a hospital. The service is to be commanded, not begged. The outside world intrudes instead of being regarded as irrelevant, and the day's hours remain in the possession of the patient. Baby declared the food disgusting, she wanted Quaker Oats, scrambled eggs, tomato ketchup. She had nothing to read, no *Life*, *McCall's*, *Ladies' Home Journal*. Nancy had before carried no responsibility weightier than arranging her father's dinner-parties. She now never flinched from managing her sister, however unsisterly it made her feel. The relationship between the sick and those who minister to them is often more complex and infuriating than marriage.

The door of the Clinique Laënnec's waiting-room opened without a knock. A tall, handsome young man with a thick moustache strode in. He wore a pair of khaki drill trousers, like a British officer in India, a Norfolk jacket of grey tweed, a soft turned-down collar and a floppy, crimson bow tie as favoured by minor poets. Under his arm was a cardboard box-file.

"Miss Janet Grange?" he said to Baby. "And you must be the sister who's accompanying her across the face of the earth?", he added to Nancy. "I'm Dr Eliot Beckett. I'm English. *Monsieur le directeur* will be along once he's finished in the operating theatre."

The sisters sat straight on the sofa, still in their hats. They had enjoyed the tea. Eliot lazily sat in an armchair opposite, long legs crossed, file on his knee. "I had a letter from Dr Hull in New York. You coughed blood, Miss Grange. When did the blow fall?"

"A Tuesday morning in the middle of March." Baby was practised in her story. "I was going to a final fitting at my dressmaker's. You see, it was to be my twenty-first birthday, we were having a wonderful ball, absolutely everyone in New York was invited."

She saw the doctor smile. "I mean, not actually *everyone* in New York, that would be four million people, wouldn't it? But everyone who *mattered* in New York. Oh, it was to be a heavenly evening." Baby's eyes shone, it could have been held tomorrow. "They'd already started decorating the ballroom, there were to be two orchestras, Viennese and a negro band – *how* I had to persuade father! The chef from Delmonico's was taking charge of our kitchens..." She stopped. "The invitations had all gone out," she ended quietly. "You can imagine, it was very embarrassing."

"I congratulate you on your sense of social obligation, Miss Grange. Giving thought to the effect of their illness upon others is an unusual quality among invalids. But why trail to Switzerland? The air is just as pure in the Appalachians as in the Alps."

Nancy replied, "My father knew the fame of Switzerland in curing the disease."

"No expense spared? You father's very rich? I could never ask an English lady that without risking a snubbing like an express hitting the buffers. In America, you're rightly proud to achieve the world's heart's desire. What's your father's business?"

"He is a banker." Nancy was irritated. The doctor talked as though on their social level.

Eliot uncapped his fountain-pen. For ten minutes he questioned Baby about her health – her weight, her sleep, the life she led, the friends she made. Did she sweat at night? Was she afflicted by catarrhs? Had any of her family suffered from phthisis? It was the first time he had named the disease.

"I heard my grandmother died of a cough."

"Can you remember what the doctor called it?"

"She had no doctor." Nancy interrupted. "She died in a slum on the East Side. She'd been in the United States less than a year."

"So? All has been amassed by your father's single-minded efforts? That's something deserving of congratulations, quite as much as writing *Huckleberry Finn*. I doubt if your grandmother suffered from consumption. She had recently arrived, and the vigilance of your immigration officers is feared across Europe."

The door reopened, admitting a tall thin man with scanty fair hair brushed from a domed brow above a pale face of hollows and furrows. He wore a long white coat, buttoned from his wing-collar to the ends of striped trousers above brightly polished black shoes and lavender spats. He bowed, introducing himself as Dr Pasquier, director of the clinic, speaking briskly with a strong French accent.

He led them through a second door, into an identical white room with fearsome furniture – flat leather couch half hidden by a white curtain on a brass rail, a white table with large bottles of coloured fluids and heavy china pots, an enamelled basin on a tripod, a tray with a white cloth bearing small shiny instruments of menacingly probing shape. A nurse was waiting, ugly and fat, in white dress, stockings and shoes, her flowing white cap with a red cross on the forehead. Nancy noticed another lidded cup on its shelf.

Eliot wordlessly offered Nancy a hard wooden chair. Removing her hat, Baby was placed in the centre on a padded leather seat with no arms, its straight narrow back reaching above her head. The nurse inserted a thermometer under her tongue. They waited three minutes. Dr Pasquier pulled a pince-nez dangling from his lapel, its black ribbon hissing from spring-loaded drum.

"Mademoiselle has a fever of thirty-eight degrees," he announced, as politely as paying a compliment.

"A hundred point four Farenheit," Eliot translated. "Even figures speak a different language here in the mountains."

"What was it this morning, mademoiselle?"

"I didn't take it." Baby looked guiltily at Nancy.

"Mademoiselle will please remove her upper garments."

Repetition had made Baby a deft and stylish undresser. Nancy suspected that she revelled in performing the forbidden with impunity, as though an artist's model rather than a doctor's specimen. The embroidered, lace-trimmed white silk camisole slipped from her shoulders, she unlaced and discarded the heavy cotton *brassière* criss-crossed with ribbons, bought with her divided stays from Bloomingdale's. Dr Pasquier was saying, "Everyone is liable to be seeded with the bacillus. If the soil is fertile, a tubercule will sprout. Many are lucky, and it falls upon

18

stony ground. Has mademoiselle been obliged to mix with many others, in a school or college?"

Nancy replied, "Our mother died at my sister's birth. We were schooled at home, and my father thought further education unnecessary."

"Has your sister performed charity work among the poor?"

"Never." She glanced at Eliot. She had taken a dislike to this abrasive English doctor. He was writing busily on his box-file.

Hands loose on her lap, thick blonde hair piled high, Baby sat with self-conscious submissiveness. Her skin was white to the wrists, her breasts smooth as lard were decorated with large nipples the colour of fresh salmon. Under the fair hairs of her armpits lay a glistening patch, the tears of her fever.

Dr Pasquier surprised her by taking both hands. "Ungues adunci," he murmured. "Clubbed fingers. You see, mademoiselle? The nails are unusually convex from base to tip, they curve over the finger's end like a parrot's beak. No one noticed it?" Baby shook her head. "Well, up here we have sharper eyes for such things than doctors who must treat an assembly of diseases."

"Will they get better?" asked Baby in alarm. "Or shall I be deformed for life?"

"They progress with the state of mademoiselle's health," he answered vaguely. He felt her neck. "No enlarged glands," he announced in his complimentary voice.

Eliot stood close beside him. Both gazed solemnly at Baby's chest, the bony birdcage of whispering lungs and ticking heart, from life to death unnoticed by its possessors as the whirling of the earth's globe beneath their feet, upon which the attention of the Clinique Laënnec was obsessively fixed and from which its income was drawn.

"The right apex," said Eliot. "Diminished movement."

Baby licked her lips several times. Head cocked, Dr Pasquier lay a finger flat under her collar-bone and percussed. Nancy suddenly saw the elderly Italian in the carefully-kept old suit who came every month to tune their pianos. Dr Pasquier produced an ebonite stethoscope, like a vase for a single rose, listening to Baby's chest with eyebrows raised and lips pursed,

19

as if savouring some excellent wine. Baby could think only of her nails turning into parrots' beaks.

"Thank you." Dr Pasquier bowed from the hips, as though Baby had just afforded him a dance.

"There is diminished breathing." He looked rapidly from one sister to the other. "With *râles* – abnormal sounds – not found by your American doctors. But as I mentioned, we have sharper eyes and ears because we hunt but one animal in the jungle of sickness. There is...shall I say, a suspicion...? of a moist patch at the very top of the right lung. We may be wrong. We must examine the sputum she coughs up, to see if the tubercule bacillus lurks therein. We shall look inside with Röntgen rays – we have every modern convenience here, you see. Meanwhile, mademoiselle is advised to enjoy our hospitality for a while."

"How long?" Baby still sat half-naked. "I've just got to be back in New York by the middle of summer."

"I assure mademoiselle that we are equally eager to lose her company." Dr Pasquier bowed again. "That day will be expedited by her not fretting about it. You will please excuse me. Dr Beckett will see you comfortably installed."

# 3

"What a pretty little room." Baby clasped her hands, eyes shining, "Nancy, it's like the one we used to share at Oyster Bay when we were kids."

It was a nasty little room.

It was a white cube, smaller than Nancy's bathroom on Fifth Avenue. The wardrobe was narrow, the white dressing-table had a plain oval mirror, the square washbasin in one corner had stout brass taps and a white slop-pail under it. The bed was in the middle, white-painted iron with a white coverlet, on large wheels with brakes. From the ceiling hung an electric bulb in a shade like a saucer, the floor was covered with more coconut matting. On the bedside commode was a nightlight with a squat candle, and another of the lidded cups. On the capacious balcony stood a long chair with folded blankets, as aboard transatlantic liners. It was one of the sanatorium's best rooms, on the ground floor, looking across the gravel forecourt with the flapping flag. It cost 25 Swiss francs a week.

"But it's freezing," complained Baby. The shadows of the conifers opposite were pointing long fingers towards the creeping dusk. Nancy laid her hand on the cold radiator.

"*Bitte? Die Zentralheizung ist zu warm.*" The fat nurse who had accompanied them shook her finger severely. "Dr Pasquier want good hygiene."

"What's that smell?" Baby's nose wrinkled.

"*Räuchern Ameisensäure.*" The nurse waved her hand. "Formalin."

They were interrupted by another white-clad nurse, young, sandy, fresh-faced, bustling, chattering cheerfully, "So here's the new arrivals? I'm Nurse Dove. I'm from London. Thank you, Fraulein," she dismissed her companion, sweeping up Baby's travelling-coat and hanging it in the wardrobe. "We'll soon get you settled in comfy. These are my rooms, along this bit of the corridor, but the Fraulein's in charge of everybody. You're from America, aren't you?" She started busily turning down the bed. "Fancy that. Mind, we've quite a few Americans here. It's a long way to come, but it's wonderful these days with the steamships, isn't it? As I always say, there's no place like Switzerland for getting you back in the pink if you've a touched lung." She closed the windows and drew the curtains. "You don't want to get into bed as though in the middle of Piccadilly Circus, do you?"

"Whose is this?" Baby picked from the dressing-table a silver-backed brush, long fair hairs choking the bristles, inscribed on the back, *To Louisa from Mummy and Daddy on Her Twenty-first Birthday*.

"Oh, dear me, that belonged to the young English lady. I must have missed clearing it out yesterday with the rest of her things."

"She's gone home to England?" Baby sounded excited.

"I wish I could say as much." Nurse Dove pounded and smoothed the pillows. "No, the poor lady died. She was a bad case, right from the start. Dr Beckett couldn't do a thing for her, she just went steadily downhill. Still, that's exceptional, the san does most people the world of good. The room's been thoroughly fumigated with formic acid," she added consolingly.

"She died?" Baby gasped. "Here? Yesterday?"

"Folk are born and folk die, that's the way of the world." Nurse Dove checked the candle in the night-light. "They're the only two things every soul must go through, and I don't suppose we realise that either has happened to us. What's the point, making your whole life miserable by thinking about your departure from it?"

"Don't leave me here, don't leave me." Baby started crying, clutching Nancy fiercely.

"You'll be all right, darling, you'll be fine, you're hardly ill at all, are you?"

"There's a lot that has a good cry when they first come in," said Nurse Dove sympathetically. "But believe me, in a day or two everything will seem so natural, you'll look upon it as your home from home. After all, there's all of us with nothing else to do except make you better. Put your sister to bed," she said to Nancy. "I'll see the porter about the luggage, and order her supper. There's always something nice."

They sat on the bed, Baby shaking in Nancy's arms, continually muttering, "Don't leave me, don't leave me... I'm so frightened, so frightened."

"I *know* you are, darling." Nancy stroked her hair. "You've been so brave, right from the start. Putting on a show, as though it was all some awful inconvenience, like pouring rain when we'd planned a tennis party."

Baby tried not to think of the golden-haired pale English miss, eaten by disease to a skin-bag of bones. "You are wonderful, being so strict, darling, saving me from myself. Now a pack of strangers have suddenly become the most important persons in my life. Don't you see? The doctors, the nurses, they're above you. Even above father."

"Screw up your courage, darling."

"It's flattering to know I have some. That's the mood everyone gets married in, isn't it?" she said, a trace of usual gaiety. "They live happily ever after, only because they don't care losing their own good opinion of their bravery."

Nurse Dove entered with the alligator dressing-case.

"Not getting undressed yet?" She spoke as to a wayward child. "You have brought a lot of luggage, but everybody does. It'll have to go in the storeroom, I'm afraid. What pretty things you've got." She held up Baby's nightdress with the air of an experienced shop girl at the counter.

"Go now, Nancy," Baby commanded. "I'm feeling stronger. I might not in a little while."

The corridor outside was empty. Electric bulbs in dish-like shades supplemented the fading light. Nancy felt relieved and guilty. As the door of the white room shut, the sisters' lives were divided. She had abandoned to professionals the responsibility and irksomeness of controlling a capricious patient on a tiresome journey. Now she faced an indefinite stay in a remote Swiss hotel with no company except an ill-tempered lady's maid, an existence to which she had afforded neither planning nor even speculation.

Nancy stopped. Behind another white door, somebody barely two yards away started coughing. It was a cough she had never heard before.

Repeated but not paroxysmal, long and rumbling, a wet, sticky uncomplaining cough, which made her imagine a sack emptied of squashed and rotten potatoes. It lasted near a quarter of a minute before ending in a sigh, a hissing intake of breath, then the sharp noise of a metal closing on metal, which puzzled her. Nancy shivered. Gripping her skirt, she hurried along the corridor.

A slim woman in a long black serge skirt and white blouse was leaving the examination room. Her face was a crimson scaly mask, the tip of her nose blunted like a boxer's, her eyelids drawn down to show their gleaming pink lining, tightly stretched skin tugging her lips and revealing her gums in a smile as gruesome as a skeleton's.

Eliot was seeing the patient out. "Miss Grange, is your sister comfortable? You're leaving for your hotel? I'll order the carriage."

He sat Nancy on the hard chair, took the ebonite-handled telephone from its cradle, whirred the handle of the wooden box beneath, and spoke briefly in French.

"Unhappily, all three of the clinic's carriages are at the station or the village, so you must wait a while." Eliot leant with his back to the radiator, hands clasped over beige shirt-front. He seemed slightly more affable.

"That poor woman has the disease in her face?" Nancy asked.

"Yes, you are right. *The* disease. It's the only one existing up here. The guests all have it, the servants have all shaken it off. Did you notice the scar on the receptionist's neck? The cunning tubercule bacillus has as many manifestations as the Devil. It can swell the neck glands like a string of blind boils. It can inflame the joints like rheumatism and gout, or hoarsen the voice like an everlasting cold. She had *lupus vulgarus*." He nodded towards the door. "Though some still dispute it, I reckon it a *tuberculosis cutis*."

"Why was my sister given a room where a woman had just died?" Nancy demanded.

"There was no other. The sanatorium is always full. To get a bed is as great a privilege as in the most fashionable hotel."

"There was no need that she should have known about it."

Eliot shrugged. "Less need to deceive her. She would have learned from another patient by breakfast. They think nothing of it, and soon neither will she. She'll make a joke of it. They develop the humour of the cannon's mouth. Why not? They are all soldiers fighting the same enemy – the tubercule bacillus. The patients give battle, not us. We are powerless. We can only provide the most promising battlefield and lay the most intelligent strategy."

Nancy began to complain indignantly, "But my sister is here for treatment – "

"Treatment? There is only one treatment for phthisis." He threw open the long window. "Fresh air. That's what your father is paying for. Paying thousands of dollars for air. If he sat and thought about it, he'd fancy himself mad or us brazen swindlers."

"Dr Beckett, your attitude is unattractive in a medical man, to whose care is committed a young lady with a disease which her family know – quite as well as you do – as dangerous to her life."

Eliot looked disconcerted. "I'm sorry to give that impression," he said with unexpected awkwardness. "Were I not driven by compassion for those who are sick, and for those who must bear with them, do you imagine I should be here?"

She was sitting straight, legs crossed under her long skirt, showing her ankles. Eliot seemed to regard her for the first time as an object worth his interest. "I could instead be turning guineas from the imaginary illnesses of London society ladies and the very real excesses of London gentlemen. Though I pity them too, but in a different way."

"How long must my sister be up here? The rest of the summer? The rest of the year?"

"We never mention time in the mountains. It does not exist. The length of our patient's sentence means nothing, compared to their escaping as cured. Pining over the calendar puts up the temperature, and is *streng verboten*."

"Doing nothing but breathing the air?" asked Nancy tartly.

"They live in it, night and day. Sleeping tucked-up on the balcony, covered with rubber sheets against the rain, guarded by iron screens from the winds. Miss Grange will be allowed exercise in strict moderation. No indulgence in exciting games and recreations, which includes the most popular game of all, *les affaires de coeur*. Our patients are thrown on each other's company as though aboard a liner at sea, and fever fires the passions like sea breezes. Are you shocked?"

"That patients remain human? Hardly."

"Perhaps the urge to flirt is an expression of *spes pthisica*," Eliot reflected. "The strange hope which our patients never lose. If I could but rid myself of this cough, they say, I should be healthy enough to climb the Matterhorn or swim the English Channel. 'The consumption is a flattering disease, cozening men into hope of long life at the last gasp.' An English clergyman called Thomas Fuller noticed that, almost three hundred years ago."

"My sister is hopeful."

"Hers is not displaced. She is a slight case. But she must surrender herself to us, as utterly as a novice to her faith."

"Surely there's some drug to speed her release?"

"Creosote? Guaiacol wafers? Koch's tuberculin, the very hair of the deadly dog?" Eliot recited scathingly. "I've tried tuberculin, but it grows the bacilli like a wasps' nest in the sunshine."

She looked at him steadily. "There *is* a drug which will cure phthisis, Dr Beckett."

"Its name would be a priceless extension of my education."

"Do you know of Munyon's Homoeopathic Remedies, of New York?" Eliot shook his head violently. "It's a company on 6th Avenue. It does business all over the world. Among my father's interests is the manufacture of medicines. After my sister fell ill, he heard from Professor Munyon that their general manager – a homoeopathic physician, trained in Michigan – had discovered a cure for phthisis."

"What's his name?"

"Dr Crippen. For the past five years, he's been representing the firm in London. I intend travelling there as soon as my sister is settled, to beg a sample off him. My father says the formula is secret, lest it be stolen by a rival firm before plans are ripe to sell it. I know the name – Tuberculozyne."

Eliot responded to this revelation only by saying, "The carriage must be back now."

Nancy remembered her coat in the waiting-room. She reached for the lidded cup on its ledge, asking its use.

"For spit." Eliot opened it. Inside, now swum in the fluid three round blobs like small oysters. Nancy's stomach turned over. "The nummular sputum of phthisis," he explained. "Round and flat, like coins. If the spit dries on the floor or a handkerchief, the bacilli waft away and look for another little nook of lung to settle into. It's the first rule up here, everyone spits into disinfectant. Doing otherwise is a social error far worse than eating peas off your knife. For patients who go out, or whose offerings we value for a lengthy look, we provide a neat pocket spitoon in blue glass with a screw cap."

The gravel was empty. The sky was almost dark. Lights burned behind the balconies. "Come and see the view," Eliot invited unceremoniously.

From the white fence, an escarpment fell two hundred feet to the village of Champette.

"We sell the purest sort of air," he told her, "better than those nests of sanitoria at St Moritz or Arosa or Davos, halfway to Heaven already. We're under fifteen hundred metres, where the atmosphere is more humid and the construction costs less. The clinic is owned by a joint stock company, you know, quoted on the Zurich stock exchange. Phthisis is good business." Nancy shivered in her overcoat. Eliot was apparently impervious to the night chill. "I think sanatoria above the tree-line, beside the regions of eternal snow, are frightening. They have to send the corpses down by sled…but you'd rather not speak of such things."

"Maybe I'll acquire your patients' hardihood, and joke about it?"

"Troops under fire prefer to scoff than tremble. Where are you staying, Miss Grange?"

"The Grand." Nancy tried distinguishing its lights below. "What's it like?"

"I've never entered it, in twelve months. I catch the dance music ascending sometimes — the valleys are enormous ear-trumpets, you can hear the cow-bells from the pasturage far down. Such a Swiss sound, as dismal as bell-buoys on rocks. I would not care for the company the hotel provided."

"Then why come to practise here, Dr Beckett? Your patients are all rich. And the company of rich people seems to affect you like that of Corsican brigands."

"I'm learning about tuberculosis on the rich, that I might apply my knowledge to the poor," he answered simply. "The labouring classes are the worst sufferers, and unfortunately can't cure themselves by seeking a change of climate. They lie in bed in their only room, spitting their germs over the family which shares it, like a cloud of deadly gas. Every single workman who develops phthisis probably gives it to a dozen more. That's not just tragic. It's uneconomical. Which should strike forcibly such a man as your father."

"Your tenderness towards the poor is admirable, Dr Beckett. Your envy of the rich is not."

Her remark seemed to jolt him. "The only people I envy are those cleverer than myself. I'm unlike you. I know both rich and poor. I'm sorry for the rich. They live an uninteresting, artificial life, because they are more frightened of the real world even than of losing their money."

"Might I suggest that you are too self-opinionated, Dr Beckett? An intelligent rich girl suffers equally with a poor one, that she cannot go to college and learn about the real world."

Eliot smiled. "Have I misjudged you, Miss Grange? I hope during your enforced stay you will afford me opportunity to rectify my mistake."

They heard the jingle of the coach, its lights flickering through the trees before it crunched on the gravel.

"When may I visit my sister?"

"Whenever you wish. We'll keep her in bed for a bit, until we see what tricks her temperature's playing. Remember, the disease is catching. Don't stand in the way of her cough."

"Why don't *you* catch it?"

"We and the nurses seem immune. Familiarity breeds contempt, I suppose." He added off-handedly, "I finish here with the end of summer. I've work waiting in London. What was the name of that American doctor?"

"Dr Crippen."

"I could look him up for you. He's probably a quack. Your rushing to England would be worse than a fool's errand. It would raise your sister's hopes cruelly."

Nancy had stepped into the coach. Eliot shut the door and turned to the sanatorium entrance, without glancing back.

# 4

Eliot was a shy young man. Reared among the rich but never of them, he had no graces to soften his resentment when thrust among them socially. The patients were easy. He had the bluff, kindly, infinitely confident and uncontradictable manner which carried the English doctor into the heart of the English family, in a nation which venerated commonsense as much as it distrusted cleverness. Their relatives he generally found boring and petulant. Nancy intrigued him. She was neither pretentious nor patronizing. She answered him back with intelligence instead of arrogance. But he distrusted his ability for small talk, he knew the likelihood of seeming rude and provoking anger. He avoided her. Rich people anyway frightened him. He had viewed too intimately their power.

When the July sun glared from the gravel forecourt and shortened the shadow of the flagpole, Baby was allowed up for lunch.

The dining-room shared the first upstairs floor with the patients' lounge, which had a grand piano, a gramophone with a horn, crettone-covered furniture and scattered small tables with magazines in half-a-dozen languages. They ate between white walls on white chairs off linen fresh every meal. Even the food seemed white – minced chicken, cream sauces, potato soup, Gruyère cheese, served by maids in white dresses whose scarred neck or limp displayed their own escape from the disease which would eventually kill many of their patrons.

Baby's day repeated itself to the minute. The monotony was deliberate. Energy of body and mind were preserved for the cure. At eight, Nurse Dove took her temperature. The morning she divided between novels from the sanatorium library and laboriously creating a spray of red roses on an embroidery frame – the clinic employed a sharp-nosed *Parisienne* to instruct their lady patients, the gentlemen enjoyed instead fifteen minutes' pounding from a Swedish masseur. There was an English breakfast and an English tea, with hot toast and Swiss cherry jam. On Sundays, her dinner-tray was decorated with a vase of bright wild flowers, which the previous week she was mystified to find replaced by the Stars and Stripes. It was July the Fourth, and all national days were monitored by *la direction*, as all birthdays were marked by a huge cream cake and a bottle of champagne with the clinic's compliments.

"I've still got *râles* at my apex, but they don't signify much," Baby told Nancy brightly. "And dullness of my infraclavicular fossa, here."

She tapped below her right collar-bone. She wore a white silk blouse and a white flannel skirt secured with huge gold safety-pins, white stockings and white kid boots. A broad-brimmed straw hat was secured on her piled fair hair with a wide ribbon of Cambridge blue. She wore the same outfit the year before, for tennis parties at Oyster Bay.

She was on the steamer chair with an open parasol, which she twirled gently over her shoulder. The balcony had a parquet floor and a white ceiling with 62 squares boxing a leaf design, which she counted everlastingly. It was afternoon rest time for everyone in the sanatorium.

"And I've cog-wheel respiration," Baby continued. "Can you imagine? Dr Beckett says it sounds like a cog-wheel jerking round, right there in my chest. But no bronchial breathing," she ended proudly. "And that's awfully good, you know."

"You *are* becoming well educated." Nancy smiled, sitting on a chair beside her.

"Oh, we all know quite as much as the doctors. And my temperature this morning was nearly normal! Wonderful, isn't it? Everyone's crazy about their temperature. The thermometer's our clock, isn't it? It measures how much longer we've got to spend up here."

"I had a cable from papa this morning." Mails were disregarded. Every morning, Nancy handed a telegram to the guard of the departing train, which the Geneva post office transmitted to New York to arrive on her father's breakfast table. She tried hard to vary her messages, generally as unexcitingly repetitive as military communiqués from a long-drawn siege.

"He's making the trip."

"The angel! When?"

"When he can. You know how it is with Papa."

"Oh, business!" Baby wrinkled her nose. "Sometimes I wonder if he thinks we're just a part of it. Look at my nails! Aren't they awful? Real parrots' beaks, as Dr Pasquier said. I'm going to send for the best manicurist in New York the moment I step off the boat."

Loud knocking came on Baby's left. The balconies were divided by screens of folding white-painted iron panels, six feet high with a decorative scroll on the top. "Darling, can I visit?" said a girl's eager voice.

Baby whispered, "Lady Sarah Pledge. She's the daughter of an earl, and the only thing she's crazy about in the whole world is fox-hunting. She's moved into the next room. We're already as close as an Indian hug. Oh, sure," she called. "My sister's here."

Lady Sarah pushed aside the screen. She was Baby's age, unnaturally slender, her eyes large and grey, her skin waxy like a lily petal. She wore a cream silk blouse and a crimson-striped cotton skirt.

"She's got a pneumothorax," Baby introduced her.

"They pump air into one's chest through a needle," Lady Sarah explained light-heartedly. "It collapses down one's lung to a little lump, so's it can heal better. You need only one lung to breathe, you know. My room still stinks of that fumigating stuff." She added to Nancy, "The Russian count snuffed it two days ago. Absolutely torrential haemorrhage, according to Nurse Dove, though she does so exaggerate in her relish about such things."

Nancy felt her stomach tighten. It was the Russian she heard coughing the day they arrived. She could not assume the inmates' easygoing mockery of death. For that, death must intrude into every day's action and thought. It was the relationship of marriage.

"I've news for you, old thing," Lady Sarah continued. "They're going to see through us. The Röntgen rays." Baby was excited. She was always eager for a new experience, and anything breaking the sanatorium's monotony was a gala. "I heard from Nurse Dove. It's quite weird down there, one sees the diapositives with one's skeleton looking like something out of a ghost story."

She broke off, coughing, her sharp shoulders shaking, her skin taking a tinge of blue. She covered her mouth with her hands, turning her back on the others in obeyance of sanatorium etiquette. As the paroxysm subsided, she took from her skirt pocket a round blue bottle, into which she spat slimy green mucus.

"What a bore," she wheezed. It was the condemnation of the English for any annoyance, from a late train to a mortal illness.

Nurse Dove shortly fussed Baby back to bed. Cards, recitals, amateur concerts in the lounge filled the evenings, but Baby had to wait like a child impatient to stay up for adult enjoyments. That evening was hot, the red cross flag dangling lifeless from the masthead. The carriage was waiting on the gravel, a white linen cover to cool the roof, the horse in a straw hat with holes for its ears. At the foot of the steps, Dr Beckett in his tweed jacket and poet's tie was chatting to the blue-bloused driver.

"I gather my sister is to be examined by the Röntgen rays?" said Nancy.

"Yes. We shall look inside to see what's going on, rather than imagining it from tapping and listening. Why should physicians be blind men?"

"Are the rays dangerous?"

"Not in the right hands."

"Do you expect to find anything disconcerting?"

"If I knew what I should see, it would not be worth the trouble of the examination." The concierge opened the carriage door. Eliot added, "You must find life at Champette dreadfully tedious."

"Not at all. I'm learning French. My maid helps with the pronunciation, though I suspect she has a vile Parisien accent. I'm also learning water-colouring from the wife of a British major. Every Monday, I go into Lausanne. All excitements in life are relative, aren't they?"

"You can't spend all your time swotting French."

"I am blessed with plenty of books, and plenty of friends who must be written to."

"Are you making new ones?"

"I prefer not making friends under duress."

"I'll come and dine with you tomorrow night." Nancy looked shocked, "I'll pay my own bill, naturally."

"You may invite yourself to dine in the hotel restaurant, Dr Beckett, but not in my company."

"Oh, come," he disposed of the objection. "If you saw me sitting on one side of the room with my inevitable *potage de legumes*, you'd invite me to join you, surely? I shall be there at eight."

He helped her into the carriage, shut the door and strode into the building.

Nancy was outraged. No man in New York dared break into her company, no more than into her father's banks. She was puzzled. She had heard that all Englishmen were desperately punctilious, so terrified of "doing the wrong thing", even if it was wearing the wrong hat.

The carriage had not rattled down the winding road before she was smiling at Eliot's self-invitation. He was as gauche as a raw college boy, but she was bored, and she was lonely. Anyway, Champette was a social desert island where no civilized rules applied.

She instructed Maria-Thérèse to press her pink chiffon gown, not worn since leaving New York. For a woman to dress up without a man to impress was like cooking a splendid dinner to eat herself. Most of her jewellery was in New York. Nancy selected the next evening from her crocodile jewel-case a triple string of pearls which had cost twenty thousand dollars, and two single black pearl earrings worth twelve hundred and fifty. She came downstairs slowly, one white gloved hand gathering her skirt, the other gently waving her grey ostrich-feather fan.

In the hall were two English couples – a major and a solicitor with pallid, scrawny wives who Nancy found indistinguishable – just returned with wild flowers from walking. There was the jolly family from Lyons on whom she practised her French, and the solemn one from Frankfurt who practiced their English to her. They stared like the urchins on the New York sidewalks watching the gorgeous rich gather for a ball. The frock-coated receptionist craned across his counter. The concierge amid a pile of luggage involuntarily whipped off his cap. She wondered if Dr Beckett would be wearing his usual shooting-jacket.

Eliot appeared in a long black cape like a cavalry officer's, its deep collar secured by a chain. He handed it to the concierge with a wide-brimmed velour hat and a small square lantern. He wore a dinner jacket of unmatchable London cut, diamond studs in his shirt front, his tie as symmetrical as a butterfly. She was amused at his startled look. The dress was cut low across her bosom, in the latest American fashion.

"May I congratulate you on your gown, Miss Grange? It must quite overawe this nation of *petits bourgeois*, as if the snow had miraculously melted and revealed the magnificent peak of the Matterhorn."

"I imagined you looked at a chest with the emotions of a watchmaker at a watch, Dr Beckett."

"Even one of that unimaginative profession is moved by a Fabergé clock. Is this the Gibson Girl silhouette we read is all the rage in America?"

"I thought everyone knew that the Outdoor Girl had replaced the Gibson Girl?" she corrected him. "Because of the automobile, you know. Women have taken to driving them. We apply freshly cut cucumber to soothe the suntan and smooth the dreaded automobile wrinkles. But *really*, Dr Beckett − would my dress shock a nation which stands idly by while fathers shoot apples off their son's heads?"

"Perhaps only the expense would. Which I suppose is necessary, to keep up with 'The Four Hundred'?"

"Only vulgar people talk about 'The Four Hundred', Dr Beckett. It was nothing but the capacity of Mrs Astor's ballroom. Are you retaining your carriage?"

"I walked. It's a splendid evening. I always take the path down the cliff to the village. They've marked the stones at every turn with white paint. I've brought an acetylene, so I shan't break my neck in the dark."

Two white-jacketed *commis* threw open the glass doors of the hotel restaurant.

"I hear that in American society, a lady considers a dress allowance of five thousand dollars a year as reducing her to rags?" Eliot resumed. "All the families in Champette could be kept comfortably on that. And I hear that two hundred million dollars worth of diamonds are suspended from the necks, bosoms and stomachs of the New York females. You could run the whole of Switzerland on that. I assume your father is a millionaire?" "Oh, there's seven thousand millionaires in America, Dr Beckett. There are millionaires, then there are multimillionaires, and then Pittsburg millionaires."

They sat at a corner table. Eliot was amused to notice everyone forget their food to stare at them. They seemed a rich and smart young couple, more likely to be encountered at some fashionable hotel on the Quai du Mont-Blanc in Geneva.

"Isn't the definition of a millionaire the ability to live off the income of your income?" Eliot asked.

"In New York, it is only spending the income of a million dollars, whether you have either. Do you know, the Granges don't even possess a two-ton bath-tub carved from solid marble, like the Astors?"

"How much wiser to watch the smart set outdoing each other with displays of wealth. That only ruins the millionaires and makes millionaires of the tradesmen."

"It doesn't prevent my father being vilified in the newspapers as a ruthless man."

"That can be a compliment. It takes the same resolution to throw a man into a river as to leap in and pull him out of it. Why did you allow me to intrude on you tonight?"

"Surely it's a social distinction to sit at table with a well-born Englishman? In New York, noblemen charge to provide that honour for eager hostesses."

"Only the Russian aristocracy do. And I'm not well-born. You're looking at my dress-studs? A coming-of-age gift from the Duke of Lincoln. Have you admired my clothes? Cut by the Duke's tailor in Savile Row, half-price. To provide a young man with impressive studs and a good tailor shows the grasp on essentials which brought the Duke's family its fortune. My father is the Duke's agent, his man of business, attending to his houses and estates. I was brought up staring through the plate glass dividing one station of life from another. I've seen balls with ladies wearing dresses far richer than yours, one woman made beautiful by fifty miserable, starving, ugly people. I've seen good food transformed into diverting shapes and pretty colours by slaving cooks. I've seen cosseted pheasants beaten into the air by half-starved farm-labourers to be shot. I've seen the cigars, the champagne, the waste. My father saved every penny that I might escape."

"And a spy never forgives his enemies?"

"The waiter is becoming impatient," said Eliot, taking the menu.

"You're very fluent in French," she said admiringly, as he ordered.

"I try not to be. Good linguists are disreputable in England, where only amateurism is trustworthy. We believe, like Aristotle, that a gentleman should be able to play the flute – but not too well."

"Don't Englishwomen speak French?"

"To their milliners." He ordered a bottle of Dom Perignon 1900 without bothering to take the wine list from the somelier.

"Why is it called the Clinique Laënnec?" It had puzzled her since leaving New York. *Is* there a Dr Laënnec?"

"Dr René Théopile Hyacinthe Laënnec," he explained. "He invented the stethoscope. He rolled up a quire of paper and listened to the patient's chest. Which saved embarrassment, applying his ear to the breastbones of plump young gentlewomen, and his hair from lice in hospital. He died a hundred years ago. From phthisis."

"Why can't my sister have a pneumothorax, like Lady Pledge?"

"Her case is not suitable."

The waiter served their *consommé à la Gélestine*, clear soup with scraps of savoury pancake.

"Is there no operation which might allow her to go home the earlier?"

"There's thoracoplasty, collapsing the chest by snipping away the cage of ribs. It's the invention of George Fowler, an American surgeon. I should have needed several months under his tuition before risking performing it. As he died three years ago, that's impossible."

"Yet you despise the remedy invented by Dr Crippen?" she accused him.

"If it works, I should buy a vat of it. In London, I intend achieving my two ambitions. First, to start a free clinic," he revealed. "Fashionable doctors learn their medicine on the poor in hospitals, and expend the knowledge on the rich. I'm reversing the process. Secondly, I'm standing for Parliament. Candidate for Holloway, in London. Labour, of course.

There's bound to be an election soon. Our Mr Asquith's ministry has been creaking far too long."

"Wouldn't you be a little young as a member of Parliament, Dr Beckett?"

"Mr Pitt was a younger one."

"My father believes that the only value of politicians is the amount necessary to bribe them."

Eliot fell silent. He was prouder than of his degrees of his selection by a committee mostly of railwaymen and the slaughtermen from the Metropolitan Cattle Market in north London. He had applauded since schooldays a line from the forgotten Victorian author, Anthony Trollope – "It is the highest and most legitimate pride of an Englishman to have the letters MP written after his name." He was disappointed the disclosure left Nancy undazzled. His bristliness was a frightened hedgehog's. He wondered if she despised him, as common.

"I'm going to London, and I'm going to find Dr Crippen," Nancy resumed. "I must do all I can for my sister."

"You've already done much. So irresponsible a patient wouldn't have survived the journey without your watchfulness."

"I know you take me for a woman who satisfies her conscience by dropping a dime every year into the Salvation Army Christmas Kettle. But you know who I admire? Your Miss Florence Nightingale."

"You could pay a call when you're seeking Dr Crippen," Eliot suggested lightly. "She's ninety, but still has people to tea."

"Hers is a life I would trade for mine."

"How singularly unfortunate for you, that the United States is not at the moment engaged in a war."

"You don't take me seriously."

"I hope you're not cross?"

"I refuse to be. Men never take women seriously. Because men wear vanity as dogs fur. Which makes life less bothersome, because we get exactly what we want by stroking it."

The five-piece hotel orchestra struck up *Wine, Women and Song*. They could barely hear each other across the table. They talked about trivial things. Both were becoming exhausted trying to impress the other.

# 5

"The whole thing's a frightful bore," said Lady Sarah Pledge. "Like sitting for one's photograph in Bond Street. When I was presented at Court last year, I seemed to spend the entire summer wearing ball gowns in the afternoon and standing in horribly uncomfortable poses while little men kept disappearing under baize cloths like parrots."

"I heard it's a witches' cavern, flashes of lightning, everything crackling and sizzling like green wood in the stove." Baby was zestful – particularly as everyone told her it did not hurt in the slightest. "Gee, I could do with some coffee," she complained.

Patients for x-ray went breakfastless, to prevent bubbles in the stomach, Nurse Dove explained.

The pair sat with Nancy in the waiting-room of the x-ray laboratory, next to the patients' writing-room with its four identical ormolu-scrolled imitation Louis Quatorze desks, refurbished daily with spotless blotters and thick white stationery. Like all rooms unlet to patients, it faced the profitless north. The last door of the ground floor corridor lay just beyond. It opened on a secret flight of steps to the basement – white-tiled, like the kitchen with its *chef de cuisine* who could have earned as much in a luxury hotel.

In the basement the bodies were stored, and sometimes anatomized, if Dr Pasquier assessed them more interesting dead than alive and the relatives could be persuaded to agree. The mortuary was reached by a broad corridor running the building's length, equally unknown to the patients. Bodies were brought down the lifts at night on rubber-wheeled trolleys by stealthy porters. Nobody seemed to die in the Clinique

Laënnec, they simply disappeared. There was a death every two or three days.

The x-ray waiting-room was cramped. It had red plush chairs and offered worn copies of *Punch* and *Gil Blas*, its starkness brightened by a framed Toulouse-Lautrec poster of Jane Avril shaking a calf at the Jardin de Paris, which Nancy thought vulgar. Opposite waited a pale, thin young Frenchman with an old-fashioned imperial, whose loose blue suit insinuated severe loss of weight. Another spitoon stood on its shelf. It was past ten, the morning after Nancy dined with Eliot. They had arrived early, but appointments were meaningless where time did not exist.

"You're not scared Dr Beckett's going to electrocute me?" Baby looked slyly at her sister.

"What a bitter man he is," interrupted Lady Sarah, who knew nothing of the dinner. "Talking to him's like biting an unripe lemon."

"Surely Englishmen are all scared of showing their emotions?" suggested Nancy charitably.

"I suppose so," Lady Sarah agreed. "That would reduce them to appearing like ordinary members of the human race."

A nurse summoned through an inner door the Frenchman, who returned after fifteen minutes, bowing politely. Next was Lady Sarah, who reappeared smiling. "Just a quick glance, not a prolonged scrutiny, which means good news." She was experienced in the Röntgen rays.

Nancy accompanied Baby. The cramped room was filled with grotesque machinery on stout wooden tables, gleaming brass festooned with white dials sprouting black wires. In the middle was a tight-stretched canvas on stout wooden legs, reminding Nancy of a circus acrobat's trampoline. Below was an electric bulb the size of a goldfish bowl, another was suspended above by wires and pulleys. It was a room of perpetual night, the windows blacked with paint, the light from a cluster of electric bulbs in shades like glass tulips. It had the dry, pungent smell which Nancy had noticed gusting from subway stations, making her wonder what it was like down there.

Eliot had shed his Norfolk jacket for a long red apron, and wore heavy gauntlets. "This useful little invention we owe to William Röntgen from the Rhineland." He had the pride of a man showing off a motorcar. "He was a dreamy sort of fellow, but one November afternoon while experimenting with cathode rays, he noticed they produced a gleam on a sensitive platinocyanide plate across the room – *with solid objects in between.* You see? A scientist does not need genius, he needs luck." Eliot's manner gave no indication to Nancy that they had ever met outside the sanatorium. "This is the latest coil set, with mercury interrupter, which produces excellent snapshots."

The nurse was helping Baby undo a pink-and-white striped blouse, with blue tie in white starched collar. Nancy's eyes met a metal cabinet bearing two grey glass plates transilluminated by powerful electric bulbs. "That's a lady's knee." Eliot indicated with the finger of his gauntlet. "You see the flat head of the tibia bone? The great hinge of the femur rolling on it, and the fibula tucked coyly behind like a shy child in a family photo? The mist all round is the flesh which excites any gentleman privileged to set eyes on it. The other disapositive is a pelvis, a female one. A man's is shaped like a pudding-basin, a woman's like a flat washbasin. Another human, perhaps a succession of them, must butt its way through that hole in the middle, to join us in this world with an eagerness which must often seem misplaced."

Nancy disagreed. "You may not enjoy every party, Dr Beckett, but it's less fun not being invited." She thought him unnecessarily sardonic that morning. Perhaps he wanted to prove himself immune to low-cut evening gowns?

Baby was examined by the skiagraph, standing against an oblong glass suspended by pullies, her breasts flattened like two cakes of dough on a cook's board.

"Please excuse my gloves, Miss Grange," Eliot said waggishly, adjusting her position. "They prevent Röntgen ray dermatitis, which would rot my hands away. Even scientific magic can turn against its sorcerer's apprentice. Now breathe as though diving into fifty feet of water. May your sister see your insides?"

The nurse clicked out the electric light, save a glowing ruby in the corner. Sparks and crackles came from the high-tension coil. Nancy found herself looking through Baby's chest. For a second her head swam, she feared she might faint, but Eliot was saying calmly, "Those twin domes at the bottom are the diaphragm, the shelf that stops the organs of chest and belly becoming mixed like salami. Everyone thought it drew air into the lungs by contracting inwards towards that long shadow of the backbone. Like the iris of your eye, in a strong light. Professor Röntgen's rays show it moves up and down like a plunger. The most welcome advances in medicine prove that our most strongly-held preconceptions are utterly wrong. Deep breath."

Nancy was intrigued by the dark shadows of ribs and spine, the trademark of the gravedigger, which no human could observe without the passing qualm of one day becoming reduced to it. In the middle, a dark shape reminded her of a squid, puffing and shrinking regularly among the seaweed, in the oceanographic institute on Long Island. "There's always something mystical about the human heart," Eliot remarked. "Though it's just a lump of muscle, no more the seat of tender emotions than the biceps." In silence, his gloved finger briefly indicated the top of Baby's right lung, but Nancy could discern nothing. The lights went on, the screen faded.

"It's no worse than a fitting at the dressmakers," Baby declared. "Am I nearer to going home?"

"We shall call for a little more of your patience," Eliot told her kindly. "But patience is not painful either, is it?"

"I'm sure I'm a total fraud." She was only half-flippant. "My temperature's the effect of my highly-strung nervous system. Everybody tells me I'm like that. Don't they, Nancy?"

Eliot sent her for a late breakfast. A second one was served in mid-morning, to match the habits of the Germans.

He led Nancy through a second door into another small white room, tiled halfway up. Below windows of frosted glass ran a long wooden laboratory bench, stained with red, blue and green dyes, at the end of a small square sink with a tap like a swan's neck. On the bench stood a brass microscope with two eyepieces, scattered round it three-inch oblongs of glass, sheets of closely-written foolscap and a pencil, as though engrossing work had been interrupted. In the middle of the room, a stout zinc-topped table was crammed with glass-stoppered bottles of light coloured liquids.

Eliot picked from the bench a wet glass x-ray plate. "Lady Sarah Pledge." He held it against the light. "You see, on the left the chest is empty, the lung deliberately collapsed like a tennis-ball. On the right...you observe that cavity? Round and fuzzy-edged, like a full moon through the cloud. She has the disease on both sides. A girl can live without one lung, but not without two."

Nancy asked, "Why must this devil take only young lives?"

"Would you like to look upon the devil's face?" He indicated the microscope. "Focus the fine-adjustment screw. You see those little red rods?"

She drew a sharp breath. "Thick as a snowstorm."

"*Mycobacterium tuberculosis*, the germ which preoccupies us all here. Discovered by Robert Koch, a *Kreisphysicus* in the Black Forest. A country doctor, bored with rough journeys and loutish patients who turned to the intellectual delights of the microscope. That was seventeen years ago, and there are plenty of doctors who won't believe him. They put it down to anything from heredity to bad drains. It's not everybody who cares to shuffle their fixed ideas like a pack of cards, even to play a more exciting game."

Taking her elbow, he turned her towards a white bookshelf, on which squat bottles were arranged like the pickles and preserves at a grocer's. "Now see the devil's handiwork."

The bottle contained clear fluid with a cone of grey sponge. "He turns the lung into cheese. A patch dies, suffers caseation, breaks down to a cavity which fills with pus. I could load these shelves a hundred times with specimens like this, if I troubled to cut them from every corpse." Eliot replaced the bottle. "The art of treating phthisis is unhappily often the art of treating the dying. Well, that's a sound subject for any doctor to learn."

"You know who will die and who will not?" asked Nancy, alarmed for Baby.

"Yes, even those who are going to take so long over it they never notice the fact. The end's a rush – when their lungs are as useless as a pair of paper bags, when they're so wasted even the worms will go starving. There's no dignity about death. No more than a dog run down by a cart. You know why your sister's lucky? The bacillus ate into an artery, the red danger-flag was hoisted early. Time will heal her. She should be grateful for that fact, not resent it."

"When I've been to London, and seen Dr Crippen – "

"Go to London and see the Astronomer Royal, if you like, he'll be as much use."

"I know you think Dr Crippen's a quack, I know you're mad at me. But my father keeps cabling. He's getting very impatient."

"May I invite myself again to dinner?"

"No"

"Why?"

"Because you are taking advantage of me, Dr Beckett. I am here friendless and unoccupied. You press your company on me."

"I thought you seemed fond of it. But I suppose my company would never do among your set in America."

She looked away. "You're being unfair."

"I'm a realist, like all doctors." He changed the subject by lifting from the laboratory bench a shallow china dish, half-filled with green lumps in a yellow fluid. "This has a better chance against phthisis than any tricks from your Dr Crippen."

"What is it?"

"Mouldy bread. I often ride round the estate with my father, gathering the duke's rents. I get to know the humble families, with whom of course the duke is as unacquainted personally as those of Hottentots. I was fascinated with their folk-remedies. They brew foxglove tea for dropsy, just like the Shropshire country people Dr William Withering was sharp enough to notice a century ago. Now of course *that* drug's been extracted and prescribed as the heart tonic, digitalis."

He spoke with warmth. Nancy felt disconcerted that he cared more for his profession than for her, and instantly felt irritated at herself.

"There's an old country rhyme about the foxglove leaf," he told her. "*The rapid pulse it can abate, The hectic flush can moderate.* You see? The cleverest man can always learn from the ignorant."

Eliot took a pinch of the slimy green bread. "They put this on septic wounds and boils, centuries before anyone had ever heard of germs. There's something in the mould which kills bacteria, I'm sure of it. Perhaps I can extract the chemical, and invent a wonderful machine to blow it into the cavities? Meanwhile, we must do with fresh air. I'm afraid that I'm keeping you from your sister," he dismissed her. "And I have a morning's work to do."

Before the mirror in her hotel room that evening, Nancy vindicated herself mentally while Maria-Thérèse silently dressed her hair. In New York, she knew sufficient young men for the companionship of a different one every week. All those Bobbies, Ollies, Charlies, Clarries — everyone's name that season seemed to end with "ie" — with their automobiles and long fur coats, their games and their hunting, their private jokes and private language composed of the latest slang from the track, the ring, even the underworld. Everyone she knew talked intently about one another, and never of anything else.

Some were vastly rich, some almost penniless. It was impossible to say in New York, when a young man would spend a thousand dollars equally carelessly if it was his last. Most of them were pleasing, or tried hard to please. Any of them would have married her, some had asked. It never crossed Nancy's mind to accept them. Her friends whispered their terror of marriage, of placing themselves overnight in ultimate intimacy with a man who was largely unknown. Nancy was more scared of being bored.

Dr Beckett had an overpowering attraction. He was the sort of man she had always imagined herself attracted to. Indulging seriously in this fancy meant forcing herself through social railings, which kept common people from a life which nobody doubted as the most delightful and fulfilling a young woman might enjoy. Or was she caged, an animal artificially kept alive in a zoo? She concluded she was right to snub Eliot. Her father was already distraught over Baby. It would be too much, coming home engaged to a penniless doctor of no family and few graces, a foreigner who wore atrocious clothes. Then she admitted that Eliot differed from the men she knew as red meat from water-ice.

Her introspection was broken by cries through the tall open windows. She looked across the hotel garden with its neatly-raked gravel and string of red and blue fairylights between the cherry and plum trees. Two men were running towards the path climbing the cliff, waiters in their shirt sleeves, an unthinkably irregular sight in the well-ordered Grand Hotel.

"*C'est un accident, mademoiselle,*" exclaimed Maria-Thérèse. Nancy immediately thought of Eliot, which annoyed her again. Taking her wrap, she went down to the garden. Through the back gate came half-a-dozen men with the hotel proprietor, followed by a blue-uniformed gendarme shouting at others to keep their distance. They bore one of the hotel's green shutters, on which lay Lady Sarah Pledge.

Nancy stopped, horrified. The party hurried past. The face was smashed and glistening with blood. The skull was crushed, pale brain exuding over her ear. One arm was twisted like a half-snapped twig. She wore the morning's white dress, she had lost her shoes, the skirt rose above her right knee to show her pink garter, until one of the bearers with sensitive delicacy smoothed it down to her feet.

# 6

"Of course it wasn't an accident," Eliot said. "You couldn't fall from that point without putting your mind seriously to it. Dr Pasquier's influence in Champette being even stronger than an English nobleman's, the Swiss authorities must say what they're told. It was all a matter of being buried in consecrated ground. Though to the *raison d'être* of any funeral, it doesn't matter if they're buried in a rubbish-heap."

"She must have known more of her condition than she let on," said Nancy.

"Most of them do."

"Yet she used to complain only that it stopped her hunting."

"Suicide's unusual in phthisical cases," Eliot remarked thoughtfully. "They're a tough army, who won't surrender. Remember, *spes phthisica*."

It was ten days later, a hot August morning, the red cross flag flapping languidly when a breeze could stir itself, the sunlight brilliant on the blue and white striped awnings of the balconies. They were alone in the laboratory. Eliot was dropping into a square enamel dish of carbolic the reddish-smeared glass slides he had been examining under the microscope. Nancy stood with hands clasped, parasol dangling. She met him there most days, when he had finished the Röntograms.

"Have the Earl and Countess gone back to England?" he asked.

"They left the hotel early this morning."

Monsieur Mittot had embalmed the body with pride. The undertaker had studied in Paris. He was a boon bestowed on Champette by the sanatorium, like trade for the shops. Sallow, fat, dark, heavily moustached, in crumpled sad black serge, he had hung about the Grand Hotel once the

Earl and Countess arrived by overnight express to Basle, with their valet, lady's maid, frock-coated secretary and the British consul acquired at Lausanne. Not even the valet took notice of him. Monsieur Mittot expected the aristocratic corpse to be shipped in a splendid coffin, most rich families paying the fare home of their dead. But he was ignorant of a tradition in the Earl's family, since Wellington's Peninsular War, of being buried where they fell. The Earl thought the shuttling of corpses by railway vulgar.

Lady Sarah was buried in the English cemetery at Lausanne, among Indian Civil Servants and City men's widows. The consul murmured to the Earl in compensation that the chaplain had been to Eton. The small, bleak church was filled with patients from the Clinic Laënnec fit enough to take the special train, weeping and coughing into their blue-glass bottles. Such emotion had startled Eliot. They shrugged at death, when it pushed past them in the corridors. A suicide – nobody believed the accident excuse – was different, real death. Dying from phthisis was the penalty of losing the game everyone played.

"When are you leaving Switzerland?" Nancy asked Eliot, as he dropped the last slide into the disinfectant.

He began washing his hands under the swan-necked tap. "Wednesday of next week."

"Taking a vacation before starting your politicizing?"

"This has been my vacation. Overpaid and overfed, the work demanding the abilities only of an earnest medical student. On my heels arrives Dr Hamish McCorquodale of Aberdeen University. A bachelor, the son of the manse – a cleric's offspring – he has sent in advance a packing-case weighty with medical books. He'll entertain you as adequately as me. Perhaps he'll bring his bagpipes."

"Can't I do any work in the clinic? You know how I've longed to help the patients, instead of walking among them like some smug neutral in a war."

"Why not come with me to London? Together we'll mount the quest for Crippen."

"Together? Imagine the gossip!"

"Oh, everyone gossips all day about the pair of us."

Nancy looked alarmed. "How can I leave Baby? She was awfully upset over Lady Sarah. Her temperature's up a whole degree."

"It'll be down in a month. She'd hardly notice you'd gone. I've never known a more dutiful relative than you, Nancy. If you don't take a holiday, you'll develop melancholia. Why not?" He was standing close to her. "Perhaps you'll return with Dr Crippen's magic, to put the clinic out of business and bring upon Monsieur Mittot richly deserved ruin."

"I cannot leave Baby," she repeated firmly.

He clasped her. "Self-sacrifice is so common in women, men take it for granted. It's not often combined with intelligence and determination. You're a woman with all the qualities I admire. Particularly when you've no more need to exercise them than to practise frugality."

This compliment seeming to come from the brain rather than the heart, she was surprised when he kissed her for the first time. She felt it seemly to offer a mild struggle.

"I'll see what Baby says," she told him breathlessly.

Baby was enthusiastic. "Go to London and see the King," she urged. "Go right now, before the fog comes down. They say in November you can't see across the street. How will I know a month's passed, darling? Counting days is like counting the telegraph poles passing the window of your train."

Maria-Thérèse decided it. When Nancy suggested a month at home in Paris, she shed tears, fell on her knees, grabbed her mistress' hand and kissed it. Nancy was startled that her maid should be equally bored at Champette. It had never crossed her mind to ask.

Nancy bought tickets from Thomas Cook's, beside the handsome Lausanne post office. A day's journey to Basle connected with the overnight express which ran up the Rhine to Strasbourg, Metz and Lille to Calais. She arranged drafts at the English-American Bank, and bought English books for the journey from Theodore Sack's shop in the Rue Central. Her father replied to her cable by offering a blank cheque for the rights of Dr Crippen's cure.

Eliot said nothing of his own travelling plans. He was preoccupied preparing his patients for Dr McCorquodale. On the Wednesday morning, Nancy crossed the square surrounded by staff from the hotel and the proprietor, so anxious to secure her return that he had been hovering outside her room with the assiduousness of Monsieur Mittot outside those of guests with dying relatives. The train was already in the station, stubby engine pluming smoke into the clear air. There was no sign of Eliot. Nancy looked anxiously up and down the narrow wooden platform. A minute before departure he appeared in his usual Norfolk jacket and a wide-brimmed brown trilby, over one shoulder a stone-coloured English raincoat and a canvas rucksack. Round his neck was a long brown knitted muffler, in his hand a cheap suitcase cracked at one corner and secured with a length of rope. He greeted Nancy casually, strolled past her and climbed into the third-class coach.

The train puffed down the mountain. Nancy grew angry. She had imagined socially difficult scenes between Eliot and herself on the journey but she had never imagined that he would travel third. Even Maria-Thérèse sitting opposite was going first-class to Lausanne.

"Haven't you any more baggage?" Nancy demanded, approaching him at Lausanne station.

"I should like to have. But this is the limit of my possessions." Eliot's eyes turned to Maria-Thérèse, fussing over the removal of Nancy's portmanteau from the van. "I found a pleasant line in my Swiss Baedeker – 'The enormous weight of the large trunks used by some travellers not infrequently causes serious injury to the porters who have to handle them.' People condemn men to a lifetime of invalidism, because they insist on moving round the world with sufficient hats and gloves and boots for a change every day."

"If you are going to draw morals from everything you see, I shall avoid you all the way. Candidly, I think you're a fool. You could easily afford to travel like a gentleman."

"I agree. Had I not better uses for my earnings than paying a bribe to discomfort."

"If a hair shirt were the price of sable, you would still buy yourself one from your haberdashers."

Eliot grinned. "Perhaps you're right. You'll be staying at the Savoy?"

Nancy nodded. "It's nine-and-sixpence a night, but there's a bath with the room. I'm surprised at that in England."

"An Englishman does not care to pay extra for a bath. He regards it as a necessity, not a luxury. I think the Savoy's preferable to the Cecil next door, which may have a thousand rooms but is growing dreadfully shabby. My ducal connections are useful in advising on such things."

"Where exactly is your Camden Road?" She had his address in her diary.

"Against the main railway lines north, near the Cattle Market and Pentonville Jail. There's always room for me at No 502. I lodged there since I was a medical student at St Bartholomew's."

"Shan't you want to see your parents?"

"They're attending the Duke in Scotland. It's barely a month since the Glorious Twelfth, and their gun-barrels are still hot. Grouse, you know," he explained.

She dropped her voice. "When may I see you?"

"The Savoy at eleven, the morning after our arrival?"

"If you're showing me the sights, I insist on paying for the excursions. I'm sure you've far, far better use for your money than that."

"I shan't be in the slightest embarrassed, when you feel in your handbag at Madame Tussaud's. The changing of the guard is viewed free."

Nancy did not see Eliot when they left the crowded Lausanne train at Basle. She dined in the station restaurant, which had a star in Baedeker. She supposed he had satisfied himself with a *casse-croûte* and a bottle of beer. She noticed him on the platform only as she was handing her ticket to the conductor of her *wagon-lit*.

"I shall feel awful, you sitting up all night," she said with concern.

"I've slept on a hard chair often enough, during night duty in the receiving room at Bartholomew's."

"We'll meet on the *quai* at Calais?"

"I trust not. Six in the morning is not a social hour. There's a customs examination at the French frontier, but as I doubt you're travelling with tobacco or cigars the *visite* will be lenient."

She boarded the blue sleeping-car, its inside subdued hues of mahogany, brass and pink-shaded lamps. It was always exciting to take possession of an ingeniously-fitted sleeping-compartment. The smooth white linen sheet of her bunk was turned down, she found the washbasin slid neatly behind a mahogany panel, she admired herself in the gilt-scrolled glass, discovered the water carafe which was protected from rattle by an upholstered bracket, the panel of sponge-rubber for a watch at the bed head. She turned a hinged brass handle expecting to find a wardrobe, and was looking into the empty compartment next door.

She rang the bell.

"*Mademoiselle desire quelquechose?*" The conductor was a sallow young Frenchman in khaki jacket and kepi, with a military moustache.

"*Donnez un tour de clef à la porte, s'il vous plait,*" she directed severely.

"*Je regrette, mademoiselle,*" he excused himself hastily, producing master-key on chain from his trouser pocket. "*Ce compartiment n'est pas occupé.*"

"*Moment —*" Nancy held up her hand. "*Parlez-vous anglais?*"

"Certainly, mademoiselle."

"Can you sell me a ticket for that berth to Calais?"

"Of course, mademoiselle." The receipt book was already from his jacket pocket. "One hundred and twenty-five francs."

"Listen — you recall the English gentleman I spoke to on the steps?" He nodded. "He is in the third class. Can you find him before the train starts?" He nodded again. She handed him the gold and silver coins, adding three francs for himself. "But will you please tell the gentleman this. That the compartment is empty, and that I have bribed you with a franc to let him occupy it free of charge all the way to Calais." Eliot would prefer to stand all night in the corridor, rather than sleep in luxury she had paid for. "All this will go no further, of course," she added reassuringly to the conductor.

He grinned and saluted. "*Entendu, mademoiselle.*"

She noticed he did not bother to lock the communicating door.

She sat on the bunk, still in her coat and hat, equally frightened that Eliot would fall for the ruse or that he would not. There was an unsubtle knock from the corridor. Eliot was outside, with his raincoat, rucksack and suitcase.

"I say, what a bit of luck," he said heartily. "I really wasn't relishing a night among people eating garlic sausage and young children of amazing energy. These railway officials are dreadfully corrupt, you know. But it was quick of you to take it up." The train was sliding from the station.

Nancy smiled. "We Yankees are sharp."

"I'll turn in, as we're up early."

"Yes, do. Sleep well."

He found the unlocked door before the train had shrieked through the station at Mulhouse. In the morning, on the gusty quay at Calais, he remembered that he owed her for the conductor's franc.

# 7

"It'll be over there. Number 272. On the corner of Oxford Circus, opposite Peter Robinson's the drapers."

"But I'm breathless!"

"Come on! While the bobby's holding up the traffic."

"You treat the fair sex quite horribly."

"All Englishmen do. We expect our women to ride like express trains and dance like butterflies, to organize our domestics with the efficiency of General Kitchener, to comfort us with the tenderness of Héloise, and to laugh at our jokes like a music-hall audience."

It was four in the afternoon of Friday, September 17, 1909. When they had reached England the previous morning, the sun gave the cliffs of Dover the sheen of an iceberg. Now the weather had changed to a malignant misty drizzle, which soaked its way through garments with the persistence of mites through cheese, and steadily cleansed the stagnant chimney-smoke of its soot for deposit on starched collars and elaborate hats.

Eliot seemed to Nancy patriotically proud of this perversity in the weather. She held an umbrella, the other hand gathering her skirt from the slimy roadway as he seized her elbow.

The London traffic was its most chaotic of the century, horsepower competing with horse. The nimble two-wheeled hansoms, the roomier four-wheeled "growlers", the smart coupé "fly" hired from the livery stable (seven-and-sixpence one horse, twelve-and-sixpence two), were being jostled from the streets by the taximeter motorcabs, far faster despite the 20 miles per hour speed limit. The horse-drawn omnibuses were being ignored for the scarlet motor ones of the London General Omnibus Company, to be stopped anywhere, the "garden seats" on the open tops advertised as freely patronized by ladies.

Stage-coaches to Hampton Court or the races churned amid excursion motors carrying a guide for the "trippers". Motor cars, electric or petrol, were hireable at five pounds a day. Everywhere dodged the enthusiastic, sporty cyclist. With its electric tramways and the underground "Tube", Eliot told Nancy imposingly, London was the most convenient of cities for getting about – so long as you had no necessity to cross the road.

Still flagrantly grasping her arm, Eliot hurried Nancy along the far pavement. Number 272 was on the sweep of Oxford Circus, a doorway between a furrier's and a trunk-maker's. The lobby inside had mustard-painted stone walls, a wooden staircase going up, an iron one spiralling into the black basement. It did not seem to Nancy likely headquarters for a man with the cure of the disease which terrified the world.

Eliot ran his eyes down a painted list of firms with offices above.

"No Munyon's. And I looked them up in Kelly's Directory this morning." He peered at the lowest line. "That's freshly painted. Perhaps they've moved?"

He took her elbow again to a shop he had noticed on the corner, marked with gold letters OTTOMAN TOBACCONISTS.

"You can find everything about any district from a tobacconist. Its craving is common to all classes of the world, but it's so uncomplicated an article to purchase everyone stops to justify their visit with a gossip."

The shop was tiny and aromatic. A wall of drawers like a druggist's were labelled *Raparee, Navy Plug, Havana Perfectos*. On the counter were glass boxes of round or oval cigarettes, a blue jar marked *High Dry Toast Snuff*. A black boy in turban and curly-toed slippers stood in eternal plaster deference. The Oriental atmosphere stopped with the proprietor, a wizened, pale Cockney with gold-rimmed glasses.

"Munyons?" he repeated in a thin voice. "They've gorn." He drew a finger across his scrawny throat. "Gorn bust."

Eliot and Nancy exchanged frowns. "Do you know a Dr Crippen?"

"Know 'im, sir? I'll say. The Doctor," he specified with respectful familiarity. "Such a nice polite gentleman. Never smoked, mind you – said it upset 'is heart and digestion. Never took drink, neither, except for a glass of beer what you and I'd 'ardly notice, sir. Used to come in and buy Turkish cigarettes for Miss Le Neve."

"Who might she be?" asked Nancy.

The tobacconist looked startled. "Ain't you one of them Yankees? Funny, so was the Doctor. Though o' course you'd 'ardly think it, 'e spoke quite like an English gentleman. You one of 'is family?" Nancy shook her head hastily. "Miss Le Neve was 'is typist, pretty young thing, always neat, luverly dark 'air. Mind, when the doctor's business went through the sieve, you could 'ave knocked me dahn wiv a fevver. Always seemed flush wiv the bees and 'oney, the doctor. Money," he explained, responding to Nancy's blank look.

"My business with Dr Crippen is urgent," Eliot stated. "Where can I find him?"

"Search me, sir. 'E used to talk of an orfice what he 'ad in Shaftesbury Avenue, opposite the Palace Theatre. P'raps 'e's gorn 'ome to roost?"

"Could you describe him?" Eliot asked.

The atmosphere chilled. "You the rozzers?"

"Of course I'm not the police," Eliot told him impatiently. "I'm a fellow doctor."

The shopman's narrowed eyes relaxed. "Well, 'e's 'ardly bigger than Little Tich, when 'e ain't dancing on the tips of 'is boots." Everyone in London knew the music-hall comic with boots as long as himself. "About forty-odd, I'd say, pink as a shrimp. Sandy 'air, bit bald, moustache. Dressed neat, even smart. Wears glasses like mine. 'E's one of them people you 'ardly takes notice of, even when they're speaking to you."

"Do you know where he lives?" enquired Nancy.

"Not the faintest, madam. I don't even know if 'e's got a trouble and strife." She assumed this meant a wife. "P'raps 'e's gorn 'ome to America?"

"Well? What do we do now?" she asked Eliot in disappointment, on the pavement outside.

"What everyone does when stymied in England. Have a cup of tea."

"Yes, lets! My friends are always talking about Rumpelmayer's."

"Rumpelmayer's? Ridiculously extravagant. Here's a Lyons teashop."

It was crowded with shoppers, men in bowlers and top hats, women in broad-brimmed, flowered or feathered millinery, glistening umbrellas at their sides, parcels round their feet. The customers sat on cane-seated chairs at marble-topped tables, while white-aproned, lace-capped waitresses served the teapots, the plates of buttered toast and the cream pastries from stout wooden trays.

Eliot searched for a place. "The weather's too miserable for tea." He grasped her arm again.

"Where are we going?" She sounded alarmed as he marched her round the corner.

"For a glass of English beer and a whet of German sausage."

The sign bore a golden crown over a Tudor rose. Eliot pushed open the door with a panel of green-tinted glass embossed, *Rose & Crown Ales Beers Stouts Wines From The Wood.*

"It's a saloon!" she objected forcefully.

"Perfectly respectable women pub it these days," he assured her airily. "There's nothing to fear, if you avoid the awful claret and hock."

She protested, "Were I seen inside a place like this in New York, it would be in all the papers."

"What devilish delights accrue by sinking from the upper classes," he teased her.

The bar was small, its dark panelling splashed with brightly polished brass, a partition with decorative frosted glass separating it from the noisy public bar next door. A red-faced man in a curly bowler hat and canvas gaiters, who smelt of oats, sat against the wall with a thin one smoking a pipe of pungent shag. The appearance of so beautiful and well-dressed a female raised their startled eyes from half-finished glasses of beer, which they were contemplating with the placid melancholy of the British enjoying themselves.

Eliot sat her at a small round table in a corner of the sawdust-covered floor. He brought from the bar a plate with sliced sausage, a brandy-and-soda and a glass of beer. She winced as she sipped it. "Two penn'oth of half and half," he explained. "Ale mixed with porter."

"At home, we wouldn't use this to drench horses."

"It sustains the working classes as faith the Church."

"I was educated that drink was an immutable evil. In the hands of the masses, naturally."

"How can a fellow-countryman of Falstaff contemplate a thought so mean? Oh, I suppose it makes a few beat their wives and gives a few more hobnail livers. One of your first failures as a doctor is making people do what's good for them. Everyone knows that cigars, pipes and cigarettes stunt the growth and rot the lungs, but who renounces a single whiff? Mankind is hell-bent on its own destruction. The German mind-doctors call it 'Thanatos'. The death instinct, as much part of us as our bones."

"That's nonsense," she told him spiritedly. "Everyone at the sanatorium submissively watched the wasted months and years pass by, in a desperate quest for life."

"The human mind doesn't know itself. No more than the complacent lady of the house knows what happens in the darkened attic bedrooms of her servants."

"Baby has not the slightest desire to die."

Eliot looked uncomfortable. In the cheerfulness of London he had overlooked the ailing sister.

"We'll hunt the Crippen," he said, to cover the gaffe. "Though I suspect his miracle cure as valueless as Mother Seigel's Syrup – advertised as indiscriminately effective against scurvy, syphilis, piles, gout, blackheads and pimples. Or Hanress' Electric Corset at five-and-sixpence, for the relief of hysteria and dyspepsia and the healthy development of the female chest. People never spend money so recklessly as on their sweethearts, their dogs or their health."

"My father believes in Dr Crippen's Tuberculozyne," she said firmly.

"A man shrewd enough to make a million dollars is generally a bigger fool over his health than a navvy. Because he can't submit to the notion of doctors knowing more than he does. He's prey to a quack like the worm to the goose."

Eliot gulped his brandy. "We'll track Munyon's to Shaftesbury Avenue. It's the new street which cuts through Soho – a rookery of French and Italian cooks, waiters, tailors and cakemakers, but the restaurants are cheap. I'll take you there tonight for dinner," he informed her.

"I may have other plans."

"That would be dreadfully foolish of you."

"Eliot, you bestow contempt as other men flattery."

"I don't. A doctor is incapable of contempt. The infinite weaknesses of human nature are his sympathetic study. You mistake it for candour. That's the quality a doctor must always direct upon himself, if kindness sometimes deflects it from the patient. Afterwards, you must come and see my lodgings. It's not much of a place, but I've a pianola."

"You've a nerve," she told him sharply. "Asking a lady unchaperoned to a gentleman's apartment."

"No one else would know," he assured her casually. "No one there would care. I live among people who share my view that conventional morality is a combination of hypocrisy, fright, and a sound feminine instinct for keeping the goods untouched in the shop window until saleable at the best price."

"If that's the view of your friends, I've no wish to meet them." He was alarmed. She had angry, pink spots on her cheeks. "Are you inviting me to play the loose woman? Or are you telling me I am one? I've suffered sufficient indignity for one day."

He grabbed her hand as she rose. "Nancy, forgive me," he asked submissively. "I talk so often for effect, but I have the tragic disability of too often believing what I say. The life I have set for myself, my unconventional ideas, my ideals – I suffer doubts sometimes that they're nothing but a passing irritation with the society I was born into. An ungrateful one, as it reared me so generously."

She stood staring down at him. He still held her hand.

"Am I Hamlet, or young Lupin Pooter from *The Diary of a Nobody*? Though I suppose they were both ridiculous, in their own way. I love you, Nancy. I loved you since I walked into the waiting-room at the sanatorium last spring." He smiled shyly. "The Rose and Crown gives hardly the most fitting echo to my sentiments. When we came in, I'd no more expectation of uttering them than my dying words. My political ambitions resolved me to stay a bachelor for years. Though *un foyer sans feu, une table sans pain, une maison sans femme* are all equally joyless, as the Bretons say."

She sat down slowly. The man in the curly-brimmed bowler had just finished a comic story, and the other was choking with laughter.

"Though perhaps you'd be right getting rid of me," he said with detachment. "It's the privilege of intelligent men and women to see the consequences of their passions, even if they often prefer to go blind. God gives us love, according to Tennyson. But love can give us murder, suicide and war. Love demands thinking about quite as much as money or health. But people don't. Even while they're enjoying it, they give it as little thought as their work on a bank holiday."

She clasped his fingers on the glass-ringed table-top. "I love you, Eliot," she said quietly. "I was brought up like every girl I know, in the same prison of conventions. It's scary, suddenly finding yourself outside."

Eliot reflected she looked like a child. The worldliness which frightened him had vanished.

"Will you come to me?" he asked timidly.

"I must go back to the hotel first. I must bring the sponge."

She had used the sponge on the silken thread, soaked in quinine, on the express from Basle. She had heard of it in whispers from girls in the corners of drawing-rooms and dinner-tables in New York. Her friends assured her that absolutely everyone used the sponge, it was as safe as a brick wall. It was so much more satisfying than the disgustingly messy manner of men diverting the stream of life at the final moment into the air like a public fountain. She had been fitted with the sponge by a respectable doctor in a tailcoat, who practised downtown in Washington Square, who Nancy told her father she was consulting for a sore throat.

Eliot said nothing, but gripped her hand tightly. Then he announced cheerfully, "We've work to do," and stood up.

They easily found the offices in Shaftesbury Avenue, but Munyon's had not leased rooms there since 1905. A grey woman in black bombazine with a pince-nez, supervising a cramped room of busy, bent-backed young typists, remembered Dr Crippen. He had left Munyon's to become consulting physician to the Drouet Institute for the Deaf at Marble Arch.

"The Drouet Institute!" Eliot groaned loudly, outside in Shaftesbury Avenue. "The devilish invention of a drunken Parisian doctor. Lead plasters, impregnated with turpentine, camphor, Spanish fly – stick them behind your ears, and you'll hear like a hare. He advertised in all the newspapers and on the sides of the buses. It was nothing but a cruel swindle on the deaf. They spent their shilling on rubbish, rather than having a proper aural examination from a doctor who'd demand guineas which they hadn't got."

Eliot continued warmly, taking her elbow across the road, "A murderous swindle. Some poor man died from a brain abscess, and the coroner's remarks put the Institute out of business. The patient deserved a statue. He saved the world more unnecessary suffering than most physicians. Not a handsome credential for your Dr Crippen, is it?"

Nancy that afternoon had become abruptly less interested in Dr Crippen.

# 8

The last Sunday in September was warm. The coals sat on their sticks and paper unlit in the well-blacked grate. A small iron kettle boiled on a gas ring in the hearth. A brown teapot with a broken spout, a pair of large white cups and the milk-bottle, stood on a dented tin tray thrust among papers and books strewn across a crimson chenille cloth on the table. A loud-ticking, circular metal alarm clock, between a pair of pied Staffordshire spaniels on the narrow iron mantelpiece, indicated four o'clock.

The room had the easygoing student air of a man with no one to impress. A black iron bed with a bright patchwork quilt stood against one wall, a worn horsehair sofa faced a chintz-covered, wing-backed armchair across a bearskin hearth rug. The bookcase was inadequate, its contents spilling haphazardly on the floor. The concession to decoration was a tawny picture, which a close look interpreted as barges in the Thames estuary at sunrise.

The pair of tall first-floor windows looked on an ill-cut lawn with rusty croquet-hoops, surrounded by thick laurels, berberis and box. The house was one of the squat grey-brick villas, which with turreted and battlemented Gothic dwellings lined the Camden Road. Outside the everlasting clank of electric trams merged with the nightly bellowing and baaing from the vast Metropolitan Cattle Market across the railway lines.

Nancy sat on the sofa in a plain charcoal dress, intently darning Eliot's sock with a wooden mushroom.

"Would you like a slice of Dundee cake? Fresh yesterday from the Aerated Bread Company."

"Fine."

Eliot fetched a basin of lump sugar from a tall cupboard containing files, more books, shoes, ties and spare bedding. "Another tune?"

"I guess my appetite's sated for Offenbach, Strauss and – may I say so? – your Sir Arthur Sullivan. Why not play yourself?"

"The piano is to me an instrument as mysterious as the ouija board," he apologised. "I simply enjoy watching the rippling keys as the music unwinds."

The pianola stood in the corner, the rolls which Eliot hired from the Music Roll Exchange in Oxford Street shared the cupboard. "My conscience disallows keeping a servant, but I've no objection to hiring a ghost as my musical valet. By the way, there's a couple of fellows coming. Did I mention it?"

Nancy looked up sharply from her darning. "I don't want to be found here."

"They find more shocking things in the world to worry them than a chap alone with a girl."

She put down the sock. "Do you know the only real disagreeableness of revolutionaries? To be entirely insensitive about the feelings of others."

Eliot grinned. "I'm sorry, my dear. But honestly, they'll take no more notice of you than of Emma."

She was the maid-of-all-work, with crumpled stockings and lank hair, raised in an orphanage. Eliot thought her barely fit to look on the outside of the asylum door. The only other occupant of No 502 Camden Road was Frau Ebert, the German housekeeper. When Nancy asked after the householder, Eliot seemed uneasy and explained that Herr Lansdorff was a bachelor of utmost respectability from Hamburg, who had paid London the compliment of living there, but was obliged to be often abroad on his business as furrier.

"Don't go," he implored. "They're nothing to be frightened of. And we've so little time."

Nancy was returning to Switzerland the following Wednesday. She was staying only two weeks instead of four. Baby's daily cable to the Savoy the previous Friday had complained of "feeling a bit cheap." Nancy at once wired Dr Pasquier. He replied that the temperature was a little raised.

There was no cause for concern. Miss Grange was obviously fretting for her sister.

"But I'll be back in London, dearest, sure I will, once Baby's settled," Nancy promised, as Eliot poured kettle into pot.

He made no reply. He knew the fragility of their friendship. It was like the solid ice bridges which formed across Swiss gullies in winter, and in summer might never have been there.

To Nancy, it was a freakish, unthinkable adventure. Once started, she gave herself to making the most of it. They spent all day and much of the night in each other's company – she insisted primly on leaving for the Savoy at midnight, though he assured her the hotel was worldly enough not to imagine the world full of Cinderellas. Eliot showed her with equal pride Buckingham Palace, St Paul's, and his own ancient hospital of St Bartholomew's in Smithfield. At the Tate Gallery, he had objected angrily to Luke Fildes' *The Doctor*. "Grossly sentimental," he exclaimed. "Look at that miserable working-class couple, cowed while the magician meditates over their unconscious child – they couldn't even afford a bed for the poor thing. Medical care is as much a *right* of the people as pure drinking water. *That* doctor clearly hasn't the slightest notion of what's wrong with his patient, anyway."

Nancy thought the painting lifelike and touching. They did not take tea with Miss Nightingale, but stared across the street at her house in Mayfair.

Nancy found Eliot hardly a pleasure-going young man. He took her to Pinero's *Mid-Channel* at the St James's Theatre, in the cheap pit when she was accustomed to the front stalls. They had "dinner from the joint" at small, busy restaurants for eightpence, or tried Appendrodt's German eating-houses, or Slater's tea rooms, or splashed a florin on a dozen oysters at Sweeting's in Cheapside. That Nancy expected anything but a life of unexciting domesticity with him seemed beyond Eliot's contemplation. That she had never been happier, she realised then and for the rest of her life.

"Who exactly are these people coming?" She took her cup of tea. She did not care for tea, but he showed no inclination to buy coffee.

"Political friends of mine. But don't expect wild-eyed men in kulak blouses with whiskers like a burst horsehair sofa and a bomb in their attaché cases. Mr Wince would pass for a prosperous and earnestly churchgoing cheesemonger. Mr Ruston was born upper-middle-class and will die upper-middle-class, a succession as certain in this country as the Crown passing from father to son."

He sat at the table, stirring his tea, long legs stretched out. "Fellows like Ruston embrace the proletariat like a wild gipsy mistress. They become horribly bloodthirsty. For their principles, they'd cut their mother's throat or dynamite their grandchildren's nursery. But they'd die before blowing on their tea or drinking their soup from the tip of the spoon. Ruston keeps a cook and would be deeply affronted if anyone hesitated in accepting his cheque. He'd never contemplate taking the five-shilling seaside excursion or living off bread-and-jam. Such people become equally boring to the class they own and the class they ape."

Nancy smiled. "You draw an unflattering self-portrait."

Eliot was surprised. "I don't find the middle-class distasteful. No more than I find the patient distasteful, rather than his disease. I operate on society intellectually, as I operate on a case. I wouldn't rush the barricades, no more than cut my throat if my patient failed to recover. Damn — !" Gesturing with political fervour, he spilt his tea over his papers. Mopping with a yellow silk handkerchief, he consoled himself, "The chapter needed rewriting, anyway."

"Why won't you ever let me read your book?" she complained.

"Wait. A woman who would cuddle a new-born baby would be disgusted by the sight of it being formed in the womb. You're privileged to learn my views from my conversation," he told her blandly. "The State has the same duty towards the health of its people as parents towards their infants. If I call my book *The Health of Nations*, I hope to startle people out of their prejudices like Adam Smith. Though as usual, they'll draw them over their heads like cowls."

The doorbell jangled. Emma showed up a tall, hollow-cheeked, fair-haired unsmiling man younger than Eliot, in a brown tweed suit with a yellow waistcoat, like a stockbroker off to the races. The other was short and fat, twenty years older, in shiny blue serge, with a pink face, sparse hair, a clipped moustache and steel-rimmed glasses askew a snouty nose. The young man had a fat manilla envelope and an Irish tweed hat, both of which he tossed on the table with an unconcern indicating familiarity with the room. Young Ruston glared aggressively at Nancy. Wince seemed amused. She continued darning the sock. "Miss Grange is from America," Eliot introduced her. The name meant nothing to either visitor. "She is the soul of discretion."

Both refused tea, sitting beside Nancy on the sofa. Ruston talked most, in a stockbroker's voice. Wince's was high-pitched, and he dropped his aitches. Both men stole glances at her.

"You couldn't have returned at a better moment," Ruston told Eliot earnestly. "You must have followed from the London papers the rough ride of Lloyd George's budget? He unveiled it last April, while the country shook in its shoes. From the outrage of the upper class over the new land tax, you'd imagine our firey little Welshman about to plunder the land like Hengist and Horsa in one."

"Got ter pay for the navy," piped Wince mockingly. "The floating bulwark o' the island, eh? A keel for a keel, one in the eye for the Kaiser."

"But the House of Lords is set to reject the budget?" Eliot stood on the bearskin, hands in pockets, looking solemn.

"Exactly what Lloyd George wants," Ruston told him. "There'll be an election on the issue before the Christmas decorations are cleared away, mark my words."

"Which'll do yer a bit o' good," added Wince. "The Liberals'll win, with the chance o' some Labour members bein' swept into Parliament by the tide."

"You and I, Eliot, know the election's like a sham battle on the stage at Drury Lane. Our object is to burn down the theatre and roast the people in it," remarked Ruston.

Nancy continued darning. Following the convolutions of British politics was wearying. She had met several lords in New York. They seemed kindly, perfectly mannered young men, who claimed an ignorance of politics as profound as of road-sweeping. Eliot had explained that the rejection of a Liberal budget by the House of Lords would be an event in British politics comparable with the inauguration of Jefferson Davis.

"It'll encourage the Holloway Labour Party, finding their Parliamentary candidate real flesh and blood. They've no more notion where Switzerland is than Swahililand," Rushton said contemptuously. "I've found a shop for your people's clinic." Eliot's face brightened. "An abandoned greengrocer's, a bit rotten inside, but I expect a practical fellow like you can fix it. There's a quarter's rent due, five pounds. I couldn't advance it. You know how difficult things are."

"For earning without spending, Switzerland's as useful as a polar expedition."

Ruston nodded towards the manilla envelope. "Need I emphasize those papers are for no eyes but your own?"

"Wot yer doin in London, love?" Wince had been rudely staring at Nancy from hair to toe.

Eliot replied for her, "Searching vainly for a Dr Crippen. Inventor of a remedy to cure her sick sister."

"Dr Crippen?" Wince equally rudely lit without Nancy's permission the large curly pipe he had been filling steadily with dark tobacco from a rubber pouch. "Oh, *I* know Dr Crippen. Lives up Camden Road, Hilldrop Crescent, I b'lieve. Leastways I knows *Mrs* Crippen better. She's a theatrical. Belle Elmore's 'er name on the boards." He struck a vesta. "Music 'all. Not that I've seen 'er on the posters. P'raps she tours the provinces? Short, flashy lady, bright fair 'air, peroxides it, I've no doubt. She ain't no spring chicken," he meditated, puffing a cloud of smoke. "But she's an 'andsome woman, I'll give 'er that. A proper Tartar in the shops along Brecknock Road, beating dahn the prices till yer'd think she'd a family ter feed on a farthing. Funny thing—" He nodded at Nancy. "She's an American, just like you."

To Eliot's eager questions he replied, "Crippen? A little bloke, mild as milk. Got a practice at the Yale Tooth Specialists, Albion 'ouse in Oxford Street. I knows that, a'cause 'e gave me one of 'is cards last week in Lipton's the grocers. Said if I'd trouble with me teeth 'e'd fix me in no time." Wince laughed. "Got an eye for business, that doctor."

The pair shortly left. Wince shook Nancy's hand heartily in a fog of tobacco smoke. Ruston's farewell was an intensely suspicious glance.

Eliot decided against ringing doorbells along Hilldrop Crescent that evening, when the householders would be settling to their suppers. He met Nancy at the Savoy Hotel the following morning. Their excitement was rekindled in the chase. It was tantalizing, fitting a face to the name exchanged the afternoon they met. They walked east along the Strand – the busiest street in London, connecting mercenary City to leisurely West End. At the foot of John Rennie's granite Waterloo Bridge, they turned north towards the crescent of the Aldwych and the new avenue of Kingsway, with the electric trains speeding tunnelled underneath.

Oxford Street that morning featured a regular entertainment upon the London pavements. They jumped to a crash of glass. A thin young woman in black, with a swirling feather boa and a fashionable hat as though a church bell had dropped on her, was vigorously breaking the window of a gentleman's hatter's with a small hammer. People shouted in alarm and rage. A red-faced workman in cap and spotted choker stood hands in pocket swearing hoarsely. Two shirtsleeved shop-assistants appeared horrified in the doorway. A small man in frock-coat and top hat tried to grab her, but jumped as she lunged with her hammer. Everyone shouted for the police.

An unhurried officer appeared through the traffic.

"Now then." His voice was father to naughty daughter, who had broken the china.

"Arrest me." Hers was Ellen Terry in the sleepwalking scene of *Macbeth*.

"Right you are. None of that there!" the policeman added fearsomely to a middle-aged woman in a black bonnet, who tried to slap the saboteur. "Come along 'o me to Bow Street."

She thrust out her wrists. "Handcuff me."

"Don't be barmy," said the policeman.

"A suffragette," observed Eliot, with his usual calmness towards extravagancies in human behaviour. The pair disappeared, the policeman holding the hammer like some item of regalia. The shop-assistants hastened to shutter the window and sweep the glass. "They use a toffee-hammer, you know, the sort that crack the slabs in sweet-shops. Does America breed such vigorous ladies?"

"Well, there was Susan B Anthony. She died about three years back."

"Susan B Anthony." Eliot quoted reflectively, " 'Men, their rights and nothing more. Women, their rights and nothing less.' They only got started here because Mr Gladstone didn't believe in women. Neither did Mr Disraeli, but he didn't believe in admitting it. Queen Victoria found them particularly objectionable."

"Surely, with Queen Victoria there was no room left in the country for a woman's movement?"

"Exactly. It must be most awkward, trying to be gooder than God in Heaven. But even a lost cause is worth believing in. Not that I've sympathy for martyrs. None at all. It's a form of political activity needing neither intelligence nor experience."

"Poor Joan of Arc. She really should have known better." Eliot smiled. "Here's Albion House – No 60."

It was an impressive four-storey cream-painted building, its tall paired windows above narrow balconies flanked by Doric columns and plaster heads. Opposite was Mudie's Select Circulating Library, which diverted and edified a million housewives. They walked up brown-painted stairs covered with patterned red linoleum. A door on the third floor announced from its frosted glass panel –

> *Dr Gilbert Mervyn Rylance*
> *Dr Hawley Harvey Crippen*
> *The Yale Tooth Specialists.*

Eliot pressed the bell.

The door was opened instantly by a peaky man about forty, in a worn blue serge suit and celluloid collar. "Dr Crippen?"

"No, his dental mechanic, sir. Are you a patient?"

"A professional colleague."

The door opened with a deferential sweep.

The room overlooked Oxford Street. It had expensive green-striped paper, green plush curtains and a thick Turkey carpet. The walls presented a pair of scarlet-sealed framed diplomas, and an etching of Sir Edward Poynter's four delicious nudes – one with a poorly foot – consulting Aesculapius.

At a green-baize covered table with telephone, typewriter, and pair of spikes bristling with paper, sat a good-looking woman in her mid-twenties, short, slim, pale, with big grey eyes, a longish straight nose and flat eyebrows. Her light brown hair was pinned high, she wore a navy serge dress. Eliot recognized her as Miss Le Neve from the tobacconist's description. He thought her mouth as sensual as a Hogarthian slut's.

With a subdued, deliberate air she apologized that Dr Crippen was at his other practice, Aural Remedies round the corner at Craven House. He saw dental patients at ten-thirty. Eliot and Nancy sat on wooden chairs, whose ragged copies of *John Bull* and *Tit-Bits* betokened the uneasy wait for terrors beyond a further glass-panelled door.

Dr Crippen appeared in a black frock-coat befitting his profession, with a bright blue shirt and a blue-spotted yellow tie in his high starched collar. A tiepin of chiselled glass the size of a schoolboy's marble optimistically passed for a diamond. His shoes were patent leather frosted with cracks; he threw out his feet as he walked, putting Eliot in mind of some music-hall comedian. He spoke quietly, with the tatters of a mid-Western accent, generously showing teeth which were a shining credit to the establishment. Eliot noticed that the bulging eyes behind the gold-rimmed glasses were grey, like his typist's.

He affably invited them through the inner door. Another to the right, painted *Dr Rylance*, emitted a steady, chilling gurgle of softly-running water. A door marked "No 91" faced them. Number 58 to their left led into a small ochre-washed room, its decorations oilcloth depictions in vivid scarlet, blue and yellow of a man with his head sliced across, a vast ear with its exposed inner workings of linked little bones, and the complete set of human teeth in a shining ring, like a grotesque galaxy.

A wooden cabinet stood in the corner, beside a marble-topped washstand on which Eliot recognized a conical measuring-glass and a medicine drop-bottle, ear speculas like confectioners' icing-cones, an angled metal tongue-depressor and a U-shaped spring for looking up noses. He saw no bowl nor bottle of disinfectant, nor even soap and water.

The metal ear-syringe struck him as large enough to stop a fire. Crippen politely invited Nancy to sit in his dental chair. There was nowhere else.

"So you're from New York, Miss Grange? Well, well! I hail from Coldwater, Michigan, myself. Though I've practised all over the States – Detroit two years, Santiago, Salt Lake City, St Louis, Philadelphia, up in Toronto." He asked Eliot, "You practise in London?"

"I practise nowhere at the moment, though I live near you, by the cattle market."

"You do? Cora – my wife – so often complains of the noise from the bullock lairs at night, and the sheep driven through the streets from the country. She's from New York as well," he informed Nancy, adding proudly, "She's on the stage, you know. Belle Elmore. You'll have heard of her."

"Dr Crippen, I have a sister in Switzerland sick with the phthisis." Nancy was impatient. Looking at him steadily, she explained, "I've come to you because I hear you've a preparation called Tuberculozyne."

"How strange you should mention it. Why, I was prescribing it only the other day. The patient suffered from scrofulous laryngitis, complicated by catarrhal pharyngitis and chronic rhinitis." Eliot noticed a glibness with impressive, if meaningless, medical terms. "She is now well on the way to recovery, I'm glad to say."

"I want some," Nancy demanded.

"Very unfortunately, that was my last sample."

"As one medical man to another, what is Tuberculozyne?" Eliot asked bluntly.

"I can't keep these formulas in my head," he lamented. "It has a basis of morphia. I perfected it from the prescription of a homoeopathic doctor I knew – he practises in Michingan, at Kalamazoo. I was trained at the Homoeopathic Medical School in Cleveland, Ohio, you know. Back in '84. Though I studied in London a while. The Royal Bethlem Hospital for the Insane. London's the greatest medical centre in the whole world, isn't it? Now my line's ear, nose and throat. I possess a diploma in the subject, from the New York City Ophthalmic Hospital," he ended in self-assertion. Eliot countered it by mentioning the Drouet Institute.

"Yes, I am a little deaf myself," Crippen replied without concern. Eliot had noticed he inclined his head to hear. "Now I must ask your pardon. I have patients waiting."

The doorbell had been ringing repeatedly. Eliot's grudging acceptance that this was truth, not an excuse to be rid of them, was strengthened by Crippen continuing genially. "But say, doctor – if you and the good lady are free, why not step across and take pot-luck tonight? No 39 Hilldrop Crescent. That's off the main road, towards Holloway Jail. My wife would just love to meet a fellow-countrywoman. Eight o'clock?"

"Yes," said Eliot shortly.

"You must be crazy," said Nancy as they descended the stairs.

"I want to find more about Tubercolozyne. If it's got morphia, it could be dangerous rather than merely useless," he told her sternly.

She signed. "Well I guess our Dr Crippen's just a fraud."

"One so transparent, it amounts to shining honesty. You must be disappointed for Baby?"

"Not really. I believed what you said about him all along. I had to see with my own eyes. There's my father to convince."

They reached busy Oxford Street.

"Besides, his wife sounds worth the trouble of meeting," Eliot suggested.

"I bet he's henpecked."

"Perhaps he enjoys it? Sometimes the male dominance in marriage is pleasurably reversed. He becomes passive, like the well-bred Englishwoman in sexual intercourse. Man-masochist mated to woman-sadist. There's a streak of both within all of us, like surliness and good humour, one or the other coming to the surface."

"Oh, Eliot! I do wish you wouldn't speak to me as though I was a lecture room."

# 9

Hilldrop Crescent made a broad sweep from Camden Road, at the crest of a hill which rose from the Midland Railway cuttings. The houses were mirror-image pairs, three storeys high, pale yellow brick, with a shallow slate roof, sharing the stack of a dozen chimney-pots. Number 39 was a left-hand house in the middle. Its low brick wall was topped with black iron railings caging a privet hedge. An oak gate between square brick pillars led to a front garden five or six paces long, shared with the neighbours and containing four London planes which were starting to turn.

Ten stone steps, flanked by a pair of cement urns sprouting marigolds, led to a portico six feet wide which shaded the brown-stained front door. Eliot was amused by the architect's embellishments to his cheap suburban villa. The tall window beside the front door had an ornamental balcony, those above were edged with elaborate moulding in cement. The next pair of houses were only a couple of yards away, a narrow passage leading past the tradesmen's entrance to the back garden.

Nancy wore an accordion-pleated navy skirt with a lace blouse, Eliot a blue serge suit and white shirt. Pot-luck in Holloway did not seem to invoke dressing. The bell instantly brought footsteps. To Eliot's surprise Crippen himself answered the door. A professional man practising even as a dubious dentist should afford a servant.

"Well, how nice! Belle will be so delighted you could make it." Crippen's affable greeting slid into the hushed remark, "Mr and Mrs Martinetti have just arrived, the famous music-hall comic singing act, you know. Retired now, and he's not altogether Al." His voice dropped further in professional confidence. "He has to be regularly dilated."

A narrow hallway with a well-varnished staircase and a hat-stand led to the parlour. It was all pink. Pink wallpaper, pink plush furniture, pink shades to the gas lamps, pink frames to the photographs on the piano, pink silk bows on the corners of the pictures and round the necks of the china cats on the pink-draped mantelpiece. At one side of the throatily roaring gas-fire sat a birdlike, bright-eyed woman in purple. Beside her stood a pale, grey, gloomy man, the comedian. Posed with one hand on a round, pink-draped table – which held a fan of theatre programmes, folded copies of the theatrical weekly *Era*, and a silver-framed picture of herself signed by Hana the theatrical photographer – was she to whom the room made a fitting compliment.

"So you're American too? Gee, it's great to meet you. I'm Belle Elmore." Advancing with arms wide apart, Mrs Crippen clasped Nancy tightly. "Which part are you from?"

"New York," Nancy told her, breathless.

"So am I! Well, I'll be darned." She had a Brooklyn accent, which Nancy had heard only from her servants. "New York!" She gazed wistfully at the pink-washed ceiling. "That's where I married Peter."

It seemed that Hawley Harvey became plain Peter at home, while everyone flattered Mrs Crippen with her stage name. She was short and fat, her face Eliot thought as exciting as the top of a steak-and-kidney pudding. Her hair was piled high in artificial curls of gold darkening towards the roots. Her broad mouth was painted, her nose flat and her eyelids heavy with mascara. She was about ten years younger than her husband. She wore a pink satin dress with pink lace at the neck and in tufts from the shoulders, so pinched at the waist that her corset whalebones seemed any instant liable to spring like a bear-trap.

Her bosom made a pink cushion to display her jewels. A semicircular brooch the size of an orange segment represented in gold and diamonds a rising fiery sun. Pearls dangled like bunches of grapes from her *décolletage*, a diamond pendant swung on a gold chain. She wore two diamond and two ruby rings on one hand, a diamond and wedding ring on the other, on her wrist was a gold watch.

The gold was not false, nor the stones paste, Eliot noticed with curiosity. That accounted for economy over a servant's wages.

She introduced Paul and Clara Martinetti. It was to be a nice little dinner, Belle explained expansively, which she had cooked herself. They were to dine in the breakfast room, immediately under the parlour, which looked across the front garden beside the steps. Eliot discovered this less pink, though the wallpaper was pink-striped and the clock-face on the mantel a pink china rose the size of the dinner-plates. He was finding the evening hugely amusing. Nancy was baffled. Was this first English home to receive her typical of the whole country? Or did all ordinary Americans abroad behave so oddly?

"I'm cold, Peter," complained Belle peevishly. The breakfast room had the only remaining open fire in the house, she had explained, sharing the flue with a kitchen-range next door, the rest was converted to gas. Crippen meekly took a black scuttle to the cellar opposite, where they heard him scraping up shovelfuls of coal. Clara Martinetti brought in roast shoulder of mutton, glistening potatoes under it. Crippen carved. He fetched a pitcher of beer from the cask they had noticed in the passage, asking Nancy thoughtfully if she preferred something else. She did. He produced a jug of lemonade, covered with muslin weighted by a fringe of coloured beads.

Belle meanwhile addressed them over the mutton like a star to reporters in her Drury Lane dressing-room. "I decided to enter the profession at seventeen. Cora Turner I was in those days. Then I met Peter, who fell in love with me like that." She snapped her fingers, ignoring the man silently slicing the meat at her elbow, "Sure, he had to marry me right away. But I said to him, Nancy – I may call you Nancy, Miss Grange?"

"Oh, please."

"I've got my artistic career to think of. Yes, sir. So I had my voice trained," she said, as if referring to her poodle. "Grand opera, that was my ambition. Carmen, Mimi in *La Bohème*, the Ring Cycle, y'know. And *Salome*. Especially Salome. I sure guess I could sing Salome a street better than Eva Tanguay right now in New York. They said in *Era* there was almost a riot, and it's been banned in Boston. She wears a stunning costume, seven veils with pearls, emeralds, rubies, diamonds, all as big as pebbles. Gee, I'd love to wear it," she said longingly, munching half a roast potato.

"But Peter just had to come across here in 1900 as manager for Munyon's." Crippen sat down to his own dinner. "And like a good, dutiful wife I followed him a month or so later. Yes, sir, that was the end of my singing lessons. *And* my career in opera. So I went on the vaudeville stage instead. Peter! You've not served the onion sauce."

Crippen hastily rose. So did Paul Martinetti, asking "Might I visit a certain room?" with a lack of embarrassment indicating the request as familiar.

Belle gave a generous smile. "Peter, put down that sauce and take Paul upstairs. Be sure you close the window. He doesn't want to take a chill. But London disappointed me," she continued solemnly. "Why, London *invented* the music hall! I'd my idea for my own sketch, I had writers and composers hired, I could have played the Alhambra, the Empire, the Coliseum, the Hippodrome, Collins', the Oxford. All I got was the Old Marylebone, the Euston Palace, the Camberwell. I've not worked for *three whole years*," she confessed indignantly. "But I got me a bad agent. Yeah, several bad agents. They did me out of money, that all. Oh, I'll get a break, it's often as long coming as Christmas, isn't it, Clara?"

"Belle does such wonderful work for us at the Music Hall Ladies' Guild," Clara Martinetti said admiringly.

"I'm the honorary treasurer," Belle told them proudly. "We've rooms in Albion House, just below Peter's surgery."

"Which Belle arranged at a *most* reasonable rent. I don't know what we'd do without Belle, honestly," Clara continued fondly. "She's at every meeting every Wednesday — aren't you Belle? She organizes our charity performances, our dance at the Cri — a really big do every February — and lovely tea-parties and fresh-air outings for the kiddies. As I always say to Mrs Ginnett and Lil Hawthorne and to Melinda May — she's our secretary and lives in Clapham — Belle's a real ball of fire." Belle simpered through this shower of adulation. Clara Martinetti explained to the visitors, "The Guild performs charity work among those of the profession who have fallen upon hard times."

Eliot hoped that few would fall upon times much harder than the three in the house. The Martinettis had faded without the limelight to the fragile paleness of dried flowers. Belle Elmore assumed the affectations and trappings of an actress, as a swindler enjoyed the fantasy of riches.

"Are you religious, Dr Beckett?" Belle asked with startling gravity, as the two men returned.

"I'm scientific, which is the same thing. I study reverently the process of life and death, and try to explain God in a chemical reaction."

"I've been a devout Catholic," she explained with the same solemnity, not seeming to hear him. "Four years now, since we moved into this house. I'm gonna convert my husband." She sounded as if still talking of converting the house to gas.

"My wife wants to choose my religion, as she does the pattern of my trousers," said Crippen humorously.

"Peter!" Belle seemed more outraged by impertinence to her than to God.

"Or his skirts." Clara Martinetti giggled. "When are you going to dress up for us again, Peter? Wearing Belle's wig, and paste on your moustache, you make a lovely lady with your figure."

Eliot's suppressed laugh at the image of the middle-aged doctor cavorting in his wife's clothes almost choked him on his roast potato. He wanted to leave the pathetic household as soon as polite. But there was the fruit pudding, then Belle said they must go upstairs for whist, adding graciously, "First I shall sing you some of my numbers."

Opening the parlour door, she explained, "Pink's my lucky colour, y'know. Lil Hawthorne at the Ladies' Guild has just gone and hung green wallpaper in her drawing-room. Gee, I told her, she'd got a real hoodoo there. She'll have bad luck, sure as fate. I won't have green in the house."

Belle sat on the pink-topped piano stool and sang *Aubery Plantagenet, the Hero of the Penny Novelette*. Then *He's a Naughty Naughty Boy*, followed by *In Sweet Ceylon*. Paul Martinetti rose and said he wanted to visit a certain room again.

The poor fellow has a urethral stricture, the late result of the clap, Eliot diagnosed. He wondered if his wife knew. The exertion of Belle's performance sent her down to the kitchen for a bottle of brandy. She poured Eliot a glass, drank one herself and had started another when Crippen returned with Paul Martinetti, and bending over Eliot asked almost inaudibly if he would care to see a certain room, too. They mounted the front stairs, Belle setting out cards on a collapsible baize-covered table.

On the landing, carpet regressed to red linoleum. Two upstairs doors were shut, through another Eliot glimpsed a capacious bath-tub surmounted by a shiny brass geyser. He saw a narrow stair ascended to servants' rooms above. Curiously drawing aside a net curtain in the lavatory, Eliot could see across thirty yards of back garden and the gas-lit rear windows of houses in Brecknock Road. Crippen waited solicitously outside.

Descending the stairs, Crippen volunteered, "I expect you'd like to talk about that preparation, Tuberculozyne, Dr Beckett?"

"Very much. Have you the formula?"

Crippen apologized in his soft voice, "It's the property of Munyon's Homeopathic Remedies, with whom I have severed my connection. I was obliged to resign because Professor Munyon considered that my wife's theatrical career diminished the dignity of his firm," he confided, Eliot suspected untruthfully. "But perhaps you've heard of Amorette, Dr Beckett? I invented it while manager of the Sovereign Remedy Company. A nerve tonic."

Eliot shook his head. The name suggested that the nerves it stimulated were erotic ones.

"Would you be interested in entering partnership with me?" Eliot's head jerked in surprise. "I'm greatly experienced in the marketing of medicine," Crippen asserted. "I can write an effective letter to a patient — whether satisfied or dissatisfied. I have quite a reputation for preparing advertising copy. And when the Drouet business failed, I acquired their mailing-list," he added stealthily. "I have £200 in the Yale Tooth Specialists — Dr Ryland contributes his experience, knowledge and skill, we split the profits fifty-fifty — which unfortunately leaves me short of capital for Amorette."

"No," Eliot told him.

"The remedies I have advertised through my professional life have given much benefit, Dr Beckett," he persisted. "I have testimonials — perfectly genuine testimonials — to prove it." He raised his bulgy eyes, staring plaintively through gold-rimmed glasses. "I guess I practise as honestly as any who prescribe remedies they know in their hearts to be useless."

Eliot struggled to be fair. Apart from digitalis for the heart, mercury for syphilis, codeine for a headache, no doctor gave any drug with sure effect. He wondered if Crippen flirted with the fantasy of being a serious physician, as Belle was wedded to hers of being a real actress.

"Perhaps Miss Grange," Crippen suggested, "who from appearance strikes me as a lady of substance — "

"Your assessment is perfectly correct. Miss Grange has a fortune. She has also a sharp Yankee eye for a swindler."

"It was impolite of me, bringing Miss Grange's name into our talk of business," Crippen apologized mildly. "I can't tell you how honoured I am, receiving a fellow doctor under my roof. To enjoy professional conversation, you know. Belle has many friends, she entertains a lot, she must keep up appearances, of course." They had reached the hall. "I hope you will not refuse my hospitality in the future?"

Eliot declined whist. Crippen was dispatched through the drizzle for a cab. Belle kissed Nancy several times. Eliot called his address to the driver, the pair of padded leather knee-doors slammed, the hansom clopped towards Camden Road.

They laughed, hugging each other with the delight of well-mannered children released from the ludicrous antics of adults.

"The opera! She'd grace the stage like a German street band in the orchestra pit," Eliot decided.

"Can you imagine them making love? Lap-dog and hippopotamus!"

Eliot recalled that it was no distance to his lodgings. "You're coming in, dearest?"

Nancy shook her head firmly. "I must go back to the Savoy. There's Baby's telegram. It hadn't arrived when I left."

"The temperature will have settled by now, I'm sure."

Nancy hesitated before admitting, "And I'm worried about the sponge. It may not always work."

"How the world has grown suddenly enlightened of its responsibilities to Dr Marie Stopes as to God," said Eliot lightly. "Science and passion make strange bedfellows, don't they? Oh, I'll visit a rubber shop. I'll spend two shillings on a dozen of their goods, constructed with the resilience of tyres on a motorbus. You should anyway wear a Dutch cap, which is safer and more comfortable."

She touched his cheek. "Dear, I still tremble to talk of such things."

"Many married couples never mention the entire business all their lives. Odd – the only bodily function they share. Creating children is the most serious thing any human being does for fun."

"I'm your fun?" She nestled against him. "How you delight in making fun of anything serious."

"Who could bear contemplating marriage with the slightest seriousness? A commonplace one hangs together for its first year through passion, for the next five through respectability, and after that from habit."

"You're lecturing me again."

"You're coming back to London?" he asked earnestly.

She kissed him. "Sure, I am. As soon as Baby's settled."

"I'd sail to see you in New York."

"You wouldn't like me there. You wouldn't like anything about me."

The horse slowed down. "Whatever happens, we shall meet again," she assured him solemnly.

"I shall cherish the idea, as sensible people of life after death. There's really no point in thinking otherwise, is there?"

They stopped. The small, square trapdoor overhead sprung open, with the customary rough and grubby cabman's hand from a frayed and greasy cuff, jerking one way and another for which passenger should pay the fare.

"The lady is going on," Eliot directed upwards. "The Savoy Hotel."

A scatter of chimes from the church clock marked midnight. Eliot had three hours of his usual working day. He lit his gas, stoked the fire, boiled a kettle for a cup of tea. Changing coat for cardigan, he uncapped his fountain-pen and resumed *The Health of Nations*.

He had been writing an hour when the front doorbell jangled violently. He took no notice. Men arrived unexpectedly at any hour of darkness — either commanding, desperate or frightened. The German housekeeper was trained for these emergencies. He heard footsteps on the stair, a knock came to his door, the maid white-faced in her shift admitted Nancy.

Her face was blotched and contorted. She threw a buff flimsy on his writing-block. Eliot read,

MISS NANCY GRANGE SAVOY HOTEL LONDON DEEPLY REGRET MISS JANE GRANGE PASSED AWAY AT SIX O'CLOCK THIS EVENING HER DEATH WAS SUDDEN AND PEACEFUL ANGLICAN PRIEST AMONG OUR PATIENTS WAS AT HER BEDSIDE STOP CAUSE OF MISS GRANGES DEATH TUBERCULAR MENINGITIS PLEASE ADVISE YOUR WISHES PROFOUND CONDOLENCES PASQUIER.

"There!" Nancy shouted at him. "She's dead. I never saw her again. You made me come to London. You told me that temperature was nothing. When I should have been at her side, I was letting you make love to me like a woman off the streets."

Nancy fell on the sofa, covering her face, starting to cry loudly. "Baby darling, Baby! How I loved you, I loved you…"

Eliot put his arm round her shoulders, but she shook it off violently. She went on accusing him, "You took advantage of me in that horrible Swiss place, advantage of my loneliness, my vulnerability, my exile. I hate you. Who are you, compared with Baby? A nobody, a nothing. My God! How I wish I'd kept you at your distance. Baby died alone among strangers, foreigners. I can't believe it, I can't believe I was such a craven fool to leave her."

"Nancy — "

"Don't touch me. I've been wicked, you've made me wicked."

The resilience and resourcefulness of Eliot's mind failed him. He sensed no point in words for his defence, or for her own. She was shedding guilt upon him before it crushed her.

"There's need for practical arrangements," he suggested quietly after some minutes. "May I help you? It's often the doctor's lot."

He knew the first boat train left Charing Cross Station, near the hotel, at eight in the morning. The night porters at the Savoy would arrange tickets and reservations to Basle. The trying business of packing could be left to the maids. He advised her to get some rest, he suggested a sleeping-draught, but she objected. She had transatlantic telegrams to send her father, to Baby's friends. His deliberately diverting her mind to expediencies calmed her. She had left the hansom at the door. He offered to return with her, but she angrily refused.

Eliot went back to his room and sat in the chair by the fire. He was still sitting there when daylight began to edge the curtains. He did not care in the least that Baby was dead. That Nancy had left him meant more than anything in his ambitious world.

# 10

Arrival of the fast liners from Europe always had impact on the social, political and artistic life of New York. The *Olympic* – 700 feet long, gorgeous inside with carved mahogany, marble and gold leaf, "the Hotel Cecil afloat" – arrived at Pier 92 in the sparkling sunshine of early October. She was the pride of the White Star Line, who could boast in their sailing notices LARGEST LINERS IN THE WORLD BUILDING, because of her even bigger sister-ship on the stocks at Harland & Wolff in Belfast, the unsinkable *Titanic*. As the passenger-list had no actors or authors, statesmen or sportsmen, the newspapers concentrated on the pair of Grange sisters, one of whom was dead.

The world relishes tragedies in wealthy families, who deserve to pay for being rich. The *Evening Sun* and *Evening Mail* described Nancy coming ashore grief-stricken, though the eyes behind her motor-veil were long ago dry in the headwinds of her journey.

Crossing the grey, misty face of Europe from the poplar-spiked fields of northern France she felt like a worm crawling through a dank garden. By the perversity of human mind, her uppermost concern was her inability to buy mourning. She would return to Campette shockingly disregardful in attire to the tragedy. The red cross flag outside the sanatorium was stiff in a cold wind, winter beginning repossession of its rightful land. The first person she saw was Monsieur Mittot, the undertaker.

As the grey-uniformed coachman helped Nancy from the carriage with customary sweep of hat, Monsieur Mittot came briskly through the double doors in his black overcoat. He stopped short on the step. Their eyes met. They had a new relationship, joined in grisly intimacy. Nancy felt shocked this man had laid hands on Baby, seen her naked. She stared at him, frightened at what he represented. The fat undertaker for once looked abashed. He raised his bowler hat an inch, nervously wiped his moustache with his fingertips and hurried towards the village path, muttering chillingly. "*A vôtre service, mademoiselle.*"

Dr Pasquier recounted, as solemnly as a priest's prayers, Baby's final illness. The rise of temperature was not thought alarming. Patients might take a chill in the clinic as in their own homes, a little catarrh need not flash urgent messages across the breadth of Europe. Headache was a common enough symptom in young ladies, surely? The bacillus had suddenly switched its attack from besieging the lung to overrunning the whole body. When Dr Pasquier himself was summoned, Baby was already in coma, her temperature had soared to 41 degrees, her breathing was snatched, the *tache cérébrale* red streak on her skin proclaimed involvement of the brain.

A silently-formed tubercule in the meningeal envelope of the brain, Dr Pasquier explained, had caused internal haemorrhage by eating through an artery. They had applied ice-bags. They had performed the operation of lumbar puncture, to inspect the blood-tinged spinal fluid. Within the hour, she had succumbed. Nothing could have been done.

"Were Dr Beckett still here, might he have saved her?"

"Dr McCorquodale is a practitioner of excellent qualifications, who enjoys my complete confidence."

He took her to the basement to view Baby's body, covered by a sheet, in a room like a butcher's refrigerator. Nancy was amazed how small she looked. Dr Pasquier withdrew the covering from her face. She was a dusky colour, her chin held up with a bandage, her eyes open the fraction of an inch, unevenly.

"Her hair," murmured Nancy. "It still keeps its colour."

The man with the scarred neck was hovering in the lobby. He made a deep bow and presented a long white envelope. It was her sister's bill.

The *Olympic* first class was full of Americans, lively, flirtatious, drunken, lustful, home from an extravagant summer in Europe. The word went about that she had a corpse down below, and people avoided her as though she was a witch. She was met at the pier by Mr Franklyn, a red, round man in gleaming top hat and astrakhan collar, one of her father's lawyers. She embraced her father in his first-floor study at Fifth Avenue. He was with Mr Bryan, his middle-aged private secretary who wore a pince-nez.

"What happened?"

John Grange was small and white-haired, with the birdlike quickness which Baby had inherited. He did deals in everything. For a meat-packer with no cash to pay a wage-bill in Buenos Aires, John Grange could raise a loan on a cargo of whale-oil in Amsterdam. If a German wanted to build a railway in Turkey, John Grange could funnel him the savings of America's Middle West. He could sink a gold mine in Canada by bankrupting a hundred farmers in South Africa, if Baltimore was sitting out a steel strike he knew how to snap up the markets for Sheffield. He neither smoked nor drank, and lived off mint tea, meat broth and raw vegetables. He was terrified of open spaces, travelled in an automobile with drawn curtains and lived in shuttered rooms with the electric light at noon.

"The funeral's on Thursday," he announced, when Nancy had repeated everything transmitted in long, anguished cables. "Tomorrow's for folk to pay their respects. There'll be a book to sign, with velum pages." The coffin would be displayed in the black-hung ballroom where Baby had last danced. "What do you intend to do, now you're home?" he asked later, when he could direct his thoughts from his dead daughter to his living one. "When you can decently appear out of mourning, that is."

"What I did before I left, I guess."

"You don't sound very enthusiastic." Nancy said nothing. "A million women in New York would give an arm to lead your life. Now Baby's gone, you mean twice as much to me. Baby was a great credit. She shone in company. She was sought in society. The boys were proud to know her, the girls fought for invitations to her parties. Baby went everywhere she should be seen, met everyone she had to know. She'd have made a fine marriage."

"I don't care to play the social game."

"For a woman in your position, it's a matter of duty."

"For a woman in any position, it's a matter of taste. I don't care to play bridge."

"You will play it, even if you don't care for it. I've got to have my daughter prominent in society. I've got to have her marry with position, money, family. That's as worthwhile achievement for a woman as making a million dollars is in a man."

"But papa! Do you need me as a decoration? A doll created by dressmakers and milliners and dancing-teachers? When everyone in New York knows and respects John Grange?"

"That's what I want."

There was another silence. "Very well, papa," Nancy said obediently.

"Did you see that fellow Crippen?"

"He's nothing but a quack."

"But he's a real doctor. I had it from Professor Munyon himself."

"He's a quack, and so is Professor Munyon."

"Pretty free with your accusations, aren't you? How can you tell who's a quack and who isn't? That takes a doctor to know."

"It was a doctor who told me."

"Doctors have a lot of professional jealousy."

"This was a doctor whose opinion I'd trust utterly."

"Who was he?"

"He's English. He was at the clinic, looking after Baby. She must have written about Dr Beckett?"

"How'd he know Crippen?"

"We met him together. Dr Beckett had returned to London."

"You'd corresponded with him?" her father asked suspiciously.

"I had become friendly with him."

"Don't go wasting yourself on doctors. I can hire any doctor in the world I like, and fire him the moment I feel like it."

"Very well, papa," Nancy said again.

Baby's prominence in New York society was increased as the centre of its most fashionable funeral that fall. For the rest of October, the compass of Nancy's mind swung too violently to plot a steady course through life. The isolated monotony of Switzerland seemed a more natural existence than the gay gregariousness of New York because it had been endured for a purpose, like monasticism or a prison sentence. To have mixed as a social equal with the unmannered and pretentious Crippens now disgusted her.

Mr Ruston and Mr Wince made her tremble at a brush with evil. But she knew that Eliot was right – "The upper classes have a far leaner time of it than a costermonger, who can revel in the unstinted enjoyment of his bodily functions." Now Eliot must be as dead as Baby.

In the middle of November, Eliot wrote to her. Nancy was alarmed, because Mr Bryan saw every envelope entering the house and would report the unfamiliar handwriting to her father. The letter began, *Dear Nancy*, and after a sympathetic half-page about Baby described cheerfully his free surgery in the greengrocer's shop.

*The municipal elections have just ended,* he informed her. *With only two of the nine women town councillors in England re-elected. You see how the suffragettes' campaign is self-defeating? Violence is a useless political weapon, unless cloaked in subtlety. They say we are in for a wet winter, the weather is filthy today, the Thames rising by the hour. I pray it will not drown the entire House of Lords before their opportunity to reject the People's budget. Then shall be my chance. Who knows, that you must put "MP" after my name, should you choose to write?*

It ended, *Yours sincerely, Eliot.* Nancy thought it as unromantic as a prescription.

Nancy nearly wrote back. She sat over her thick, cream wavy-edged paper, fountain-pen uncapped. It seemed dereliction of duty towards her father. Instead, she accepted the invitation to a dance with Clarrie Burgess.

Clarrie was three years older than her, heir to a railroad fortune. When Nancy had begun accepting the shower of invitations after Baby's funeral, Clarrie's eagerness in courting her, she suspected, indicated society's relish for a fresh face. Within a week, his presents had escalated from flowers and chocolates to a diamond bracelet. The same evening, John Grange called her to his study. He did not mention Eliot's letter, but with the air of offering sound advice to an investor declared that Clarrie Burgess would make her an excellent husband.

"He would not," said Nancy.

"Why?"

"He has a scented moustache."

Her father was too puzzled to reply.

In the *New York Times* two mornings later, Nancy found half-a-dozen columns about phthisis. It was as common as drunkenness or lice among the crammed tenement dwellers of the lower East Side. Her knowledge of pulmonary tuberculosis, its progress, its treatment, was singular among the untrained women of New York. The notion of turning this to some use was exciting. It would restore the purpose to her life which had died with Baby.

Everyone had heard of Lillian D Wald's Visiting Nurse Service. The charity attracted the generosity of Nancy's friends as more genteel than the Salvation Army. Nancy telephoned for an appointment at 265 Henry Street. She drove to the lower East Side in a hansom, remembering that in the same squalor her mother and her relatives had met hastened deaths. Was she lucky to have risen from such society? Or wicked to tolerate it at all? As political thought always turned her mind to Eliot, she left the question open.

The Henry Street Settlement was housed in a brownstone, with shutters and window-boxes, a tree outside protected by railings, half-a-dozen children playing on the front steps, staring and giggling as she banged the big brass knocker. She was taken to a small, square, linoleum-floored semi-basement with faded yellow wallpaper and pair of hanging gas-globes. A roll-topped desk was jammed against a stout cupboard, library shelves along one side were filled with neat piles of pink lint, rolled bandages, basins and heavy metal boxes. In the corner stood a small washstand with basin and pitcher, the middle had a board and a flat-iron. There was a flower vase standing empty, and a mirror in which she felt no one bothered to look. The decorations were photographs of nurses in groups, a sombre picture of President Lincoln and a framed red-and-white card ordaining DO IT WELL.

Two mature women sat on rush-seated chairs, both in blue-and-white check cotton dresses with flared skirts, a black tie and a broad white belt. The one with the centre parting and the bun was Lillian Wald. The other, with the upswept hair, her partner Mary Brewster, wife of a general.

Lillian Wald told her bluntly, "You're not the first society lady who's come here, filled with good intentions. But unfortunately, even the best intentions aren't good enough. Once they find the nature of our work — and the nature of the folk we work among — they generally find their disgust hard to swallow. Maybe it would be better for both of us if you expressed your desire to help by writing a cheque?"

"However big a cheque, it wouldn't buy me an easy conscience. And I have come to you with the selfishness expected of my set. I want something useful in my life."

The reply seemed to excite curiosity. "But why occupy yourself with the sick? Here at the Nurses' Settlement the work's mostly hard, and always unpleasant till you're used to it. Some ladies never get used to it. You could go across to the Travellers' Aid Society on West 54th. You'd do as much good, saving vulnerable young working women arriving in New York from moral corruption."

"But I'm interested in medical matters. Particularly phthisis. I've just lost a dear sister from the disease. I was so close to her in a Swiss sanitorium, I felt that I had nursed her myself."

"Oh, I recollect the item in the newspapers," said Mary Brewster.

Miss Wald became less forbidding. "I'll accept you as a do-er rather than a do-gooder," she decided after more questioning. "I only take trained ladies, you know. It's public health nursing, for the ultimate good of the whole community of New York. I will not bestow nursing care as a charity upon our patients. That is a derogation of human dignity to the recipient, however inflating for the donor. I enrol a few nurses' aides, which you can try for six months. If you last, you can take regular instruction as a public health nurse. That'll be at Teachers College, in Columbia University. I'm starting a training programme there next year."

Nancy was as delighted with her uniform as with her acceptance – the same check that Lillian Wald wore herself, with dainty buttoned shoes protected by black spats, a black straw skimmer hat, a wide apron for work, the promise in summer of a white muslin cravat. She carried a black leather bag with two handles, accompanying one of the nurses from tenement to tenement, generally over the rooftops. The poorer you were on the lower East Side, the higher up you lived.

Her job was mostly cleaning and cooking. The squalor, filth and decay neither shocked nor deterred her. Nor that one in ten of the adults she saw every day, perhaps one in six of the infants would before long end in an unembellished pine coffin in Potter's Field. The well-fed patients in the clean and comfortable Clinique Laënnec were equally surely condemned to die, and Eliot had taught her that the only real tragedy in life was death. The tubercular sufferers sought fresh air as shipwrecked sailors water. Some lived in tents on the roof, through burning summer and winter snow. Nancy consoled herself that many of the East Side immigrants – or their children – would pull themselves from the human mire. And that many others kept their families clean, fed and temperate in such discouraging surroundings. And that many more had left straw-floored European cellars and garrets no better, and the air tainted with political oppression.

Her father had at first objected with unexpected mildness. One evening in late November, he called her to his study. "Mr Bryan saw this in the *Herald*."

He picked up a newspaper cutting. The column was headed, JOHN GRANGE'S DAUGHTER IN SLUMS. "You spoke to this reporter, Nancy?"

"I asked Miss Wald's permission. I thought what he wrote would make you proud of me, papa."

"I am not. Why should my only daughter spend her days in filth? You could be molested, attacked."

Nancy sat in a straight-back chair opposite. She slowly smoothed her grey satin skirt. "I should never be. In my uniform, I am like a queen in her robes. I am respected, welcomed and loved." She reminded him, "I asked and you gave your permission."

"I did not give you permission to penetrate such places. I naturally imagined that you would be a nurse to people of social standing."

"Women of my own age – those I work among – do things far more evil every day without troubling their fathers at all. Don't you see, papa? I'm your best publicity agent. You're far too hard-headed, not to recognize there are many who do not overlove you."

"I make enemies with every deal. I don't give a damn. I make as many friends, so long as it's successful."

"A rich man is disliked by people who know absolutely nothing about him, except that he's rich."

"That's unreasonable."

"No more than a man with no coat hating the wind. You can no longer play Mr Vanderbilt and say, 'The public be damned.' When you talk of the public now you mean its newspapers, and they're incapable of damnation. If they tell New York that your daughter tends the sick and the destitute, you will be thought of the kindlier."

John Grange sipped the mint tea resting on the arm of his leather chair. "That's not what your life's for. I could hire a hundred clever dicks to make me look the sweetest man in town. Baby understood that. She'd never stray from her proper position."

"Can't you understand? I would never work with the nurses if it wasn't what I want to do most in the whole world?" He said nothing. "Oh, papa! I know you want me to be a success in society, to marry the man whom every other girl in New York would long to wed. But surely you love me enough to let me find my own happiness?"

"I love you with all my heart, Nancy, but in this world we must put our tender feelings behind armour-plate if we want to be successful."

There was a long silence. He rose abruptly, leant over and kissed her. It was the end of an inconclusive interview. Nancy continued at Henry Street. She knew it distressed her father. She knew her response to his distress must shortly end her employment.

He never mentioned her work, but asked searchingly after the invitations she received and accepted. Nancy refused any but the smallest parties where she was unlikely to meet eager suitors. Her set said she was never the same since Baby's death. They shook their heads that she was developing the same oddities as her father.

# 11

"I'm going to try something entirely new." Eliot's voice had more enthusiasm than he usually allowed himself the luxury. "Or more correctly, something extremely old, which nobody has bothered themselves to think about intelligently."

The patient sitting on the bench was pale, wizened, bright-eyed, sharp-nosed, skinny, growing bent. He wore a coarse woollen pea-jacket with two rows of buttons like a sailor's, a greasy choker, the patched corduroy trousers flopping over his boots held by a broad, brass-buckled belt. Stained cap and stubby clay pipe lay on the bare floor. Though before eight in the morning he reeked of beer.

His sleeves were pushed to the elbows, displaying forearms red, weeping, pitted with yellow pustules down to the wrists. He looked at Eliot with the cheerful scepticism of Cockneys, who throughout London's history have found people trying to sell them second-hand goods or political and religious ideas with comparable passion.

"Wot is it?"

"Mouldy bread."

"Luv a duck!"

"It's been used for centuries by country people for the best of scientific reasons — it worked. There's always been lightning in the heavens and steam from volcanoes, Bill. But it needed imagination to turn them into electric light and railway engines."

The old greengrocer's bell clanged as the door opened. Eliot was startled to see Crippen in a drenched bowler and long waterproof coat.

The streets of London were struggling to become light on the blustery, teeming morning of November 19, 1909. The People's Surgery had been open a month. Single-handed, Eliot had scrubbed and sawn, banged in nails, licked with paint the rickety shop in Brecknock Road, which still smelt of rotting cabbage. He had wheeled in a handcart bits of furniture from the pawnbrokers in the Caledonian Road. An old lace curtain from his lodgings discouraged the curiosity of passers-by through the shop window. The second-hand examination couch stood in a small inner room, with the bowls and bottles, the bandages, tow and oiled-silk. His own savings and £5 from the Holloway Labour Party could provide only essential dressings. He perceived that he would be offering advice rather than treatment, most common remedies being beyond the pockets of his patients.

It was his first encounter with Crippen since the day Baby died. Eliot congratulated him on being about so early. "I generally leave home round eight," Crippen said in his usual quiet, absent-minded way. "I get my own breakfast, and maybe take Belle up a cup of coffee. I've a long working day. Seven-thirty's my usual home hour." He shook the raindrops from his bowler, standing among the wooden forms facing the fire, inspected curiously by a dozen waiting patients – porters, slaughtermen, drovers from the Cattle Market, just off work or just out of the pub. "I just had to see the surgery that everyone in the neighbourhood is talking about."

"Not all of them kindly. The local doctors are furious at my robbing them of poor people's shillings. I'm expecting them any moment to smash my window with toffee-hammers. They say I'm insane, working for nothing. Or devilish clever, buying votes by free medicine instead of free beer."

"I so enjoyed your company, I hoped I might meet you and Miss Grange once more." Crippen seemed to have forgotten Eliot's remark on the stairs. "I honestly don't recall passing more than a word with other medical men all the twelve years I've been in London. I don't join societies and all that, you know. They're a bit high-falutin' for me."

"Miss Grange is back in New York," Eliot told him. Partly to change the subject, partly mischievously, he said with the solemnity of addressing a

Harley Street specialist, "Perhaps you'd give me a second opinion on this case?"

Protesting he was a throat man, Crippen followed the pair into the inner consulting-room.

"You may think it a case of Bockhart's impetigo?" Crippen had never heard about the German physician Max Bockhart, Eliot knew, or the disease he described of pustules bursting from the hair follicles. But flattery of assumed knowledge was a courtesy among doctors so widespread it amounted to professional etiquette. "Bill Edmonton here works at the slaughterhouse in the Cattle Market across at Copenhagen Fields. He's picked up a staphylococcal infection from handling the meat, which I intend to treat somewhat unorthodoxly."

"I ain't a slaughterman, doctor." Bill sat on the spoke-backed kitchen chair beside Eliot's deal table. "A slaughterman can touch two 'undred pahnds a year. I'm only a boilerman." He grinned. " 'Poupart's Piccadilly Potted Meat. Londoners Love It'."

Eliot remembered the newspaper advertisements of clerics, army officers, goggled aviators, mortar-boarded schoolmasters and other persons of authority and energy, mouthing forkfuls of its slippery slices like famished Children of Israel savouring manna.

"What do Poupart's pay you?" It was a question the patients grew to expect from Eliot.

"Depends." Bill looked sly. "I gets paid by the meat wot comes aht of the boiler. And the sacks of meal wot I finish wiv, from grinding the marrow-bones. I can make meself a good ten bob a day, a'cause my governor don't use just wot comes from the slaughter-ahses, 'e buys cheap bits and bones left over by the butchers, even from the big ahses in the West End."

"I suppose if it's all boiled, it kills the germs," said Eliot resignedly. "I'd like to take a look round the Market one day, Bill. A doctor should know the working conditions of his patients. Most know as little as of those in a young ladies' seminary."

"Come on a Monday morning," he invited with pride. "It's the best day. There's two thasand bullocks an' ten thasand sheep sold on Mondays, so they say."

"Perhaps I'll come tomorrow."

From a glass bell on an upturned orange-box Eliot took two slimy green squares on a strip of cheesecloth. Crippen peered curiously through his gold-rimmed glasses.

"Mould," Eliot explained. "Which ruins leftover bread-and-cheese and last Sunday's cold mutton. It's a fungus named penicillium. It was first mentioned in that famous book by Mordecai Cooke, *Fungi, their Nature, Influence and Uses*. That was published fifty years ago." Crippen looked vague. Eliot might have been talking of the Vulgate. "It's a tangle of filaments, a lacework as familiar through my microscope as the tramway map of London."

Eliot pressed the mould on Bill's pus-riddled forearms, covered it with a square of oiled silk and secured it firmly with bandages. "Now pass a specimen of your water in this jam-jar, Bill. Boils can be associated with diabetes, can't they, Dr Crippen?"

"Undoubtedly," said Crippen, to whom the connection was clearly as novel as between water and ice to a South Sea Islander.

Bill left, cap on head and pipe in mouth, wearing the expression of awe shot with distrust of any Cockney finding himself the object of learned attention. Eliot washed his hands with yellow soap in a tin basin on another upturned crate. He told Crippen, "I'm not running this surgery to cure Holloway's aches and pains, but to show what *must* be done. This is the most generous city in the world – you've only to look at *Fry's Guide to London Charities*, there's two thousand hospitals, asylums, dispensaries, homes, orphanages. Not to mention Bible, tract and missionary societies. All with a total income of *twelve million* pounds a year. The British aren't mean. They're class-ridden. They'd share their last crust with a beggar, but if he demanded half as a human right they'd rather toss it down the sewer."

Eliot wiped his hands on a towel hanging from a nail. "Oh, I know there're plenty of medical clubs, but they have to compete with the burial clubs, and the Cockney prefers the prospect of a good funeral to that of postponing it."

Crippen seemed unstirred by social injustice. He enquired, "Were you free for dinner tomorrow?"

Eliot excused himself promptly. "Tomorrow's the Lords' vote on the Budget. I'll be in Parliament Square to see any fun. Please apologize to Mrs Crippen."

"I shall not be with Belle. You remember Miss Le Neve, my typist? We have been acquainted since '03, when I was consulting physician to the Drouet Institute, and she came to us straight from Pitman's College, only seventeen. We often have dinner together at Frascati's in Oxford Street. They have a nice winter garden with beautiful music, and you can get a good little table d'hôte for five shillings." Eliot felt admiration at such dalliance in the ogreish shadow of Belle. "I'm sure that Ethel would enjoy the company of a medical man so cultivated as yourself, quite as much as I do."

Eliot rang the compliment on the counter of cynicism. After some persuasion, he agreed. It might be amusing to observe Crippen without Belle. Frascati's made a change from the Caledonian Road. Crippen was so pathetically pleased, his watery eyes seemed likely to spill over. As he turned to leave, Crippen reached for a thick green book beside the bell-jar on the orange-box. "Walsham and Spencer, *Theory and Practice of Surgery*," he murmured reverently.

Crippen turned the pages. "*Trephining the Skull... Rhinoplasty... Fracture of the Shaft of the Femur... Strangulated Hernia*," he read aloud. "Do you know, I've still my surgical instruments? I keep the case at home, behind the books. Belle doesn't like to look at them. She calls them a hoodoo. She had an operation once," he disclosed quietly. "An ovariotomy, in New York...oh, over ten years ago. They left behind the womb and the Fallopian tubes, so the scar's not too ugly."

He took the other volume from the orange-box. "Gray's *Anatomy*, Fifteenth Edition by Pickering Pick, FRCS, of St George's Hospital," he read out, as though the title page of the Bible. "Such a wonderful book. I came across it while studying operations here in England, back in '83."

"Borrow it if you wish," Eliot invited handsomely.

"May I? I shall find nothing more satisfying than renewing my knowledge of the human body," Crippen told him gratefully. "I'll keep it from the rain under my waterproof. I've only a little walk to catch the Underground at Camden Road Station. I really called to ask if you'd be interested in a little proposition?" Eliot stared, unbelieving after Crippen's last feeler. "I hold the patent of a remedy called 'Ohrshob—'"

"Called *what*?"

The German for 'ear' with 'shob' from 'absorb'. A good name, I think? It's an ear salve, for deafness. If you could dispose of a gross among your patients, I'd be most liberal with the commission—"

Eliot clapped him on the shoulder. He felt no anger nor contempt for this threadbare physician. Only sorrow and amusement. He later reflected this attitude brought the failure of his early life and the success of his later one. "My patients could never afford your remedies. Might I suggest an alternative? Spare them a mite yourself."

Crippen seemed neither offended nor unresponsive. "I shall draw a cheque, Dr Beckett. Frascati's at eight tomorrow."

The door jangled, and he stepped into the rain.

It was still raining hard at six the next morning, when Eliot arrived at the Cattle Market. It was almost an hour before sunrise. The Market was vast, 70 acres, 50 years old, a monument to the practicality which illuminated the Victorians' life as gloriously as their religion.

A 100-foot high, white stone clock tower, surmounted by a gold dragon wind-vane, dominated as majestically as the campanile in Florence a crushed cloister of shops and offices, the post office and telegraph station. Around massed rows of iron-railed stalls for the 750,000 cattle which lowed their way through every year. Along the edges stretched the sheep and bullock lairs, low buildings with slate-and-glass roofs split for healthy ventilation, open-fronted with slim iron pillars, a three-foot deep cobbled gully along the back for hosing away each morning's dung. Victorian expedience incorporated a pub at each corner, identical Italianate four-storey square buildings, the *Lion*, the *Lamb*, the *Bull* and the *White Horse*, open all night.

Eliot had sent a boy to Bill Edmonton at Poupart's meat works, saying to meet him in the *White Horse* — Bill certainly could not read a note. Eliot bought him three-ha'penn'oth of porter, but insisted leaving the warm gaslight before Bill became hopelessly drunk. They entered a broad gate in the blue-painted ten-foot railings. Under the naphtha flares, the sight struck Eliot as a brownish, choppy sea, with mooing for the sound of waves. Whistling and clanking of trains came from the huge triangular Great Northern goods depot against the Regent's Park Canal, where truckloads of cattle and sheep from the Midland shires and Yorkshire moors were shunted about all night.

The iron rails which confined the beasts hemmed the humans into narrow lanes. Butchers in bowler hats and heavy topcoats, landowners in deer-stalkers and Inverness capes, farmers wearing old-fashioned varnished flat waterproof hats, drovers with long sticks and leather-strapped corduroys who had walked ten miles from the Home Counties during the night, uncountable Cockneys with caps and mufflers and their hands in their pockets, and as many dogs, barking, snapping and sparring, seeming to enjoy the morning better than any other living things in sight.

Small, tight groups of better-dressed men with notebooks and pencils directed at the cattle sharp looks honed on experience, a nod sealing the bargain for another restless knot of animals to sizzle in the ovens or grills of Londoners. The repetitive large-scale transformation of living organisms into dead edibles chilled Eliot's imagination. To Bill, the Market was only an area which filled and emptied in the early morning, and needed hosing down before the next.

Bill conducted him across the broad, cobbled Market Road which bisected the pens. A pair of men in oilskins like sailors' goaded cattle into a long shed with a platform some six feet high running its length, on which stood a pair of men with sledgehammers.

Bill leered. "The killing pen." They mounted the platform as the gate clanged shut on a packed, snorting, heaving line of cattle. " 'Ave a look at the knockers at work."

Unhurriedly, the sledgehammers fell on the flat of the animals' heads, with a steady crack like a sportsman's gun. The knockers never missed. The beast fell, or sagged against the flanks of its fellows. Once the line was silent, and still save for mortal spasms, the knockers rested sweating on their hammers, the far gate was opened, and a team of men with hooks dragged the carcases into the brightly gas-lit building beyond.

Were they dead, Eliot wondered, or merely stunned? In the next building, it made no difference. All were raised by their hind hoofs on chains from the roof, and had their throats cut over buckets. The room was filled with men engulfed in leather aprons like a blacksmith's. They decapitated the animals with a stroke of a cleaver, tossing the heads like footballs into iron bins. They spread the carcases on the flagged floor, shackling their hooves to short iron posts, and dextrously rid them of their hides. The shiny, bloody torsos were shifted by handcarts to worn wooden tables, where more aproned men chopped them to bits, separating the entrails into separate round bins of liver, kidneys, lungs, guts and tongues, with a final bin for all the rest.

Poupart's was hardly more than a shed, impossible to see across for steam. Bullocks' and sheeps' heads, bones with fragments of meat, bits of internal organs which had escaped becoming sausages, were dumped in boiling vats. The meat was sieved and minced, seasoned fiercely and packed into tins under heavy weights. The liquor went for pea soup, the skimmed fat for lard, the bones were crushed through steel rollers for meal to nourish the roses in London gardens.

" 'Londoners Love It,' " Eliot ended with a smile, after recounting his investigation to Crippen and Ethel Le Neve at Frascati's that evening.

"In Chicago," Crippen said with quiet pride, "they've got slaughterhouses so efficient, they say they use pretty well everything in a hog but its squeal."

"Peter! You'll put me off my dinner," Ethel dabbed her forehead with a tiny lace-edged handkerchief.

Crippen looked delighted. "Ethel my dear, when you dine with two doctors, you must be ready to hear strange things. Isn't that so, Dr Beckett?"

"Perhaps I should never have mentioned it at dinner at all, Miss Le Neve. But the Market made so strong an impression on me. There's a broad, tumbling Styx flowing into the heart of London," he said dramatically. "None of those beasts will ever return to their lush fields and flyblown byres, no more than we can reverse the torrents of the River Severn."

"Yes, it is sad," said Ethel. "Ever so."

Frascati's was large and handsome, a café and grill-room with the plush-curtained, palm-fringed winter garden upstairs. Ethel was prettier than Eliot remembered. She wore a plain cream blouse and a navy serge skirt, befitting the desk rather than the dinner-table. Her pearl necklace Eliot assumed a sham. When Crippen had introduced her with muted effusiveness, she shook hands in a ladylike way, whole arm delicately raised. Her expression seemed consciously subdued, a lively young woman wrapping herself tightly in a mantle of modesty to suit the company. She differed from Belle as a bunch of violets from a bunch of bananas.

Conversation continued untaxingly with Ethel's enthusiasm for her new typewriter. "A Smith Premier, with complete control from the keyboard," she explained triumphantly. "It has a combination paragrapher and column finder, with removable and interchangeable plattens, a stencil key, a ribbon-colour change and a back-spacer."

Eliot gravely congratulated her on command of such advanced machinery. Then Crippen said unexpectedly, "Did you know, Dr Beckett, that Belle is my second wife? I was married to an Irish girl from Dublin, called Charlotte Bell," he reminisced pleasantly. "A student nurse at the Manhattan Hospital. I was an intern. A pretty usual combination, isn't it?"

"Peter has a son," Ethel added.

"Yes. Otto. He's in California now. My wife had a fit and died in her next pregnancy. That was in Salt Lake City, in the winter of '91."

"Peter makes the perfect husband," Ethel said with sudden spirit. "He had no vices, and Belle can do what she likes with him. Their house is an absolute disgrace, Dr Beckett. She *won't* keep a servant, you know. The gas stove's rusty and the kitchen's covered with cooking stains, there's dirty dishes, knives, flat-irons, saucepans everywhere, mixed up with Belle's false hair and even her precious jewellery. And as like as not, some beautiful white chiffon gown that Peter's paid a fortune for, tossed over a chair with his collars and shirts. Once she even took in lodgers," Ethel said indignantly. "*Germans,*" she emphasized the horror.

Crippen murmured in mitigation, "Four young students." He paused. "I had to black their boots."

"Why, she's even had Peter make a cage for the cats, for fear they'll be put in the family way." Ethel stopped abruptly, pink from the outburst. She added firmly, "Of course, Belle and I get along very well together. Sometimes we're like sisters."

"Belle has an extravagant temperament," Crippen excused her. "She's Polish."

"Really?" exclaimed Eliot. So she was one of a million Central Europeans who had jumped out of the frying-pan into the melting-pot.

"Her father had a fruit-barrow in Brooklyn — as we'd say in London, a costermonger. Her mother was German. She called herself Cora Turner, and only after we married did I discover she was really Kunigunde Mackamatzki," he revealed in a mild voice. "She was nineteen. I had to win her from the protection of a man called Lincoln — "

Crippen broke off his sentence. The orchestra began the waltz from Franz Lehar's *Merry Widow*, which gave George Edwardes a *succès fou* at Daley's in Leicester Square in 1907. Crippen put his hand on Ethel's and exchanged a look of dreamy sentimentality. "Our favourite tune," he explained to Eliot. "All that is needed to put the crowning touch on our happiness."

Eliot stared down at his plaice — rather than sole, it was the five shilling dinner — to avoid laughing at a pathetic little doctor who created romance from a tinselly restaurant, a banal tune and a commonplace typist with pretty eyes. He had a talent for *Gemütlichkeit*, Eliot thought. He suspected suddenly that Crippen had invited him to meet Ethel, had indulged in such confidences, to enrol him as an ally against Belle. He remembered his father's advice, never be inveigled into marital conflicts or the beds of young married women. He spent the rest of the meal talking mostly about the House of Lords. It bored Ethel, but Crippen seemed to draw from it intellectual uplift.

Over the fruit-salad, Crippen passed Eliot the promised cheque. He saw it was for a guinea. "You're very generous," he said warmly.

"The most generous man in the world," Ethel agreed. "You've only got to look at Belle's dresses and jewels, haven't you?"

It was approaching midnight when Crippen hailed a hansom. Ethel lived in Constantine Road on the southern edge of Hampstead Heath, barely a mile beyond Hilldrop Crescent. Eliot avoided a lift on the excuse of some excitement in the streets of Westminster. He strode towards the river down Kingsway, intending to take a tram along the Embankment to the Houses of Parliament. He heard the newsboys shouting a special edition. He thrust a ha'penny at a ragged urchin for the *Evening Times*, eagerly scanning the front page under a street lamp in the rain.

On Lord Lansdowne's resolution, the House of Lords had rejected the House of Commons' Finance Bill by 350 votes to 75. Eliot crammed the paper into the pocket of his raincoat. "There'll be a general election," he exclaimed excitedly. "A general election as soon as the year's out."

He walked with a springier step, seeing himself as Dr Eliot Beckett, MP.

# 12

"Well, you made a bit of a fool of yourself," said Major Beckett.

"I misjudged the revolutionary passion of Englishmen," Eliot told his father. "It boils, but only as porridge boils. It plops sedately, then cools to a stodgy mass. Perhaps stodginess is our national genius? The French and Italians are like pans of fat, igniting and burning out the kitchen every so often."

Major Beckett frowned. He was a tall, spare, man who wore his frock-coat and starched collar and cuffs like a uniform. His son had developed a clever way of speaking, which he enjoyed in women and distrusted in men. He supposed those who played politics needed to wrap their opinions like Christmas presents, or their hearers would discern them no more intelligent than those of the man beside them on the omnibus. "You did very badly."

"Obviously, sir, as I lost my deposit. When I was canvassing with my red rosette, every working man in Holloway swore to support me. In the end, they chose the Liberal against the Conservative. They knew where they stood with both parties. They don't trust Socialism, because it's new-fangled. No one is more conservative than the British lower classes."

It was noon on Monday, January 24, 1910. They sat in the smoking room of the Imperial Club at the corner of Pall Mall and St James's Street, a cavern hewn from mahogany and leather. Eliot sipped his sherry, his father being old-fashioned took madeira. To soldier away half a life in India made a man confident of election to the club. A factotum to a nobleman invited the sneering mutterings which could provoke blackballing. Colonel Beckett has risked it. He believed that the agent of a duke enjoyed

103

a standing above that of a lord or even earl, like duke's servants taking precedence below stairs when their masters were guests at country houses.

"Had it occurred to you, Eliot, the working men might have given their vote were you one of them, and not of a higher social station?"

"Should I have sported a cloth cap, like Keir Hardie?"

"I'm not suggesting you played the hypocrite."

"Why not, sir? We're a nation of hypocrites. We created an Empire rather brutally. We stand appalled at foreign accusations of drawing economic and political strength from enslaved nations. We say we're only bringing them the advantages of Christianity and drains."

"I suppose you politicos have faith in your ideals as a salesman in his samples, however shoddy." Feeling his political antagonism had displaced paternal affection, the major added, "It must have been a bitter disappointment for you."

"The blackest of my life. And wasted work always torments me, whether it's an experiment which fails, or a patient who dies. I spent the wettest winter that London has known, tramping the Holloway streets from the hour men leave for work before daylight to the hour they return well after dark. I spoke every night in cold halls smelling of damp clothes and unwashed flesh, only quarter-filled with people who were either indifferent or hostile and generally stupid. I hope the carnival didn't embarrass you? I got a good deal into the newspapers, who seemed to find a medical man as a socialist an interesting freak. What did the Duke think?"

"His Grace was quite amused. He is not particularly interested in electioneering. He knows that the important issues in the country are all decided by a dozen or so men like himself. I excused you by suggesting you'd grow out of it."

"It's a poor fighter who throws in the towel after a pummelling in the first round."

"Or a wise one? Your profession passes well in society today. Doctors have been knighted, and of course Lister is in the House of Lords. Look at Dawson, the Duke's doctor. On the Duke's recommendation he's now the King's doctor, and set for his knighthood. The Duke has a soft spot for you, Eliot. And you're damned clever. Give up this politicking, set up your brass plate in Harley Street. A word from the Duke could bring you the patients which could bring you a fortune."

"I don't want a fortune."

"You will when you're married. Your wife will see to that."

"The marriage bed is for me an article of furniture as elusive as a seat in the House of Commons."

The major raised his eyebrows, but seemed diffident about pursuing this remark. "You mustn't starve yourself of the normal pleasures for a young man. I recall my own time as a subaltern…mind, London was a rougher place in the seventies, with the Middlesex and the Oxford music halls going strong. There were houses in the Haymarket and Covent Garden where a young serving officer, deprived by duty of feminine company, might take a year's compensation in a single night."

"I'm going to the music hall tomorrow night," said Eliot, looking amused. "One of the turns is a lady of my acquaintance. I move in theatrical circles, you see."

His father was curious. "What's her name?"

"Belle Elmore."

"Never heard of her."

"She is the wife of a confrère. A funny little man called Dr Crippen, who lives round the corner."

"Of course, I've taken little interest in such things for years."

"How's mother?"

"She has bred a new begonia."

Mention of Mrs Beckett was an understood signal that one or the other had suffered enough serious conversation.

When Eliot opened his front door with a latch-key, Emma appeared from the basement to say there were "gen'men upstairs". He found Ruston impatiently pacing the carpet, Wince on the sofa smoking his pipe and reading his *Times*.

"Where have you been?" Ruston greeted him.

"The Imperial Club." Ruston looked outraged. "Surely a fellow may lunch with his own father? I could hardly have invited him to the Holloway Socialist Workers' Club." He tossed his wide-brimmed hat on the iron bed. "Why have I this pleasure? After my resounding failure at the polls, I imagined you'd want no more to do with me."

Ruston made an impatient gesture. "Elections are a farce, and the result in Holloway proved as much. The political parties of this country are as irrelevant as a literary tea-drinking society. All talk, gentility and selfishness. We shall achieve nothing without force."

"And patience." Wince turned a page of the paper.

"I'm giving you a chance to prove what you're made of," Rushton said.

"Such courage as I have is at the disposal of the cause," Eliot told him.

"We don't want your courage," Ruston asserted. "We want your respectability. A doctor will provide cover. We plan to achieve all we hope in one sharp blow."

"What? Assassinate Mr Asquith?" Eliot asked derisively.

"The German Emperor."

"Oh, that's quite ridiculous."

"That is for others to decide, not you."

Eliot felt a strengthening of his feeling that Ruston was mentally unsound. "Have the practical difficulties occurred to your friends? That we are in Holloway and he in Potsdam? That he is surrounded by a bodyguard who would esteem it a privilege dying to the last man?"

"Emperor William has been on the German throne almost 22 years. Do you know how many times he has visited this country? Eleven! As the King's nephew he's popular here, even if his country isn't."

"If you shoot Kaiser Bill on his next trip, it won't prevent war, but provoke it."

"That's the 'ole idea," said Wince, still reading the paper.

Ruston had been striding the room while talking. He stopped, hands in the pockets of his tweed trousers. "We know our Prussians. They've constructed the most wonderful military machine, which they're itching to get moving like the proud possessor of a brand new Rolls-Royce. The Kaiser killed in Britain! Think of the excuse it gives the hotheads in Berlin. Once von Moltke's General Staff have started the engine and released the brake, nothing can stop it."

Eliot sat abruptly next to Wince, who was relighting his pipe. "And what use will a war be to the English working-man? Apart from ending his miseries by permitting him to be killed in it."

"War brings revolution. The country's seething as it is. Look at the trade unions – gaining half-a-million members a year. Look at the wave of strikes. They're startling the old fuddy-duddy union leaders, scaring the bosses and terrifying the Government out of its wits. The election meant nothing, nothing. Both parties were the bosses' party. The workers are impatient for power. They're scornful of compromise. They're impatient to tear down the plywood barriers in their way."

"Tonypandy," added Wince lugubriously. "The 'ole of the South Wales' coalfield's out. The workers 'ave rejected the advice of their own leaders, 'oo are acting a bunch o' cowards."

"The bosses are using the one weapon they know and love," Ruston continued forcefully. "Starvation! I hope they'll succeed. They'll have the whole working class up in arms."

There was silence broken by the bubbling of Wince's pipe. "I disagree with you", said Eliot.

"You are not entitled to disagree with me. About anything." Ruston picked up his umbrella and Irish hat. "I only want to be reassured I can rely on you when the time comes?"

"I gave you my loyalty five years ago. I'm not the man to withdraw it the first time it's tested."

They left Eliot with his legs stretched out, staring at the neglected fire. He had joined the British Revolutionary Movement while a medical student at St Bartholomew's. Like other young men, he wanted to see the world changed not in his lifetime but before he was thirty. He stirred uneasily on the sofa. If Ruston was not mad, he lived among political lunatics isolated from the real world like the inhabitants of H G Wells' *Country of the Blind*, which he had just read in a magazine. In the cold, misty afternoon he was sweating. He was afraid of no one, but the prospect of helping murder a fellow-human, whether emperor or helpless cripple, terrified him. Had his father met the Kaiser, he would have courteously invited him to sherry at the Imperial Club rather than blowing his head off.

It was growing dark. Eliot threw coal on the fire and lit the gas. He wrote distractedly for a while, then threw down his pen and reached among the music-rolls for Beethoven's Sonata No. 14, the Moonlight. He sat on the sofa, staring into the flames. The music induced a dreaminess which he felt wickedly voluptuous. He pulled out his watch and sighed. In half an hour he must leave for the Metropolitan Music Hall, three or four miles away across Regent's Park in the Edgware Road.

Crippen had called at the surgery the previous Friday with a pressing invitation to share his box. Belle had a fortnight's engagement, an agonized week had been passed turning over her wardrobe. Eliot readily accepted. Watching Belle on the stage promised the fascination of watching Blondin cross Niagara Falls on a tightrope. He had picked up his hat and Burberry for the theatre when the doorbell jangled loudly. He wondered if Ruston had returned with a plot to kill the Czar as well. There was a timid tap at his door. He threw it open to reveal Nancy.

They grasped each other. For a minute, they were unable to speak.

"Why didn't you write or cable you were coming, dearest?" Eliot asked, still incredulous as they stood holding hands, staring at each other and laughing.

"Oh, I don't know... I wasn't sure I could go through with it, until I'd actually rung your doorbell."

"You took a gamble. You might have found me living with another woman."

"I didn't think you'd possibly find another to suit you. If you had, I'd have bowed out happily. After me, she would need to be a paragon."

"How long are you staying?"

"I don't know."

"Where?"

"I'm installed at the Savoy."

"Move in here."

"All right."

Startled by the impulsiveness of invitation and acceptance, Eliot said, "But your father. He wouldn't care for it at all."

"I'll write I'm in clean lodgings for single ladies. He'll accept that. He accepted me walking the East Side slums this winter, climbing across tenement roofs with no more protection than a nurse's uniform."

"You *have* made your life complicated."

"Being in love with someone always brings complications. Otherwise, wouldn't there be empty shelves in the circulating libraries?"

"Now we're going to the music hall."

"*What?*"

He took her arm, as he had when firmly piloting her round London. "I'm committed. I never chuck up my obligations to my friends."

"Surely you could find somewhere more romantic?" she protested.

"Tonight's a memorable theatrical occasion. Come on."

They hurried downstairs. Ruston, Wince and the Kaiser vanished from Eliot's mind.

They laughed all the way in the hansom. The attraction was Belle, Eliot explained, sparkling in the footlights after three years in the domestic dark. The reason for her revival was apparent in half-a-dozen ladies wearing long fur coats and elaborate hats, standing in a line with top-hatted gentlemen outside the brilliantly lit music-hall facade. Placards declared OFFICIAL PICKET, MANAGEMENT UNFAIR TO ARTISTES, PLAYERS NOT PAUPERS. Eliot's preoccupation with the oppressed masses overlooked that they included the music-hall performers.

There was a national music-hall strike. Like all strikes, its causes seemed to outsiders mystifyingly trivial. An arbitrator had awarded the artistes matinée pay at one-seventh of the evening performance rate in one-show-a-night houses, one-twelfth in two-show-a-night houses. "Barring" an artiste for a fortnight, from appearing again within a mile radius, was to be abolished for those earning under £40 a week. The music-hall managers rejected it. A National Alliance of artistes held a mass meeting in The Surrey Theatre, Will Crooks MP in the chair rousing them to "Stand up and stand firm."

The managers determined on strike-breaking. "The names are not those of artistes as well known as those which it is customary to find in the bill," *Era* wrote of the music halls which stayed open. Hence Belle's chance, Eliot realized. Hence the picket-line evoking curiosity and amusement from the public as it pressed leaflets on them with the cheerfulness actors and actresses can never submerge in their activities, even attending each others' funerals.

Crippen was waiting in the foyer. He had a new grey frock-coat with a bright orange tie and a lilac waistcoat. He was delighted to see Nancy. How gratifying for Belle to be viewed by a fellow-countrywoman on her great night. "Haven't you noticed Belle's strong resemblance to Marie Lloyd?" he asked, leading them up the red-carpeted stairs to a two-guinea box. "Do you know why she took the name 'Belle Elmore'? Because Marie Lloyd first appeared at the Royal Eagle calling herself 'Bella Delmere,' " he told them proudly.

They sat on red-plush chairs. The quack doctor leaves threadbare gentility to bask in the tarnished sun of his wife, Eliot thought. Ethel Le Neve inhabited the real world, which the audience had entered the theatre to forget.

Nancy sat squeezing Eliot's hand. Before Baby's illness she was a regular New York theatregoer, always in a large party, all beautifully dressed, aware of affording pleasure to the ordinary men and their wives peering at them through opera-glasses from the cheaper seats. It was a social gathering, Nancy could barely remember the plays. She supposed this theatre of faded plush and scratched gilt resembled that her friends' fathers recalled fondly, "The Rialto" on Broadway south of 42nd Street.

The "Met" was large, a 4000-seater, fifty years old, built over the White Lion pub, which had a reputation among Cockneys for sing-songs and knees-ups. The performers were in competition with its generous furnishing of bars. The West End theatres seemed as formal as visiting relatives on a Sunday afternoon. The flickering displays in the picture houses as lacklustre as a dance of ghosts. The music hall was like a Bank Holiday outing, when everyone expected to enjoy themselves.

The songs and sketches went to the audiences' hearts, because they exalted, lampooned or consoled their everyday joys and pains. All of them felt the relationship with lodger or landlord, mother-in-law or pawnbroker, what it was like to be stoney broke or rolling drunk. Everyone ate kippers and went to the seaside, knew husbands who were henpecked, or roving or cuckolds. Everyone knew they peopled the greatest country on earth, and that all foreigners were ridiculous, particularly as unable to speak English. When the Great Macdermott had his audiences at the London Pavillion thundering back, "We don't want to fight, but, by Jingo, if we do!" it was a threat which deserved Britain's enemies taking seriously.

Moustached and brilliantined, the conductor rose amid his stiff-shirted orchestra, bowing deeply to the whistling and clapping. After a perfunctory overture, the electric candles of the chandeliers dimmed, the red curtain rose on a man in furs outside a stage-property igloo, with six seals who tossed brightly coloured balls to each other, played tunes on a rack of rubber-bulbed motor-horns, climbed ladders, performed acrobatics and jumped into a glass water-tank.

Nancy was puzzled. She had steeled herself for an evening of blue jokes and girls with slashed skirts, like the burlesque shows in the Bowery, where she was no more likely to find herself than at a boxing-match. Nothing could be more respectable than performing seals. Crippen sat engrossed, hand limp on the plush edge of the box. Eliot fancied he had seen the same act as a carousing medical student, but perhaps it had been performing dogs.

The seals were followed by Weldon Atherstone, the monologuist, with top hat, tails and ebony cane. Perfect tailoring was his trademark, like the black half-moons of George Robey's eyebrows, or Albert Chevalier's suit of Cockney costermonger's button-covered "pearlies". He did Fagin in the condemned cell from *Oliver Twist*, the music hall falling as silent as a church.

"The black stage, the cross-beam, the rope..." Atherstone's low voice seemed to ooze from him. "All the hideous apparatus of death."

Violent applause. Only forty years ago, Eliot reflected, this audience in its ancestors' shoes waited excitedly through the night for the morning's execution outside Newgate Jail. Calls of "Blackleg!" came from half-a-dozen voices − planted by the strike committee he suspected. Next appeared a pair of Chinese wirewalkers in kimonos and plate-like hats. Then the orchestra struck up Yankee Doodle. Belle had not seen the pinnacles of New York for thirteen years, but an American act was thought so smart on the London stage, some natives changed their accent to Brooklyn and their costume to Wild West. Eliot saw Crippen's hand tighten on the plush.

Belle's waist was so pinched between bursting bosom and spreading hips, it looked to Eliot in danger of exploding like the bound-up barrel of some ancient siege-artillery pressed back to service. The skirt of her green silk gown foaming with lace trailed a yard behind her. Her hair was in bright blonde curls, as tight as the head of a cauliflower. Her heavy face was vivid with greasepaint, dusted with powder like an apple-dumpling with flour.

She stood between two vases of artificial red roses, holding a mirror edged with gold tassels, which she flashed along the stalls. Fixing on a sallow-faced man with a limp moustache, she started to sing, *Who'll be My Sweetheart Tonight?*.

The thin notes fell into the auditorium like shot sparrows. "Blackleg!" and "Scab!" came from the same seats, whistling and hissing from the gallery. Belle interpreted the noise as shouts of approval and hoots of delight. She favoured her audience with repartee – not the daggered Cockney wit of Bessie Bellwood, the rabbit-skinner's daughter who lived with the Duke of Manchester, but "Oh, you naughty boy!" and "Wouldn't you like me to hold your hand?" Expression and utterance had the mawkish combination of ardent promise and coy chastity in equal proportions.

The conductor was looking nervously over his shoulder. Belle stopped. The house was in uproar. She nervously exchanged a word with him, smiled bravely and began *Something to Warm your Feet On*. Ha'pennies started to fly across the footlights. The strikers had come well armed. Coinage was augmented by eggs, one cracking against Belle's skirt. She burst into tears, rushing from the stage still clutching her mirror. The curtain fell. The noise coalesced to a chant, "We want our money back!" Three rough-clothed men had quit the frustrating remoteness of the gallery to climb over the footlights. A rousing roll came on the drums.

"Stand up," Eliot hissed at Nancy.

"Why?"

"The National Anthem. Always played after a show."

Everyone in the house, even the intruders on the stage, stood stiffly while the orchestra on their own feet played *God Save the King*. The conductor cautiously signalled for another drum-roll and repeated the verse. The tension had gone. A heavily moustached man in evening dress appeared gingerly through the curtain to announce hastily that money would be returned at the box-office.

"Belle's talents aren't suited to these audiences," said Crippen. "She was born for opera."

His face was pink, his bland expression blighted with disappointment and shame. The evening had done Ethel good, Eliot thought.

# 13

"Well, Belle dear, I forgive you, though I daresay hundreds wouldn't," said Clara Martinetti amiably.

"Oh, gee, don't go on about it," Belle told her curtly.

"I shan't dear, I promise I'll not utter another word, now I've had my say. But you *are* Honorary Treasurer of the Music Hall Ladies' Guild, aren't you, dear? And to go strike-breaking – "

"Wasn't Belle punished enough on the night?" Paul Martinetti asked charitably.

"Getting the bird is the worst punishment in the whole world," Clara agreed. "I'm sure Peter could see that."

"Oh, yes, I'd much rather be hanged," Crippen assented mildly.

"But Clara sweetie, don't you see? I only got hissed because I was a blackleg. There were folk planted in the house for no other purpose than to wreck my act. I'm not downhearted, no sir!" Belle's voice rose. "I've had offers last week from the Euston, from Collins' across in Islington, even from the Hippodrome. And I could take my pick of the provincial touring companies tomorrow. Couldn't I, Peter?"

Clara's expression indicated sour disbelief sugared with politeness.

It was a week later, just before ten on the evening of Monday, January 31, 1910. The four sat in the downstairs breakfast room at Hilldrop Crescent. They had just finished dinner – loin of pork with jacket potatoes, followed by blancmange with strawberry jam. Eliot and Nancy had been asked, too.

Crippen had called at the surgery with the invitation the morning after the fiasco. Eliot had politely declined it – he had stomached enough of the grotesque Crippens – but asked sympathetically after Belle.

"Not in bad shape. Mr Atherstone was wonderful last night, you know, comforting her. She bounced back, she's like a rubber ball." He paused. "Sometimes she's like a tiger." He looked round the bleak consulting-room, sitting in the spoke-backed chair. "Do you use henbane in your practice, Dr Beckett?"

"Luckily, I have no maniacal patients."

"I first learned of it at the Royal Bethlem Hospital for the Insane," Crippen continued quietly. "It's given a good deal in America, you know, in asylums. I've prescribed it as a nerve remedy, in a homoeopathic preparation. Very diluted, in sugared discs. Naturally, in its pure form, which the chemists call 'hyoscine'. The dose would equal 1/3600ths of a grain."

"Extremely minute."

"As demanded by the laws of homoeopathy," he asserted. "I bought five grains from Lewis and Burrows' chemist shop in Oxford Street last Friday."

"Five grains!" Eliot exclaimed. "That's enough to kill a platoon of guardsmen."

"I also find it useful for spasmodic coughs and asthma," he explained. "And I am persuading Belle to take it." He hesitated again. "I can satisfy her demands in the way of clothes and jewellery. Others I cannot. You understand, Dr Beckett? I'm not a young man like you. And it is Ethel and I who are proper hub and wife." He continued solemnly, "Our wedding day was December 6, 1906. Seven years had passed since Ethel and I first met. It's a date I can never forget. It was a Thursday. It was the time Belle finally got rid of the Germans. It was rainy, but it was all sunshine in our hearts."

His colleague's double life seemed to Eliot more sickly than exciting, and he had a roomful of waiting patients.

"Since then, we have had one long, lovely honeymoon. We have an absolute communion of spirit. It is not a love of a debased or degraded character, it is a wonderful good, pure love," Crippen continued with muted passion. "Her mind is so beautiful to me. Ethel will always be my wifie, not even death can come between us. We meet in the afternoon, once or twice a week, at King's Cross station, and go to one of the little hotels for railway travellers."

Crippen fell silent. Eliot began to look upon him more kindly, as a patient. To share a man's secrets was to fractionize his mental tension.

"We were to have had a little one, you know, Ethel and I," Crippen divulged in his flat voice, "in the early part of last year. But poor Ethel suffered a miscarriage. No one knew at the office. Ethel was so often away from work because of her health. Her parents did not know. Only Mrs Jackson, her landlady. Ethel went to her aunt in Hove for recuperation. We so wanted the child to live. It would have been part of us both. That was something Belle could never give me, not after her operation. Belle has a gentleman, you know."

Eliot was not surprised. "An American, in the real estate business at Chicago." Crippen's bulgy eyes fixed Eliot's. "He was an actor, on the music hall, called Bruce Miller. He met her when I was visiting America, I'd left Belle in rooms at Guildford Street, over the river in Lambeth. He was across the herring pond for some business with the Paris Exhibition, so it must be ten years ago. He's often here, he writes almost every month. 'Love and kisses to Brown Eyes,' I've seen some of the letters. I've never met him. He calls when I'm out, I stay away from his path. I'm easygoing. I don't care for fuss. I'm sure that one fine morning I'll find Belle has disappeared, gone to join him in America."

"Which would be a solution to your difficulties?"

"I cannot give Belle what he does," Crippen said simply. "Do you know why I was attracted to her? I expected Belle to be a great favourite on the stage, thunderous applause, flowers across the footlights, delightful suppers... That's a vanished dream. Mind, I enjoy the company of stage people, like the Martinettis. But they're so excitable, so emotional. They're not cultivated like Miss Grange and yourself."

The dinner which Eliot declined ended with the two men going upstairs to prepare for whist, and Clara following Belle with the dishes into the kitchen.

"Put the bones in the sack under the sink," Belle directed. "Peter takes them to Poupart's in the Cattle Market. What's the point, missing a few pennies which are there for the taking?"

"How Peter does look after you," Clara said admiringly. She touched Belle's rising sun brooch, adding playfully, "If you're ever tired of that lovely thing he bought you, you can just pass it on to me."

"Ain't there more to a husband's job than keeping his wife dressed?"

"A whole world more, dear."

"Peter and me have had our own bedrooms since we moved in here."

"Oh, I know that."

Belle carefully gathered the four bottles of stout, with a farthing returnable on each. "Peter ain't no good to any woman. You can't blame me, can you, for looking around?"

Clara said sharply, "I don't think that relieves a woman of her duty to her husband." She set her load of plates on the greasy wooden draining-board, beside a sink already piled with dirty crockery – some smeared with egg, she noticed, unwashed since breakfast.

"Peter doesn't mind," Belle said casually. "But what's the good of a home and a husband if you've got talent? If the stage is in your blood, you don't care much for the washtub and the dustpan."

"That's true, Belle," Clara agreed, though sounding sad that she had to. They found Crippen alone in the parlour, adjusting the gas fire. "Where's Paul?" Belle demanded.

"Gone to the smallest room."

"What, by himself? Why didn't you take him?"

Crippen straightened, blinking. "He knows the way. The light is always on."

"I'm sure Paul doesn't mind," Clara said. "Why, this house is like our second home."

"It's common politeness." Belle sat in a pink armchair by the fire. "Peter's taken to leaving the light on all night, because he has to get up," she explained unkindly. "Perhaps he's the same trouble as Paul? Peter, I'm cold. Fetch my shawl. And pass round the chocolates," she commanded, as Paul slipped back to the parlour. The box was a condolence from the

Martinettis. Belle took three of four, holding them in her palm and gobbling them one after the other.

They all turned, hearing Paul gasp. He had idly picked up a large book and flicked the pages.

"What is it, Paul?" Clara was puzzled.

"Things not for the eyes of ordinary men."

"Gray's *Anatomy*," Crippen remarked. He helped himself to a chocolate. "Dr Beckett loaned it me."

"You shouldn't leave an awful book like that lying about," Belle complained. "You've upset Paul."

"No, it's interesting." Clara had her fingers in the pages. "Oh, what a spooky picture!" she exclaimed. "What is it?"

Crippen leaned between the Martinetti's. "That's your lungs and your heart, with the great blood-vessels rising beside your windpipe."

"It looks like some ship with two billowing sails," observed Paul more discriminatively.

"Oh, mercy! Is *that* my leg?" Clara cried.

"Those are the muscles," Crippen explained. "Separated very prettily in the picture, aren't they? Like the petals of a flower."

Clara turned more pages. "And *that*?"

"The womb."

"Peter!" snapped Belle. "What language."

Crippen took the book from the Martinettis, snapping it shut with unusual assertiveness.

"Weren't we playing whist?" Belle asked sarcastically. "Set up the table and bring the cards, Peter."

They played until one in the morning. To theatrical people, night is the working-man's afternoon. None needed be up in the morning – except Crippen, at seven. At half past one, Belle opened the front door. Paul was in overcoat, silk muffler and top hat, Clara wrapped in furs. "Gee, it's freezing," Belle announced. "Sure you wouldn't care to pass the night?"

"We'd best get back to Shaftesbury Avenue, Belle. Paul's better sleeping at home. He's not at all well, you know."

"Peter, fetch them a cab. There'll be one on the rank round the corner in York Road."

"Not at this hour," Crippen said doubtfully.

"Surely you can pick one up in the street?" Crippen hurried into the sparsely gas-lit night, without overcoat or hat. The three waited in the hall, chatting until hooves clattered up the Crescent. The hansom stopped, lamps like bleary eyes over its pair of wheels, horse snorting, muffled bowler-hatted cabby with whip on his perch, breath of man and animal a cloud in the still, frosty air. The knee-doors flew open, Crippen stepped out and politely waited to help his guests in. Clara noticed him shivering.

"Good night, Belle." She kissed her hostess fondly at the top of the front steps.

"I'll come down to see you off."

"No, don't come down, Belle. You'll catch your death."

The driver cracked his whip. The Crippens stood waving in their lighted doorway as the hansom drove towards the Camden Road, from where they could hear the lowing of cattle gathering for sale and slaughter in the Metropolitan Market.

Crippen shut the front door. Belle returned to the armchair by the fire. He reached to dim the gas-globe.

"Why are you turning the gas down?" she demanded.

"Economy. The company's left. The curtain falls."

He remained standing in the middle of the room. She pulled her shawl round her, looking at him curiously. "That's a strange thing for you to say."

"Is it? But a social performance is like one on the stage. We all play our parts. We can generally tell the others' lines before they speak them. With the Martinettis, I feel like the manager of a theatre."

"*I* don't play a part, not in my own home." He said nothing. "Aren't you getting me another glass of brandy? Or don't you want me to have a wink of sleep?"

Crippen descended the stone steps to the kitchen. The brandy was in a cupboard with the bottles of stout, all bought from the grocer's in Brecknock Road. He reappeared with a squat glass containing over an inch of dark spirit. Belle took it without a word. She sat sipping while he folded the green-baize cloth, collected the cards, and moved the square table against the wall.

"This brandy's scented, I guess."

"It's a new bottle. I got it on my way home. It's cheaper, which accounts for the stronger taste. The grocer told me the best brandy is almost tasteless, like drinking liquid fire."

She held the empty glass out. Crippen disappeared. She heard him knock over something in the kitchen below, which smashed on the floor. "It was the gravy boat," he announced, reappearing with more brandy. "It was cracked anyway."

"There's something funny about you. You don't usually break things."

"If we had a housemaid, I suppose she'd break much more." He stood facing her, back to the gas-fire, hands under the tails of his grey frock-coat. "Why did you talk to the Martinettis tonight of engagements offered you at the Euston and Collins'? You knew they were lies."

"Don't dare call me a liar," she said stridently.

Crippen kept his impassiveness. "You have been lying much worse to yourself. You never had the slightest prospect of being a success on the stage. Not from the moment I first set eyes on you. When you came into my office, while I worked for Dr Jeffery in New York. When you'd just had a miscarriage."

She opened her mouth, but instead of speaking screwed her eyes up. "You're sort of shimmering."

"You've drunk a lot of brandy. It's slurring your speech. I paid for your voice training. With a proper coach, right after we were married, till the hard times came in the winter of '92 and the money ran out. I paid for your gowns. I paid for your jewels. I paid for that show you were in, back in '99. As Cora Motzi in Vio and Mitzki's *Bright Lights,*" he derided her daringly. "Bright lights! You never dazzled anyone in the world, except me. Last week at the Met I saw what you were worth. Nothing."

Her only response was to say in a dreamy voice, "Gee, I'm kind of dry. My throat's burning. Get me a glass of water, Peter."

When he returned from the kitchen with a tumbler she was asleep. He stood staring at her. She opened her eyes suddenly. "Where you been?"

"To fetch you a drink."

She took the glass. Crippen resumed his stance by the fire. "When are you going to see Bruce Miller again?"

She choked, unable to swallow. "Shut your mouth about Bruce Miller."

"What about Richard Ehrlich? The German student who was your lover under this very roof. Did you ever see *him* again?"

"What if I did? You're no use to any woman."

"I am to any normal woman."

"What are you saying? I'm not normal?"

"You suffer from nymphomania." Belle started to laugh. It became wilder, then uncontrollable. She swung about in the chair, gripping the arms. Crippen watched her. "I intend to treat you for it."

"Treat me?" She stopped laughing, staring at him fixedly. "I like that! How, I'll ask?"

"With henbane."

"That's a poison!" she shouted.

"All drugs are poisons, unless taken in the right doses."

"Why don't you treat Ethel Le Neve?" Belle asked thickly. "Le Neve," she sneered. "She was born plain Neve, her father's a coals canvasser, who gets drunk in the pubs and gets arrested."

"You're drunk yourself."

Belle half-rose, gasping. "That table! The one we played cards on. It moved. Look!" She gave a hoarse cry. "There's something under it. A dog, a huge black dog – "

"I can't see anything," Crippen said mildly.

Belle slumped back, holding her forehead in both hands. "My face is burning. I'm sick, I guess. Help me to bed."

Crippen suddenly leant over her, gripping her arms. "How many times have you threatened to leave me?" he said with unknown venom. "Threatened! It would be the happiest release for me and Ethel. You could take your jewels. You could take our whole £600 in the Charing Cross Bank. You could go off to America to Bruce Miller, to whoever you cared. But you wouldn't. You found me too useful here, working my heart out at Munyon's, the Drouet Institute, the Tooth Specialists. Providing you with clothes and comfort, a slave for anything you fancied. You've your own friends. Your own pleasures. You leave me here lonely and miserable. The only sympathy and affection I've ever had in the world is from Ethel."

He straightened up. She sat looking dazed, slowly rubbing her arms. "All right. All right, I'll go," she mumbled.

"It's too late now."

"What d'you mean?"

"I don't know. My head is full of bees," he told her abruptly.

She half rose, face shot with terror. She screamed, "It ain't a dog, it's a bear — "

He glanced quickly at the drawn curtains of pink velvet. They were thick enough to muffle the sound. The neighbours were anyway used to Belle's outbursts. "There's nothing there. You're seeing things."

"Oh, Peter…" She looked at him piteously, clutching her breast. "My heart…my heart…it's flying from my body."

"You're drunk. You had three glasses playing cards. Maybe that brandy's not only stronger in taste?"

She rose unsteadily from the chair. Her mouth opened, no words came. She staggered, clutching the mantelpiece, pulling the pink cloth, smashing a china cat against the gas-fire.

"Peter!" she screamed. Crippen continued staring, hands under coat tails. "I'm dying…" He did not move. "I'm going next door, to Mrs Harrison…" She tried to walk, knocked over the small table, clattering the framed photographs on the floor. She crumpled. She lay face down on the carpet, giving a huge gasp. Crippen stayed immobile.

"Belle," he said quietly.

He hesitated.

"Belle — "

He crouched and turned her half-over. Her face was dusky, her mouth slack, her eyes partly open. He stood up. "So," he said. He gave her chest a gentle kick, partly inquisitive, partly insolent. "Belle has left me," he murmured. He sounded unbelieving. He walked quickly round the room, hands in pockets. He stopped suddenly, righted the overturned table and carefully replaced the photographs. He rearranged the pink mantelpiece cover, picking up the fragments of china from the carpet, cupping them delicately in his left hand, leaving the room for the kitchen and tipping them into the round bin under the sink where Belle had scraped the leavings from their dinner plates.

He returned to the parlour, strode straight past Belle, crouched and switched off the gas-fire. Then he turned Belle on her back with his foot. He raised her eyelids, revealing pupils like black full moons. He felt her wrist for a pulse, noticing the forearms drawn in spasm, the fingers clawed. "So Belle shall vanish," he said. He began to undress her.

He unbuttoned her yellow silk gown down the back, unlaced the waist, pulled the bodice from her crooked arms and tugged the skirts from her feet. The cotton underskirt was soaked with urine. He remembered that Belle had not visited a certain room since dinner. He tugged off the black ankle boots with pearl buttons up the side, and unbuckled the black lisle stockings from suspenders stretching halfway down her fat thighs. He loosed the tape of her cotton knickers, which ended in six-inch frills over the knee. He unknotted the lacing of her stays, ripping them off her wobbling buttocks. She had only an undervest with six buttons, which he loosed from wallowing breasts. He had not seen her naked for five years or so. She always had him come to her in the dark, like an animal. He noticed the scar running from navel to pubic hair, the incision for the ovariotomy which turned her barren.

He unpinned the rising sun brooch, unclasped the gold chain of a lozenge-shaped diamond pendant from the fleshy, blue-tinged base of her neck, slipped off her gold wristwatch, pulled the two diamond rings from her right hand and the ruby from her left, placed them among the photographs. Her broad gold wedding ring would not budge with determined tugs. He noticed a sticky thick smear of vomit on the carpet, noting to mop it with the kitchen dishcloth later.

Crippen hung his frock-coat over the back of a chair. He pulled Belle by her feet across the carpet into the bare-boarded hall. The clocks chimed half past. It was only an hour since the Martinettis had left. Gripping her ankles, he pulled her up the stairs, her head bouncing from step to step, tortoiseshell combs spilling from her hair. He was sweating. He tugged her across the line into the bathroom. Grunting, he bundled her into the bath. There was a gurgle, and faeces oozed through her flaccid anal sphincter. He wrinkled his nose, turned on the cold tap, used the rose-patterned pitcher from the marble-topped washstand to swill it down the plughole. He went downstairs, felt for his leather-covered case of instruments behind the books, and stuck Gray's *Anatomy* under his arm.

Belle filled the bath, breasts slid sideways, her stomach slack rolls of fat, her face blue. Crippen loosened his cufflinks and turned up his sleeves. As he moved her head, long muscle-scalpel in hand, she made a low groan. He jerked up, shocked. Was she still alive? He decided it was a post-mortem effect. He dug the scalpel into her neck to the left of her windpipe, trying to sever the tendinous end of the sternomastoid muscle from the top of the breastbone.

He pulled the knife out. It was ridiculously blunt. He inspected the edge, noticed his razor-strop on its hook below the window, and honed it for some minutes. He was delighted to find that it cut flesh like the tenderest chicken. He severed the big carotid arteries and jugular veins, blood stickying his fingers as he slit through her windpipe and gullet. He must decide the next step. He opened Gray's *Anatomy* on the cork-seated white bathroom chair, seeking the section *Osteology*, bloodying the pages as he turned them.

Crippen's anatomical knowledge was skimpy, but principles learned in the dissecting room remain in the mind, like the principles of Christianity to the theological student long left the seminary. He found the subsection *Vertebrae Cervicales* under *Columna Vertebralis*. He dug the knife through the skin and fat of the neck, severing the elastic ligaments which join one vertebral bone and the next, like the segments of ox-tail in a stew. As he lifted Belle's head into the air, something clattered against the enamel of the bath. A circular metal Hinde's curler, with three or four inches of bleached brown hair twined in it. Belle had overlooked unclipping it with the others when she dressed. He wondered if the Martinettis had noticed it.

Reaching for a pair of long pointed scissors from the instrument case he cut the curler free, clanging to the bottom of the bath, where the headless body had trapped pools of blood. He decided to take the hair off, snipping into the rose-patterned wash-basin until the head was as bare as a nun's. He would burn the hair in the kitchen stove, with his shirt and *Gray*. Hair did not rot. The teeth, too, could be an obstacle. He could extract them and drop them into the bin at Albion House, unnoticeable among the day's crop.

Osteotomy forceps, like a stout pair of nail-clippers, severed the ribs. As though pulling apart the picked carcass of a chicken to boil for soup, he tugged the severed gullet and windpipe from the hollow of the corpse. He cut the flat muscle of the diaphragm which separated chest from belly. He slit the guts from the filmy, blood-gorged, fatty mesentry, which secured them to the trunk like a string of sausages in a paper bag. He had blood to the elbows, and leaning over the bath was backbreaking. He freed the sloppy, brownish, gleaming liver, the kidneys dangling from their springy arteries, the spleen like a huge red mushroom, the bag of Belle's stomach still containing her roast pork, her potatoes in their jackets and her blancmange, the brandy stinking like an uncorked bottle.

He severed the top of the rectum, where it joined the big pipe of the gut. Gripping the joined organs by the gullet and windpipe, he pulled them with a glug and a squelch from the husk. He wondered what to do with them. He dropped them between Belle's legs. He rinsed hands and forearms under the cold tap. From the hook on the door hung his green-striped flannel pyjama jacket, forgotten that morning after shaving. He wrapped it round the organs like pastry round the meat of a Cornish pastie. He remembered Belle's womb. It would never do, leaving *that*.

He clutched it in the basin of her pelvis. Her bladder squirted the last of the urine between her legs. With one cut, he had her womb and most of her vagina. Her ovaries had gone to another knife, seventeen years before. The clocks chimed four. Completing the job could wait until tomorrow. It was cold, Belle would not go "off" any sooner than a joint freshly bought from the butcher's. Would the neighbours be curious over the bathroom light? They were familiar with the gas burning in the smallest room next door. He had forgotten the wedding ring on her third finger. Reaching for the scalpel, he adroitly severed the finger through the little joint at its base, pulled off the ring and tossed the digit into the empty body.

# 14

No 39 Hilldrop Crescent was equidistant from the church in Oseney Crescent across Brecknock Road, and another at the angle of Camden and Caledonian Road. With the laziness of London clocks, each chimed in succession, not synchrony. Crippen woke as usual while they were announcing seven. He was so late to bed, he had set the double-bellied American alarm clock for seven-thirty, and he fumbled to press off the switch.

It was over a half-hour till sunrise. He felt for a vesta and lit the bedside candle. He was in clean pyjamas, one of the three identical green-striped pairs Belle had bought at the winter sale of Jones Brothers, Shirtmakers, Holloway. He lay still on the narrow brass bed in the cold small room with pink dog-roses twining up the wall-paper. Was it a dream?

He reached for his round, gold-rimmed glasses, stood up, stretched, crossed the line to the bathroom. He lit the gas. It was clearly not a dream. Belle's clipped head stared at him from between her feet, the pile of entrails peeped glisteningly from the wrapping of pyjama jacket. His problem was where to shave. He collected his razor, turned off the gas, and descended to the kitchen.

By seven-thirty he was dressed, his steaming cup of Camp coffee wedged among last night's dirty crockery on the kitchen table. He felt Belle was as usual asleep under the bright pink coverlet of her bed with pink bows on the corners. As far as the world would know, she was. By his usual homecoming time she would be going to America. It was fascinating, living her life for her.

He bolted the tradesman's entrance and locked the front door behind him. No one would call. Mrs Harrison visited only when invited. As they used condensed milk the milkman knocked only on Sunday, the baker left a loaf on the side step Wednesdays and Saturdays. He took his usual way to Caledonian Road Underground station, skirting the Cattle Market. He arrived before nine at Aural Remedies at Craven House in Kingsway. Miss Ena Balham, thirtyish, in black serge, with pince-nez and a faint moustache, was behind her big, square black typewriter.

"Did you say 'White rabbits'?" Crippen looked mystified. "It's February the first," she chided him.

He took her inch-thick sheaf of newly opened letters. Aural Remedies was a correspondence clinic. People with bad ears responded to advertisements in *Tit-Bits* or *John Bull* – enclosing postal order with stamped addressed envelope – and Crippen dispatched the remedies. He flicked through them silently, pencilling code-numbers for which letter Miss Balham should write, or which bottle of eardrops dispatch.

"You quite well this morning, doctor?" she asked kindly.

"Perfectly."

She gave a slight laugh. "You seem so quiet. Not your usual self."

"I've some urgent business at the Tooth Specialists."

He hurried towards Oxford Street. A few minutes, and he would be seeing Ethel. Now they were really hub and wifie. They could live under the same roof. The future shone like a summer sunrise.

The shiny black leatherette cover stood on her machine. "Where's Ethel?" he asked explosively.

The office contained only Miss Marion Curnow, the middle-aged manageress, in white blouse and check skirt. She looked surprised. "She just phoned from Constantine Road. She's a little poorly this morning."

Ethel was often poorly. They called her behind her back, "Not Very Well, Thank You."

"Well, doctor, it's an important day in your life."

Crippen started. "Why?"

"You're freed from slavery to Munyon's."

Crippen nodded distractedly. He had drawn dwindling commission as an agent since Munyon's office in Oxford Circus failed.

"You don't take it hard, doctor, my continuing as Munyon's London manageress?" Miss Curnow accepted his manner as pique.

"No, not at all. The money was hardly a king's ransom." He paused. All four who worked in his office knew that Crippen had been short of funds since Christmas. His wife's dresses alone... Miss Curnow had thought severely. "I'm expecting quite a considerable sum coming in from America."

Crippen went to his room.

He left before noon. "Tell Dr Ryland I shan't be back today," he instructed Miss Curnow.

The head would be a difficulty. It needed cutting into fairly small bits, and he had not the luxury of time. Perhaps some other approach would suggest itself. The limbs should sever easily at the joints, with assistance from the *Arthrology* section in *Gray*. He hurried to Shaftesbury Avenue, turned into No 1 King Edward's Mansions, and rang the bell of the Martinetti's flat.

"How's Paul?" he asked Clara at the door.

"He's just gone into a nice sleep. If you don't mind I shan't waken him. How's Belle?"

"Oh, she's all right."

"Give her my love."

"Yes, I will."

The next day was Wednesday, and the weekly meeting of the Music Hall Ladies' Guild. The morning was bitter and overcast, gas flaring in the shop windows as Crippen made his way to work. He went directly to the Tooth Specialists. Miss Curnow was unpinning her hat. He set a packet on Ethel's typewriter, and left immediately for Aural Remedies round the corner.

Ethel arrived ten minutes later. She wore under her overcoat a blue serge costume trimmed with black braid. She sat at her typewriter, unhurriedly opening the packet. Inside was an envelope addressed to her. "Well I never!" she exclaimed. "She's gone to America."

"Who has?"

"Mrs Crippen."

"Hasn't she been threatening to for years?"

Crippen's note asked her to pass an enclosed package to Miss Melina May, secretary of the Music Hall Ladies' Guild on the floor below. He would look in later. They could have a pleasant little evening.

The errand seemed un-urgent. Ethel passed over the package at ten to one, on her way to lunch. "Mrs Martinetti's just telephoned," remarked Miss May, at her desk with her typewriter and wire baskets of correspondence. "She can't come to the meeting, her husband's still poorly."

Miss May opened the packet. She was dark, pale, pretty, once broke her leg, developed a limp, had to renounce the stage. She was surprised to find the Guild's cheque book, pass book and paying-in book. Two letters were addressed from Hilldrop Crescent and dated that day.

*Dear Miss May*, said the first.

*Illness of a near relative has called me to America on only a few hours' notice, so I must ask you to bring my resignation as treasurer before the meeting today, so that a new treasurer can be elected at once.*

She frowned. The writing was not Belle's. She looked at the foot.

*Yours,*

*Belle Elmore, p.p. HHC*

Miss May resumed,

*You will appreciate my haste when I tell you that I have not been to bed all night packing, and getting ready to go. I hope I shall see you again a few months later, but cannot spare a moment to call on you before I go. I wish you everything nice till I return to London again. Now, goodbye, with love, hastily.*

"Well, really!" complained Miss May.

The other letter was longer, addressed to the Committee –

"Dear Friends" – explaining the sudden flight, submitting Belle's resignation, urging the rules be suspended for election of another treasurer that very day, sending "my pals" her loving wishes. It was in the same handwriting as the other. Miss May was cross. Everyone liked the ebullient Belle. Anyone merited sympathy over a sick relative. But suddenly changing the treasurer meant enormous unnecessary fuss.

Crippen had two mornings' work in one at Aural Remedies. Eardrops must be made up and packed in their pasteboard cases. The January accounts needed sending to Eddie Marr – the New York advertising man who put up Aural Remedies' money. He longed to see Ethel but dared not reach Albion House before the Music Hall Ladies' Guild dispersed at about four. He strolled down Oxford Street to Attenborough's, with the three brass balls outside. He pawned seven diamond rings, a pair of diamond earrings and a diamond brooch, taking the £195 in banknotes. He signed the contract note readily. He was well known in the pawnshop. He often brought Belle's jewellery for repair.

It was only three-thirty. He turned the opposite way to Albion House, towards Shaftesbury Avenue. He was surprised to find Mrs Martinetti in, not at the meeting.

"Well, you're a nice one," she greeted him at the door. "Belle gone to America, and you didn't let us know anything about it. Melinda phoned from the Guild. I couldn't leave Paul in bed, though he's much better."

Crippen came into the flat, which was small, mahogany-panelled and embellished with framed photographs of other theatricals, all ebulliently and lovingly autographed. "Why didn't you send us a wire?" She was more curious than scolding. "I would have liked to go to the station, and bring some flowers."

"There wasn't time. The cable came late last night. I had to look out a lot of papers – legal and family papers. The rest of the night we were busy packing."

She said with resignation, but unable to suppress annoyance, "Packing and crying, I suppose?"

"We have got past that," he said vaguely.

"Did she take all her clothes with her?"

"One basket."

Clara was amazed. "But that wouldn't be nearly enough, to go all that way."

"She can buy something over there."

Clara stood holding the rounded back of a chair. Crippen was edging towards the door. The doctor was always busy. "Belle's sure to send me a postcard from the ship," she said more agreeably. "Or she'll write when she gets to New York."

"She doesn't touch New York. No, she goes straight on to California."

"Whereabouts? To your son?"

"Around Los Angeles." He made a broadly embracing gesture. "Up in the hills. Right up in the mountains."

Clara concentrated perplexity and irritation into a small sigh. "I suppose you won't be wanting tickets for the Benevolent Fund Ball now? It's the twentieth, Sunday fortnight. At the Criterion, as usual."

"I'll take a couple anyway," he said generously.

She picked up a book of tickets from the cloth-draped mantelpiece. "They're half a guinea each."

He opened his wallet, taking care she did not see the pawnbroker's £5 notes. "Perhaps somebody else would like to go," he suggested absently.

He waited until five before reappearing at the Yale Tooth Specialists. Miss Curnow had gone home. Ethel was alone with two men in office suits, who were peering earnestly at the magazines while waiting for Dr Rylance. She arched her eyebrows. "She's gone?"

"When I got home last night, she'd vanished."

"She'll come back."

"I don't think so."

Ethel's eyes flicked towards the patients "What about her luggage?"

"I suppose she took enough." Why do women ask so closely about trifles like luggage? he wondered. He added in a low voice, "She left a note saying I must do what I could to cover up the scandal."

They looked at each other deeply for some seconds. All they longed for had unexpectedly, unbelievably happened. Remembering his note, she asked, "Did you want to go somewhere this evening? Frascati's?"

"Perhaps I'd better get home this evening. There may be a wireless from the ship."

"There must be a lot to clear up."

He nodded.

"Can I come and help?"

"Wait till Monday. We can go to the theatre then. It'll cheer me up."
He placed his hand upon hers by the typewriter, clasped it fiercely and
left.

By Saturday, all was done. Sunday was Crippen's bath day. He closed
the window, lit the geyser and lay in the hot water, gazing through the
steam into the bright morning sunshine, deliciously *gemütlich*. His only
concern was the Gray's *Anatomy*, burnt in the kitchen range, with Belle's
womb and vagina wrapped in the *News of the World*. He wondered if Dr
Beckett was expecting it back. It would be polite to enquire.

When Crippen did call upon Eliot, a couple of months had passed.
Towards two o'clock on the afternoon of Saturday, April 2, he appeared at
the People's surgery – which everyone in Holloway called "The Free
Medicine Shop." Nancy had a coat over her blue-and-white striped nurse's
uniform, specially made by Liberty's in Regent Street. She was going with
Eliot to the Brecknock Dining Rooms, which served beefsteak pudding,
cheese and tea on marble-topped tables for sixpence.

Their usual patients were augmented that morning by venturesome
newcomers from the most unfortunate of British classes, the genteel
lowest of the lower-middle, who fiercely upheld their distinction from the
workmen. They could read. Friday's *Daily Mail* had given a whole page to
the surgery, with an inspiring photograph of Nancy – the young and
beautiful daughter of a New York millionaire, sleeves rolled up to bandage
and poultice the blemishes of the poor, called throughout Holloway "The
Angel from America." Eliot had directed, "Cut it out and send it to your
father. Let him enjoy his philanthropy by proxy."

Eliot greeted Crippen with a started look. The usual colourful tie was
replaced by a black one, a broad band of black crêpe ringed the sleeve of his
light grey overcoat, his expression was of strained solemnity. He removed
his bowler. "I have bad news. I thought you would care to know, as you
were acquainted, and live so near. Belle is dead."

"I'm so sorry." Eliot used his professional condoling voice. "When did it
happen?"

"The Wednesday before Easter. March 23."

"I'm sorry, too, Dr Crippen," said Nancy "When was the funeral?"

"Oh, Belle didn't die here" Crippen came into the shop, which reeked of the crowd that had packed its benches since seven in the morning. "She died in California. She suddenly had to visit a sick relative, she took a chill on the boat going across, and never shook it off. I was shocked at a letter from her relations, saying she was very ill. Then I had one from Belle herself, telling me not to worry, she wasn't so bad as people said. I didn't know what to think. My head was full of bees," he complained pathetically.

"Next thing, I had a cable saying poor Belle was dangerously ill with double broncho-pneumonia. I had to consider going over right away. But of course, it's more difficult for me to leave London overnight like she did," he sighed. "I sat at home, fearing every minute for another cable saying she was gone. Sure enough, that came the following day."

Nancy remembered Baby. "It's always a shock, isn't it? Even when you've grown used to a dear one being gravely ill."

"Bronchial pneumonia is so more surely fatal than the croupous variety," Eliot said sympathetically. "The fever persists so long, and there is nothing we can do except prescribe a jacket poultice, a steam-kettle and spoonfuls of brandy. Everything turns on the skill of the nursing."

"Perhaps you would care to see her obituary notice, which I inserted in *Era*?"

Crippen took from his overcoat pocket a folded newspaper the size of *The Times*. Eliot noticed he held some envelopes in an elastic band, addressed in his cramped writing and edged with the thick black line of mourning.

Crippen opened the paper called "The Actor's Bible". Its first two pages were filled with narrow columns of dignified advertisements by players. All were "Mr" or "Miss" and gave their speciality — "Soubrette" or "Juggler" or "Trick Cyclist" — often followed by the telling words, "Available" or "Disengaged" or "At Liberty". Inside was news of shows in the West End, on the road, in New York, Berlin, Paris, even Australia. It reported meetings of the Actors' Union, the Stage Benevolent Society and the Showman's Guild. There was always a serious editorial — the issue which Crippen unfolded doughtily defended the dry-eyed flippancy of Louis Dubedat's death in *The Doctor's Dilemma*. It had advertisements for depilatory powder, bronchial troches and Roze-la-Valla wrinkle remover. Each week carried its list of deaths, with ages, and birthdays without. The paid obituary announcements filled a separate half-column. Crippen's finger indicated – *Elmore – March 23, in California, USA Miss Belle Elmore (Mrs H H Crippen)*.

"As sad a loss for the Ladies' Music Hall Guild as for myself." Eliot said nothing. He wanted his lunch. "I'm leaving Hilldrop Crescent when the quarter's notice expires in June – how could I live in a house with so many strong memories of Belle? She seemed to express her character in the decorations, the furniture. Miss Le Neve has meanwhile kindly arranged to leave her position at the office and come as my housekeeper."

"Why double your grief by enduring solitude?"

"I've just been for a nice little holiday to Dieppe," Crippen revealed. "After what happened to Belle, I needed some change of air. Oh, your anatomy book, Dr Beckett. It seems to have been mislaid in the fuss of Belle's departure."

"I'm sure I know all the anatomy I need."

Crippen was feeling inside his jacket. "I should like to make another donation."

The cheque from his wallet was drawn on the Charing Cross Bank for £5.

"That's most generous of you," Eliot said honestly. He seldom had enough to keep the surgery open more than two or three weeks ahead. He refused more from Nancy than his other supporters – he disliked feeling her father's client, and it was important politically to spread patronage and responsibility as widely as possible. "We have a tough job, screwing money out of trade union officials, clergymen and the brewers who contribute so much to what we treat."

Crippen gave Nancy his gentle smile. "I read the *Daily Mail*. Very touching. I wish I had done something of this nature when a young man, instead of going to Munyon's. Then, perhaps, people would remember me gratefully after my own death. As I'm sure Belle will be remembered. Good day."

The following Friday morning, a well-dressed woman appeared in the surgery, whom Eliot did not at first recognize against the sunlit street.

"We met at the Crippens," she introduced herself. "Mrs Martinetti." She looked nervously round the waiting patients on the benches. "Might I speak to you, doctor, in confidence?"

Eliot led her through the inner door. Nancy was on her daily round of bedridden patients. He wondered if she was consulting him for some disease unfit for the ears of her husband. "I heard the sad news that Mrs Crippen had died," he told her.

"She has *disappeared*." Clara Martinetti sat on the kitchen chair, vast hat on head, back straight, gloved hands clasping the horn handle of her umbrella. "You know Dr Crippen well — "

"Not particularly." Eliot sat at the deal table, which was covered with papers, medicine bottles and jam-jars sealed by oiled-silk containing lumps of mouldy bread for his patients' boils.

Clara looked surprised. "He always made out so. When I read about you in the *Mail* I decided to come and see you, because I'm terribly worried about Belle." She hesitated. "I'm wondering if the story of her death is true."

"Why shouldn't it be?" asked Eliot in surprise. "To catch cold on a boat and die of catarrhal pneumonia six weeks later is tragic, but perfectly reasonable. The patient even has spells feeling much better as the temperature falls — exactly as Mrs Crippen wrote to her husband. The disease may clear in one part of the lung, you see, only to break out afresh in another. I have seen many cases, and I can tell you that none recovered."

To Eliot's irritation, she stayed unconvinced. "I heard of it yesterday fortnight. I had this telegram. It was sent from Victoria Station."

From her crocodile handbag came a buff form stuck with paper strips. Eliot read —

BELLE DIED YESTERDAY AT SIX O'CLOCK PLEASE TELEPHONE ANNIE SHALL BE AWAY A WEEK PETER.

"Annie is Mrs Stratton, one of our committee. Like Mrs Smythson and Mrs Davis and Miss Way, we're most concerned. We called at Albion House directly after Easter last week, to offer our condolences and ask where poor Belle died. Dr Crippen said in Los Angeles, with his own relations. We asked the address because we wanted to send a letter of sympathy and an everlasting wreath. He said it wasn't necessary. None of Belle's friends in America would ever have heard of the Music Hall Ladies' Guild. Really!" Eliot felt that Crippen's gravest offence.

"Anyway, he gave us his son Otto's address in Los Angeles – you knew the doctor was twice married?" Eliot nodded. The woman was stealing time from his patients. "He said his son was with Belle when she died. Naturally I asked about the funeral. Would you believe what he said? She wasn't buried. She was cremated. He was having the ashes sent over. He said we could 'have a little ceremony then'. Cremated! It's unnatural."

"They're very go-ahead in these matters in America."

Her voice accelerated under the steam of her indignation. "I asked him what ship Belle went by. He said it was the French line, something like *La Tourenne* or *La Touvée*. The doctor speaks French of course. So I went down to the offices of the French Atlantic Shipping Line in the City. Oh, yes, they had a liner sailing from New York to Havre called *La Touraine*. But it hadn't arrived on February the second. That was the day Belle left. And it went straight into dry-dock for repairs," she ended triumphantly.

"But Dr Crippen is always vague, and must have been dreadfully agitated," Eliot told her impatiently. "He simply got the ship's name wrong."

Clara leant over the table. "That telegram was sent as Dr Crippen left for Dieppe with his lady typist, Miss Le Neve."

Eliot nearly laughed. "To save your embarrassment, I know all about Miss Le Neve."

"I don't think you do, Dr Beckett. At our Benevolent Fund Ball in February – after Belle had left, before there was the slightest suggestion that she was ill – the doctor appeared with Miss Le Neve. She was wearing one of Belle's dresses, magenta silk, I recognized it beyond doubt. She had Belle's fox fur. Belle's muff. Belle's earrings. And Belle's brooch she was so fond of, the one with the rising sun. She wore it the evening you and the nice American lady came to dinner. And Belle's gold watch. A ring with four diamonds and a ruby, Belle's I swear. And a wedding band."

Eliot rose. Any woman felt outraged at a friend who was ousted by another prettier and younger than them both. He put his arm round her shoulders. "It's easy to think terrible things when someone you love dies far away in the lawless wilds of California. But we are men and women of the world, Mrs Martinetti. Surely the theatrical profession well knows the temptation of a pretty girl to an older man? To use his wife's ornaments to decorate her is appalling bad taste, but nothing worse."

"She's moved in with him," she exclaimed accusingly.

"A man must have a housekeeper. After twenty years of married life, you can hardly expect Dr Crippen to 'batch' it, surely? Weren't Mrs Crippen and Miss Le Neve perfectly friendly? It's only natural the doctor should turn to her for condolence." Eliot opened the consulting-room door. "Why, you'll be suggesting the good little doctor murdered his wife."

"No, I'm not suggesting that." He felt she made her reply unnecessarily thoughtfully.

"A gossip, a malicious gossip," he pronounced to Nancy that evening.

Eliot sprawled on the sofa in Camden Road, Norfolk jacket off, in his red socks, reading *The Times*. The sunny day brought an evening cold enough for a fire. They now had two rooms in the big house – always empty except for the visitor who arrived unexpectedly, stayed secretly and left hurriedly.

"What misery is occasioned by people who stir the mud in the murky little puddles of others' lives," he commented.

"And what pleasure." Nancy was at the table, writing an order for Allen and Hanbury's, the surgical suppliers across at Bethnal Green.

"I have the utmost compassion for people with stunted bodies, but not with small minds," Eliot observed into the pages of his newspaper. "Belle was a nymphomaniac," he revealed.

"What's that?"

"Morbid uncontrollable sexual desire in the female. The deranged women furiously embrace every man they can get at. It's been a well recognized condition for over a century. Dr Crippen had to dose her with hyoscine. That's the usual drug, it's either a sedative or a strait-jacket. They get in awful trouble with the law otherwise." He turned the page. "Crippen's was a happy release."

"I'm not so sure. I've seen a woman crazy with grief across the body of her husband, killed in an East Side knife-fight. Yet everyone in the

137

neighbourhood heard her screams, night after night, when he beat her up."

"Dr Crippen is like a divalent atom, with two combining powers. He chose to link himself with a pair of elements as different as the violently explosive fluorine and the totally inert platignum."

"What's Miss Le Neve like?"

"I believe she's a very good typist."

# 15

Three weeks later, on the morning of Wednesday, April 27, 1910, King Edward VII arrived at Dover from Calais in the royal yacht Alexandra. He had journeyed by train across France from Biarritz, with his usual pause in Paris. Biarritz saw the English king a week or two every spring. He ate, drank, smoked cigars, played bacarrat, strolled the promenade in the Atlantic breezes which sprayed the sea along the rocky coast, drove into the Pyrenees in his Mercedes, the royal motor-engineer Mr Stamper sitting next to the chauffeur, poised to jump out for the breakdowns.

The machinery of State meanwhile clanked round the King. Mr Asquith had kissed hands on appointment as Prime Minister in the Hotel de Palais. The King's suggestion that a British cabinet meeting be held the following week at the Hotel Crillon in Paris, was thought placing the convenience of the Monarch too noticeably above the proprieties of the Constitution.

King Edward returned among rumours of Mr Asquith's demand he create sufficient new Liberal peers to swamp the House of Lords, and bring it to the prime minister's bidding. A royal threat was enough. The House of Lords would fight for their right to throw out budgets, but not at the price of being overwhelmed by a pack of upstart bounders. He returned also to a buzz about his health.

The King went to the opera, he saw Lord Kitchener and the pictures at the Royal Academy, he went to the opera again, he went to Sandringham and to Mrs Keppel's house in Grosvenor Street. On Thursday, May 5, he failed to welcome Queen Alexandra back from her Mediterranean cruise, and Buckingham Palace announced that he was suffering a severe cold.

The next morning, the King's doctors declared that he gave rise to anxiety. His horse *Witch of the Air* won the 4.15 at Kempton Park. They sent for the Queen. The Queen with sublime understanding sent for Mrs Keppel. At six o'clock, the doctors proclaimed his condition critical. Saturday morning's *Times* appeared with thick black lines separating all its columns.

His people were shocked. The reticence of the bulletins had drawn knots instead of crowds to the Palace railings. The King had worn the crown of scandal, but earned the affection of his easygoing, race-loving, self-indulgent subjects as deservedly as his nickname "Tum-tum." He was crowned with France and Russia his country's implacable enemies. He died leaving them enduring friends.

"You'll enjoy the royal funeral," Eliot told Nancy that Saturday evening. "We do those sort of things terrifically well."

Eliot heard the doorbell. There were hurried footsteps on the stairs. The door flew open without a knock. Ruston appeared with Wince, who carried a brown attaché case. Both stopped, staring at Nancy. She sat on a stool between the fireplace and Eliot, who stood unmoving, hands in pockets, resentful of the interruption.

"We're just going out to dine. Can I offer you fellows a b and s?" Ruston's gesture brushed aside brandy and soda. "I want to speak to you, Eliot. In confidence."

"Miss Grange's discretion is as remarkable as her intelligence."

"I must insist on seeing you alone."

Ruston sounded angry. He called every week, his business trivial — generally chiding Eliot on not distributing the movement's tracts among the doctors, lawyers, ministers of religion and similar professional men who might afford him confidence. Eliot objected that he was too busy patching the sick poor to ring middle-class doorbells. He knew that Ruston himself wrote the tracts, and thought them intellectually powerfully persuasive.

Nancy stood. "I've anyway to see Frau Ebert about our Sunday dinner," she said accommodatingly.

"Why must you keep company with that woman?" asked Ruston peevishly as the door shut.

"Marat was married and even the incorruptible Robespierre was not celibate."

"Women interfere." Wince laid the attaché on the table, unlocking it with a key on a bunch from his trouser pocket. "And talk."

"What we are to say mustn't reach another ear, Eliot, even in a whisper. You'll swear to that?"

"I can hardly give my sacred oath if we regard the Bible as capitalist propaganda. You can't have it both ways."

"It makes no difference if you agree or not," Ruston told him impatiently. "The only way to keep a man's mouth shut is assuring him that his head will come off if he opens it. You know we can do that, don't you?" he asked menacingly. "Remember what happened to Thompson."

Thompson was a young schoolmaster Eliot had known in the movement before leaving for Champette. While Eliot was in Switzerland, Thompson's body had been found in Hackney Marshes with a bullet in the brain. Neither Eliot, nor seemingly Ruston, nor certainly Scotland Yard, had a precise notion of the murderer or the motive. But the reference was enough to make Eliot uneasy.

"I'd never tell my old woman so much as the time o'day." Wince was spreading on the table the yard-long sheet of an Ordnance Survey map. "She'd always look out someone to pass the news to."

"Well, Eliot, now's a chance to show what you're made of."

Ruston's smile was more sarcastic than inspiring. "His Imperial Majesty Kaiser William II will soon be within our shores. Our fat King's funeral is May 21, a fortnight today. As his nephew, the Kaiser's importance in the ceremony will be separated only by our new King George from that of the corpse."

Wince nodded, producing his curly pipe and tobacco-pouch.

"I don't think anyone knows at the moment when the Kaiser will leave Berlin, not even the Kaiser himself," Ruston continued. "He's due to attend a lecture next week by the outspoken Mr Theodore Roosevelt at Berlin University, and he won't miss the chance of presenting himself as a man who can appreciate American politicians. Particularly one demanding Britain to get out of Egypt. What we're pretty sure about is our friend's route. The Imperial yacht *Hohenzollen* will berth here at Sheerness, on the north-west corner of the isle of Sheppey."

Eliot looked obediently at the map. The oval island in the Thames Estuary, some ten miles by five, was separated from the north Kent coast by a narrow reach of sea choked with sandbanks. To the west lay the mouth of the River Medway and Rochester, reminding Eliot of Charles Dickens. To the east, the tiny port of Whitstable, reminding Eliot of oysters.

"We shall know when Kaiser Bill arrives with no more trouble than reading the newspapers," Ruston resumed enthusiastically. "We'll know the time his train leaves for London, because there'll be a reception committee in feathered hats at Victoria. That'll be announced in advance by the newspapers as well."

Wince held a match over his pipe-bowl with one hand. "Bin spyin' out the land for just this chance the past three years. Sheppey itself we can ferget. It's a military area, see? Barracks up there, at Garrison Point." He indicated with a stubby finger of his free hand. "Railway runs straight sahth for three and a 'alf miles, crosses the water at King's Ferry Bridge. It's all marshland, flat as yer 'and. They'll station a platoon up 'ere on Barrows 'ill ter keep a sharp lookout on anyone moving abaht."

Wince seemed to Eliot an unlikely military man. Then he recalled some remark by Ruston of Wince in Dusseldorf on a month's training "for active service." Perhaps Wince's shambling personality was a careful disguise. Eliot knew that he spoke fluent German and French, and had a quicker head for figures than himself.

"The branch line joins the main London, Chatham and Dover tracks just 'ere, another three miles further sahth. It's still flat an' covered with orchards – as you'd expect in Kent – so you can't see far. Then it runs west for five miles, nearly all in cuttin's, 'ard against the old Roman road ter London. See that curved cuttin' there, ahtside a village called Cold 'arbour?" Puffing clouds of smoke, Wince tapped the map decisively. "That's where we're going to do it."

"Do what?" asked Eliot.

"You're being deliberately obtuse," said Ruston irritably. "Blow up the Kaiser."

"You're mad."

"What do you mean, Eliot?" he demanded angrily. "Are you with us, or aren't you? You've known perfectly well that's our plan, since January. You chose to live here cheaply and in comfort, and now you're asked to do something in return you're showing up as a coward."

"I'm not a coward. It's just that I'm not interested in murdering people."

"Oh, damn you!" Ruston banged the table. "We're going to change the history of the world. And you're no more serious about it than a cricket match."

"I don't see why you should pick me to do your dirty work."

"Let me explain our plan." Wince seemed unconcerned with the argument. "We've got a couple of blokes 'oo'll be in the firin'-line. Railwaymen, from the Great Northern."

"Members for ten years, utterly reliable, both been to Dusseldorf and trained with explosives," said Ruston warmly.

"There won't be nobody watchin' the line most o' the way. Stands to reason, don't it? They'd need 'arf the army. An' wot's the point? The Kaiser's a popular chap, the King's cousin. They'll send a tank engine ahead o' the royal special, so if anyone's provided a rather generous detonator, or removed a rail or two on the sly, the driver and fireman'll get it in the eye, not 'is Imperial Majesty. Our men will set orf the charge as the train goes across, then run for it."

"They won't run far," Eliot said.

Wince continued calmly, "There'll be a carriage an' pair with another of our blokes, getting them to Chatham along the main road in less than an hour. In Chatham, we've an 'ahse they can lie low in, as long as they like."

"Where'll you get the dynamite from?" Eliot asked. "You can't buy it at the Army and Navy Stores."

Ruston smiled smugly. "It's under your feet."

"So far, there seems nothing for me to do, anyway," Eliot pointed out. "I don't care going along just for the excitement."

"You are the hub of the operation, Eliot. Your orders are to take a room in the *Bull and Mouth* inn at Sittingbourne for the week of the funeral. Sittingbourne is exactly where the two railway lines join. Our two railwaymen are heroes of the people, but they are unschooled. They can barely read and write. We need an intelligent man to pass messages, to free the snags, to extemporize should anything go wrong. A well-spoken fellow like you will create not a breath of suspicion. You won't use your own name, of course. Choose any you like," Ruston ended generously.

"Lenin?" suggested Eliot.

"You must take this seriously," Ruston repeated angrily.

"I take extremely seriously the certainty that I shall be arrested and hanged, as colonel of a regiment of two illiterates."

"Then you will be a martyr," Ruston assured him solemnly.

"Why not go instead? Wouldn't you like to be a martyr, too?"

"To be frank, I am too important to risk."

"I've thought of another objection."

"What's that?"

"My father will undoubtedly be sacked by the Duke."

Ruston glared. He checked what he was about to say. "I interpret this foolish attitude as embarrassment at having to perform your duty, when you had every intention of avoiding it. We shall be back tomorrow." Wince began folding his map. "I have important things to accomplish tonight."

"And I am becoming late for my dinner."

Eliot was evasive about the visit until sitting in the corner of a narrow French restaurant in Soho. It was one of the few open, the evening after the King's death. The tables were crude, the floor sawdusted, the walls lined with scrolled mirrors, the ceiling over the gas-globes thick with dead flies. Eliot said it served the best veal in London.

"They wish to change my duties from pushing political tracts through clergymen's letter boxes to blowing up the German Emperor," he announced.

Nancy stared, mouth agape. "Oh, God save us," she muttered. "But it's crazy."

"I know. The only effect of the plan will be the locking up of its perpetrators."

"There's a lot about this movement you've never told me of, isn't there?" She was more frightened than reproachful.

"There's a lot I don't know myself. You must have guessed the house is a staging-post for comrades from the Continent? Scotland Yard certainly has our address, but as we're doing nothing illegal I don't give a tinker's cuss. There's German money behind it, which probably accounts for the Kaiser's privilege as the target. Communism's a German phenomenon. Marx and Engels were Rhinelanders, remember. Over there, it's a voice demanding to govern. Here it's just a voice, to which the British workers are as deaf as to the street-corner evangelists."

Eliot reached for her hand across the zinc-topped table with paper cloth. "I can't forgive myself for getting you mixed in this, dearest. I should have told you at the beginning, but of course I was scared you'd just fly off."

She was concerned only at his being mixed in it. He said ruefully, "When I joined, I suppose I'd have blown up the Duke and my father with him. Now my ideas upon the British revolution are as gentlemanly as Carlyle's on the French one. I still want a revolution, but only in the abstract."

The fat proprietor in his tight alpaca coat presented the burgundy. Eliot sniffed, sipped and nodded. "Ruston's probably as appalled at the scheme as I am, but too frightened to admit it. I've the idea that Wince is the boss, really. Everything is so devious in a revolutionary body, I suspect for the fun of it."

"We must leave the house at once," Nancy said firmly.

"*You* must. You're going home to New York by the next boat."

"Of course I'm not."

"Nancy, my darling – love is sweet but life is sweeter."

She looked scared. "You mean we're in danger?"

"If they're ruthless enough to kill the Kaiser, they certainly are to kill me."

The proprietor served their *blanquette de veau à l'ancienne*. "Ruston tried to scare me about one of our comrades who was found shot," Eliot resumed. "Though I doubt for ratting on the movement. He was a young man afflicted with the same malady as Oscar Wilde. He had strange business with important men who would have mourned him by cracking a bottle of champagne."

"I'll go to New York if you come too. That'll solve everything."

"I can't leave overnight, like Mrs Crippen. No more than Dr Crippen could. I've patients depending on me."

"They can go down the road to the Royal Free Hospital. They survived before your surgery was there."

"They'd think poorly of me. And I don't care to run away. It would blow a hole in my political career."

"Why not stay in New York? There'd be no trouble, fixing you a licence to practise."

He was silent for some time. "No," he said.

"Do you suppose the whole plan's a fantastic dream of those two men?" Nancy suggested more cheerfully. "My father gets threats against his life every month. Nothing happens. He just passes them along to Pinkerton's."

"I shall emulate Gilbert's admirably sagacious Duke of Plaza-Toro in similar circumstances," Eliot decided. "I shall send my resignation in, the first of all his corps, O!"

"Go to the police," she suggested eagerly. "You know enough about Ruston and Wince."

"Enough to get them both hanged on the same morning. But I can hardly denounce them without incriminating myself."

They decided the safest plan was an anonymous letter to Scotland Yard, warning of an attempt upon the Kaiser during his train journey to London. Eliot calculated it would line the railway with policemen, to scare away the two unlettered assassins. They must move house instantly, Nancy insisted. Eliot recalled Crippen's remark about leaving Hilldrop Crescent. He suggested they bought the fag-end of the lease. Nancy agreed. Scrubbed and stripped of its pink hangings, the house was tolerable. "At least, there's no dynamite in the cellar," Eliot told her.

Preparing the anonymous letter on Sunday morning was a fresh experience as alarming to Eliot as preparing to blow up the royal train. He tore a sheet from a cheap exercise-book, wrote in pencilled capitals, and took the Metropolitan Railway to post it in the City. That afternoon he walked with Nancy up Camden Road to Hilldrop Crescent. A dark girl about sixteen in a brown dress and an apron opened the door. The antipathy to servants had died with Belle.

Eliot gave their names. The girl shrugged, and called into the house, "Madame!" Ethel appeared, smiling. "I read about you in the paper," she said admiringly, remembering Nancy. "This is Mademoiselle Valentine, the doctor and I brought her over from Boulogne last week."

Eliot brought a smile from the girl by addressing her in French. "Oh, I do wish I could speak like that!" Ethel clasped her hands together. "Valentine is living with us *au pair*, as the French say."

On starvation wages, as the English say, Eliot thought.

"I hope she'll improve my French conversation. The doctor speaks the language perfectly, of course. He's out, seeing Mr Marr at Aural Remedies," Ethel apologized. "Even on a Sunday, would you believe it? But Mr Marr's very useful to the doctor. Do come in."

She led them into the parlour, with comfortable assurance as mistress of the house. The room was still pink, but the bows had gone from the picture-frames, the photographs were cleared away. It was full of clothes — a fur coat, overcoats in brown, black and cream, a feather boa, jackets and skirts, an armchair filled with lace-edged silk blouses and coloured underskirts, another with pink nightgowns, stockings and stays. Eliot counted seven pairs of shoes lined across the carpet, black, blue, black-and-white and pink. The card table was piled with hats. A square wicker basket used by performers "on the road" stood empty, its side stencilled in thick black letters BELLE ELMORE. Before the fireplace was a dark, middle-aged woman in a brand-new heliotrope costume made for someone shorter and fatter.

"This is Emily Jackson." Ethel's voice was fond. "She was my landlady at Constantine Road. I was giving her some of poor Belle's clothes. It seems such a shame, just having them eaten by moths, doesn't it?"

Nancy made a sympathetic remark about Belle dying so far from home. "It was a great shock," said Ethel solemnly. She looked quickly from Eliot to Nancy. "Mrs Jackson was more of a mother to me than a landlady. She knows all about me and the doctor before…before…"

"The doctor's one of the nicest men I ever met," asserted Mrs Jackson warmly.

"And now the poor King too has gone to his rest," sighed Ethel. As this seemed to raise death from a personal to general subject, Eliot mentioned his interest in the house.

"Yes, the doctor *did* give notice, for sure," Ethel said. "But now we're thinking of staying till September. It's so difficult, finding somewhere nice. And the doctor's getting a bit more cheery now. A few days in Boulogne did him the world of good, even though somebody stole his luggage going across. Would you believe it! It was his leather hatbox, one moment it was there, the next it had vanished. I told him to inform the French police, but he said they'd never lift a finger to help an Englishman. If you're looking for a place, why not ask the house agents we pay the rent to? They're Lown & Sons, 12 Ashbrook Road, at the bottom of Highgate Hill."

Eliot thanked her. "They haven't wasted much time, dividing the spoils," he remarked, as they walked back to Camden Road.

"Do you suppose he'll marry her?"

"Oh, yes. He's dreadfully sentimental."

They left Camden Road two days later, a moonlight flit with a couple of cabs, one full of Nancy's luggage. Lown & Sons had found them a furnished terraced house opposite the Postmen's Office with the Royal Arms over the gate, in the road running east from Hilldrop Crescent to Kentish Town railway station. Nancy immediately engaged two servant girls and a cook. Eliot knew Ruston could find him any morning at the surgery, but had grown a shell of indifference. He did not somehow feel the sort who ended up on Hackney Marshes.

"This ghastly plot has disillusioned me about anything done in the name of 'The People'," he confessed to Nancy, in their new living-room with the green-striped wallpaper and plants in brass-pots. "Who are 'The People'? The humans I treat every day in the surgery. Not very worldly, not lettered, full of prejudice and superstitions, stupid but shrewd. Often noble – a man will crack a joke rather than infect his family with his terror of coming death. Our democracy is the benevolent management of their organized misapprehensions, that's all. They need leadership for their own survival, not the survival of their leaders. But Ruston talks about 'The

People' in the arrogant abstract, and seeks an easy ride to political power on their backs. I'll always support the underdog, but not one only ambitious to be the top dog."

At seven in the evening of Wednesday, May 18, the *Hohenzollen* anchored off Sheerness. She had been escorted from Flushing by the cruiser *Könisberg* and the despatch-boat *Sleiper*, by four British destroyers from the Shivering Sands buoy. The Kaiser travelled with Dr Neider his personal physician, Count Eulenburg his Master of Ceremonies, General von Plessen and Vice-Admiral von Muller, and Baron von Reischach his Master of Horse. Reading this roll call in *The Times*, Eliot wondered if all six would shortly be shot in fragments into the Kentish air. The newspaper mentioned to his discouragement that Scotland Yard had received a hundred anonymous warnings of assassination attempts against the Kaiser, which they took as malicious hoaxes.

On Friday, Eliot's paper told him the Kaiser would leave Sheerness at ten, to be met at noon by King George at Victoria station. Eliot walked down Brecknock Road for his usual morning's work. At eleven, he abandoned the struggle. Nancy had returned from her rounds. He left her the patients, found a cab in York Road and directed the driver to Victoria.

The crowd in the triangular station forecourt would reassure the Kaiser that his popularity exceeded that of his country – if he arrived, Eliot thought. The newspapers had laid cosy emphasis on the rulers of Prussia and Britain being cousins for the first time since George II and Frederick-William I. Eliot pushed his way towards the scarlet-tunicked guardsmen, their officers with black crêpe armbands, drawn behind the cordon of policemen. He nervously imagined the stir among the officials in gleaming top hats and morning coats beyond. He already heard the whisper through the crowd which swelled into the horrified cry, "The Kaiser – killed!" He saw himself tortured with remorse, agonized with fear for Nancy, awaiting the knock on the door for policemen to bundle him into the black Maria, to join Ruston and Wince in the dock of the Old Bailey, and with luck breaking stones on Dartmoor for the rest of his natural life.

King George arrived in a landau, with an escort of Household Cavalry. He entered the station. Ten minutes later he reappeared with the

Kaiser in a black overcoat. Eliot cheered so loudly that people started looking at him.

The funeral was the spectacle Eliot had promised Nancy. The silent crowds were so thick in St James's that fainting ladies were succoured on the pavement by vinegar-soaked sponges suspended from the balconies of White's club, ladies not being allowed inside in any condition. The Kaiser rode on King George's right, immediately after the gun-carriage. Behind the monarchs of Europe and Mr Theodore Roosevelt, King Edward's favourite terrier Caesar was led by a gillie in Highland dress, a white Scottie interloper joining them in Piccadilly all the way to Paddington Station, where the coffin was slid into the white-domed mortuary saloon of the Royal train, last used for Queen Victoria, on No 2 platform for Windsor.

The Kaiser left after the weekend. His farewell lunch at Buckingham Palace continued with earnest talk to his host in Victoria Station waiting-room, though twice informed his train was ready to leave. Next morning's *Times* reported his arrival at Port Victoria, a few naval buildings and a coastguard station, the rail terminal against a jetty over the river Medway. He changed aboard the *Hohenzollen* into Admiral's uniform to receive officers of the Royal Navy, and at 6 on the morning of Tuesday May 24, he left British shores. The Kaiser never saw them again.

At item at the bottom of the account caught Eliot's eye.

## RAILWAYMEN IMPRISONED

*George Horace Clem, aged 35, and Henry Teacher, 42, both of Holloway, London, labourers employed by the Great Northern Railway, were each sentenced to 3 months detention by the Chatham magistrates on Saturday for drunken and disorderly conduct. They were arrested outside a Chatham public house on the night of Friday, where they were shouting abuse about the German Emperor. The chairman said their conduct was despicable towards a personage of such importance.*

Eliot rubbed his chin. It looked as if the assassination scheme had been hatched, to produce only a dead chick. On his way to the surgery, he stopped at a small shop in Brecknock Road, which combined a subscription library with selling stationery, newspapers, sweets and books.

He bought a school atlas, opening it in the shop. "Port Victoria," he murmured. "I wonder – "

The mouth of the River Medway was a mile across. The railway from Sheerness, which Wince had indicated on his Ordnance Survey map, ran across the Isle of Sheppey on its east. The separate railway from Port Victoria traversed the Isle of Grain on its west, joining a different main line far away at Gravesend on the south bank of the Thames. Both the railway terminals of Sheerness and of Port Victoria were the same distance by Admiral's launch for a yacht anchored in mid-river. Wince had chosen one terminal, but the Kaiser another.

Eliot laughed aloud, startling the half-dozen customers. "Saved by the London, Chatham and Dover Railway!" he announced mystifyingly.

He tucked the atlas under his arm and strode jubilantly along the pavement. So much for the military genius of the British Revolutionary Movement, he thought. It could draw a blueprint of Utopia, but could not even start a fight in a public house. That it would fail disastrously once it stopped talking and started acting he had always suspected. Perhaps that was the reassurance which drew him to it.

"I'm resigning as socialist parliamentary candidate," he told Nancy that night. "I can do far more good in medicine than a dozen MPs in Parliament. Personally, I suspect the Duke has done more for British workers than Marx and Engels and Rosa Luxembourg combined. And your father for American ones. Why, he can create a thousand jobs with half-an-hour's cleverness on Wall Street. Amazing."

Nancy kissed him.

"Aren't you surprised at me?" he asked.

"No. Only at how long you've taken."

"They threw the dynamite into the river," Ruston told Eliot with his sarcastic smile. "I had the strongest suspicion it was useless, anyway."

That was seven years later, when they happened to meet as Ruston halted his company at a crossroads beyond Poperinge, the day before he was killed in the third battle of Ypres.

151

# 16

On the Friday morning of July 8, a girl wearing a black dress pushed into the surgery. Eliot vaguely recognised her. The "Free Medicine Shop" was crammed as usual. The warmth of patients' praise lit hopes in others, who came far across London, on foot if they could not afford the tram. Eliot found himself playing Christ at the Pool of Bethesda. He cured where he could and comforted where he could not. He felt that his miraculous aura reflected poorly on the abilities of the rest of the profession.

"*Vous vous rappelez, docteur? Mademoiselle Valentine Lecoq.*"

"*Ah, oui! Vous êtes chez Crippen.*"

The *au pair* had called with an envelope. It contained a letter of four pages, which Eliot opened in the consulting-room.

*39 Hilldrop Crescent,*
*Holloway,*
*July 8, 1910*
*Dear Dr Beckett,*

*I am sorry I was not at home when you called two months ago, because I always enjoy conversation with you, who are such a credit to our profession. I should like to see you very much at this moment, because of some troublesome affairs of a personal nature, on which I would welcome your advice.*

*My position has been made very difficult by Mrs Martinetti and Miss May and the other members of Belle's old committee. They always question me closely about Belle whenever we meet, and of course I cannot cut old friends easily, particularly when their office is so near mine at Albion House. Things came to a head last month when my son Otto in California replied to Miss May's letter enquiring about Belle's last hours etc in his home at Los Angeles,*

152

*where I had informed her that she died. Otto replied that he had heard of his stepmother's death only through me, and that it occurred in San Francisco.*

*This caused Mrs Martinetti and Miss May to cross-question me about the place of Belle's death, and I explained that she died in fact in a little town near San Francisco with a Spanish name which slipped my memory. When they pressed me about the crematorium in which she was disposed, I said something about there being four crematoria in San Francisco, and that I had the ashes in my safe at Albion House, with the death certificate.*

*So far as I know, Belle did not die, but is still alive.*

"Great God!" exclaimed Eliot, so loudly the patients outside the door looked up.

He continued reading.

*After our little dinner on January 31, my wife abused me for not taking Mr Martinetti up to the lavatory. She said, "This is the finish of it. I won't stand it any longer. I shall leave you tomorrow, and you will never hear of me again."*

*She frequently threatened to go right out of my life, to the man better able to support her than I was. I took this to be Bruce Miller in Chicago. On this occasion, Belle did say one thing which she had never said before, viz, that I was to arrange to cover up any scandal with our mutual friends and the Guild the best way I could. When I went home between five and six p.m. that day, I found she had gone.*

*I sat down to think it over, I wrote a letter to the Guild saying she had gone away, which I also told several people. I afterwards realized that this would not be sufficient explanation of her not coming back. I told people she was ill with pneumonia, and afterwards I told them that she was dead from this ailment. I only put the advertisement in Era as I thought this would prevent people asking a lot of questions.*

*The Music Hall Guild ladies seemed upset that I took Miss Le Neve to the Benevolent Fund Ball, with my wife's brooch and furs. Belle had so many clothes, I do not know what she took away. As for the jewellery, I had bought it all. Whenever Belle threatened to leave me, she told me she wanted to take nothing from me.*

*You know how I have looked upon Ethel as my wife these past three and a half years. Now she can take her rightful position in my home. But Belle's old friends do not care for this. They are treating me with such suspicion I am most uncomfortable. I am managing to conceal their unpleasantness from Ethel, who thinks like the rest of the world that Belle is dead.*

*As you can understand, my head is full of bees. I do not know where to turn. I shall, of course, do all I can to get in touch with Belle, so as to clear this matter up. I shall insert an advert in the Chicago papers, offering twenty-five dollars reward for information of her whereabouts.*

*I want nothing more than to discuss the whole unfortunate matter with a clear-headed professional man, none better than yourself. I am writing this before business — Ethel is not up. Will you take luncheon with me today in the Holborn Restaurant? I shall be in the foyer at one o'clock sharp. I shall be very pleased and grateful to find you there.*

*Yours sincerely,*

*Hawley Harvey Crippen.*

Eliot's response was a laugh. "Poor little man!" Crippen had covered his shameful abandonment and adultery with an elaborate piecrust of gentility, which crumbled to the prod. He wondered about the recipients of the black-edged envelopes. Anyone would anger at tears spilt over a corpse still enjoying life in Chicago, and liable to resurrection with a postcard.

He left Nancy to finish the surgery, found a passing hansom outside in Brecknock Road and arrived at the restaurant early. The elaborately decorated foyer was busy as a railway-station with dark suited men and a few ladies, staring curiously at Eliot's Norfolk jacket and loose tie. He pulled out his watch. Dr Crippen was quarter of an hour late. Eliot looked up, to find his host approaching through the plate-glass doors. On one side was a burly, beef-faced man in his mid-forties with a heavy moustache, wearing a bowler hat and a blue serge suit. On the other, a younger, thinner pale one in a dark tweed suit with a cap.

Crippen smiled to them. "This is the friend I was expecting — Dr Beckett, of Holloway. May I introduce Mr Walter Dew?"

The older man shook hands. "Didn't I read about you in the papers, sir?"

"And Mr Mitchell." Crippen continued politely. "Both are from Scotland Yard."

Eliot looked startled. Crippen continued in his affable way, "They called this morning at Hilldrop Crescent, and Miss Le Neve brought them along to Albion House. We are all three trying to clear up the mystery of my wife's leaving home. It takes a deal of time, as everything must be written down and read over and signed — isn't that the case, Mr Dew? But we still need our lunch, before we go on. Perhaps we should eat alone, if you'd excuse me?" he apologized to Eliot.

"That would be best, Dr Crippen," Dew agreed.

"I'll be glad when the whole business is cleared up for good and all. That's why I'm so pleased that Scotland Yard is taking a hand in it," Crippen ended admiringly.

"I smell a rat," remarked Nancy that evening. She was reading Crippen's letter.

"Why? He's living with his typist, exactly as I'm living with you. It shows a refreshing disrespect for middle-class convention."

"The police wouldn't be interviewing him if they didn't smell one, too."

"The police don't take suspected criminals out to lunch."

"Don't they in London? They're so awfully polite."

When a man is last seen in the company of detectives, his future movements grow in interest. On the Saturday afternoon, Eliot strolled to Hilldrop Crescent with a notion of the tête à tête denied them at the Holborn Restaurant. Valentine opened the door, in her brown dress without the apron. She seemed distressed. The doctor and madam had gone out, she explained in French, leaving her a letter to deliver. The envelope she took from her skirt pocket Eliot saw was addressed to Wm Long Esq., The Yale Tooth Specialists, Albion House, London W, with *By Hand Urgent* underscored on the top. Valentine deplored she knew nothing of London, having ventured barely past Regent's Park. Eliot felt the envelope. It contained a door key. He was curious. He comforted the girl that he would take it by cab himself.

Long was the only one in the office.

"I'm worried about Dr Crippen," he said at once. "He was here when I arrived at nine — most unusual for him. When I asked what was up, he said, 'Only a little scandal.' We had police officers here yesterday — " He started opening the envelope. "But only to find if Mrs Crippen had any estate to pay taxes on."

"Who told you that?" Eliot asked sharply.

Long looked surprised. "Why, the doctor. Then this morning, he sent me out with a list of clothes to buy." His voice grew puzzled. "A brown tweed suit, a brown felt hat, a couple of shirts and collars, tie and boots. And braces. All boy's size. I put them in the back room, No 91. When I came back from my lunch they'd gone. Instead, there was the hat which Miss Le Neve was wearing. I haven't seen either of them since." He gave a whistle, reading the letter. "Looks like the doctor's done a bunk."

Eliot took the closely written page of Yale Tooth Specialists' paper.

*Dear Mr Long,*

*Will you do me the very great favour of winding up as best you can my household affairs? There is £12.10s due to my landlord for the past quarter's rent, and there will also be this quarter's rent, a total due to him of £25, in lieu of which he can seize the contents of the house. I cannot manage about the girl. She will have to get back to France, but should have sufficient saved to do this.*

*After the girl leaves, kindly send the key with a note explaining to the landlord c/o Messrs Lown and Sons. Thanking you in anticipation of fulfilling my wishes. I am, with best wishes for your future success and happiness, yours faithfully,*
*H H Crippen.*

"There's another addressed to Dr Rylance." Long continued looking startled. "Do you suppose it's all right to read it?"

Eliot glanced at the second letter, which started, *I now find that in order to escape trouble I shall be obliged to absent myself for a time...* The other dozen lines were on business, and ended with Crippen's kind wishes for his continuing success.

"What's the game?" asked Long nervously.

"Mrs Crippen is not dead."

"Cor!"

"She ran off to a lover in America. Dr Crippen put about the story of her death to save scandal, but it stirred up more scandal than ever."

Long stood open-mouthed, trying to steady himself in the social earthquake. "Where's he gone?"

"Perhaps to America, too. He could make a fresh start."

"But why the boy's clothes?"

"Miss Le Neve's obviously gone with him. It may not be thought entirely proper for a doctor to travel with a lady not his wife."

Long's face brightened. "Come to think of it, Miss Le Neve was a bit of a tomboy. There were times she'd put on one of the doctor's suits, and go out in the street for a lark."

On Sunday, Eliot had promised Nancy an excursion to Canterbury. Monday, July 11, was bright and hot, promising a "scorcher" to Londoners tramping in their bowlers and boaters to work. Concerned about Valentine, Eliot rang the bell at Hilldrop Crescent on his way to the surgery.

The girl received him conspiratorially. *"Voilà, docteur—"*

He stared through the back window. There were the two Scotland Yard men from the Holborn Restaurant. Both had their jackets off, and were digging the garden.

On Thursday, "The North London Cellar Murder" was created. The newspapers proclaimed that human remains had been found at No 39 Hilldrop Crescent, below loose bricks under the coal. MYSTERIOUS PURCHASE OF SUBTLE DRUG BEFORE TRAGEDY, read the headline of the *Daily Chronicle*, facing its editor with contempt of court. By Saturday, every London police station bore a poster headed MURDER AND MUTILATION, followed by descriptions, photographs, handwriting specimens of Crippen and Ethel, for whom was offered £250 reward each.

"So much for your innocent little doctor," said Nancy over the breakfast table.

"But he is. I'm sure of it," Eliot insisted. "He was giving his wife hyoscine, to dampen her sexual demands. He told me as much. He was so appallingly ignorant, he probably gave her a lethal dose by mistake."

"Then why did he cut his patient up and bury her in the cellar?"

"He'd still face a manslaughter charge over the hyoscine. Which would have kept him away from the tender Ethel a good few years, if not for the rest of his natural life. Think of the scandal! He's as sensitive towards that as Mrs Keppel. And maybe he had some dark, primitive idea that Belle should silently vanish from the face of the earth, as she so often threatened."

"It seems a rather drastic way of achieving it."

"Perhaps he enjoyed it? There's no knowing what strange bats flit in the dark corners of the human belfry. Perhaps he just panicked. It makes human beings do the most wildly illogical things, you know. More die in fires from trying to get through the exit all at once than roast to death."

"So if he'd rushed out of the house and confessed to the first policeman in sight, everyone would be saying this morning, poor man, how tragic to have slain his own dear wife in error? Rather than calling him the biggest monster since Jack the Ripper."

"You're perfectly right. And cutting her up wouldn't signify much to him, anyway. You mentioned once at Champette how a doctor sees the body as a watchmaker a watch. He was simply taking a timepiece to bits."

"You're just making excuses, because you liked him," Nancy objected.

"But look how perfectly the scheme worked," Eliot persevered. "If he hadn't decamped with Ethel, Belle would have lain in rest until they demolished the house. If the police hadn't believed his story, they'd have arrested him over the cheese and biscuits at the Holborn Restaurant."

"Supposing we *had* moved into the house, Eliot?" Nancy shuddered. "Supposing we'd found the body?"

"Oh, we'd have invited the Martinettis – 'Come to dinner, we think we can dig up Belle Elmore'."

Nancy sighed. "You never take anything outrageous seriously, thank God. Even blowing up the Kaiser."

# 17

Crippen was everywhere. At Vernet-les-Bains in the eastern Pyrenees with a youth. At Llangranog in west Wales with a young lady. At Stonebridge in Sussex, he was arrested. Seeking lodgings with his companion at Willesden in London, he needed rescuing from a fierce crowd by the police.

A young female found drowned at Bourges in central France, and many others elsewhere in Europe, were weightily announced by the police forces as *not* being Miss Le Neve. The Battersea Flat Crime, the Slough Murder, the Train Murder were outshone in the newspapers. *The Times* gave Crippen four columns and invariably called him "Dr" in inverted commas, which infuriated Eliot. The William Atherstone who comforted Belle after her disaster at the Metropolitan shot himself in Battersea. The coroner relished the coincidence, and the next day dropped dead himself.

In the North Atlantic, shortly after midday on Friday, July 22, Captain Henry Kendall of the 5,000-ton Canadian Pacific Line's *Montrose*, sent his white-jacketed "tiger" to present his compliments to Dr Stewart and invite him for a peg before lunch.

A ship's captain's life is as lonely as Diogenes'. He intrudes among his officers like a headmaster amid his boys. The passengers who are not wearisome provoke jealousy among the others from invitations to his cabin. Engineers prefer their own company, and he can no more sit with his purser than a lord with his butler. His only irreproachable companion is the ship's doctor, trusted confidant of everyone on board.

The captain's quarters in the *Montrose* shone with teak, brass and leather, in the style of supreme marine comfort. The ship was ten years old, 250 steerage passengers segregated by sex with bunks in her converted hold, twenty saloon class with cabins and meals at the officers' tables. She had sailed two days before, from Antwerp for Quebec.

"Mr John Robinson and Master Robinson." Captain Kendall swivelled in his leather chair. He was middle-aged, square-jawed with a long mouth and protuberant ears. "Have you noticed anything about them?"

"The son is a wee bit overweight," observed the doctor over his whisky. "I saw a couple of safety-pins holding his trousers together at the back. He's going to California for his health. I haven't been invited to inspect his chest."

"I should think not!" exclaimed the captain. "They booked through our Brussels' agents, just before sailing. Their luggage consists of a handbag bought in Belgium. Their clothes, the brown suits and canvas shoes they stand up in. I examined their hats while they were at lunch yesterday," he continued significantly. "The rim of the boy's is packed with paper."

The doctor thought it odd that the captain should go about spying on passengers' hats.

"My suspicions were aroused before we left the Scheldt. I saw the boy squeezing the father's hand immoderately upon the boat deck. Unnatural for two males."

"Unnatural, but not unknown."

The captain leaned towards the doctor, who sat on a leather bench against the bulkhead. "When I spoke to Robinson just now, he said they'd laughed all night over the comic ditty at the smoking-concert, *We All Walked Into the Shop.*"

Smiling, the doctor recollected in song, "*One night while out with several pals, 'Twas raining hard outside, we saw a card in a milkshop window, Families Supplied...* How's the chorus go...? *We ordered a couple of kids apiece, Then we all walked out again... We all walked into the butcher's where The Meat was hung on pegs, The fat old butcher kept shouting out, I've got some lovely legs —* "

"I told Robinson a funny story," the captain interrupted. "To make him laugh," he explained. The doctor looked lost. "To see if he had false teeth. And he *had*," said the captain triumphantly. "He has no moustache, but is growing a beard. It makes him look more like a farmer every day. His nose has marks. Yet he wears no spectacles. Well, doctor? What do you make of that?"

"I can't make anything of it, sir."

"*I* make of it that Master Robinson is a girl." The captain folded his arms. The doctor said nothing. Like many captains, his was a spasmodic eccentric.

"A girl," Captain Kendall repeated, delighted with the mystification. Insatiable with detective stories, he revelled in playing the detective. As a junior officer, he was scourge of the ship's cardsharpers. "Haven't you seen the 'boy's' hands? Soft and white. Nails carefully manicured. And how refined and modest he is, how under his father's thumb. And his endearing smile?"

"Well, I noticed the father cracks nuts for him."

"This morning I called, 'Mr Robinson!' on deck. He paid no heed, till the boy had the presence of mind to make him turn."

Captain Kendall tapped the pile of crumpled newspapers Dr Stewart had observed on his desk. "Why do you suppose I had the chief officer collect every English and Belgian newspaper on board? They must not suspect their deeds are discovered – they might do something rash. They must not suspect what I suspect. That the Robinsons are *Dr Crippen and Miss Le Neve.*"

"Good God," exclaimed the doctor. "Shall you put them in irons?"

"On the other hand, they may not be," the captain admitted lamely. "Which could land me in all sorts of trouble with head office. So I prepared this for the Marconi operator."

The doctor read the pencilled form from the captain's desk drawer.

PIERS LIVERPOOL HAVE STRONG SUSPICIONS THAT CRIPPEN LONDON CELLAR MURDERER AND ACCOMPLICE ARE MONG SALOON PASSENGERS MOUSTACHE TAKEN OFF GROWING BEARD ACCOMPLICE DRESSED AS BOY VOICE MANNER AND BUILD UNDOUBTEDLY A GIRL BOTH TRAVELLING MR AND MASTER ROBINSON KENDALL.

"This very morning," Captain Kendall continued impressively, "Robinson – Crippen – sat looking aloft at the wireless aerial, with the crackling electric spark of the messages, and said, 'What a wonderful invention it is!' But time is running short. Our wireless has a range of 150 miles. We are already 130 miles west of the Lizard. Should I send it?"

"Undoubtedly," urged the doctor. "Now you mention it, I *have* noticed how the girl's under his hypnotic influence, how she follows him everywhere. Though from her lack of distress, she must surely be utterly ignorant of the horrible crime committed?"

"Do you know what he's reading?" The captain grinned. "A shocker by Edgar Wallace, *The Four Just Men*. It's about blowing up Parliament. The villains have £1000 on their heads – two hundred and fifty apiece, the same as our friends the Robinsons. Another peg?"

"Thank you, sir. Only a chota peg." It was seafarer's Hindustani for a small drink.

The Morse of Captain Kendall's message was received at 3.30 that Friday afternoon by Crookhaven Wireless Station on the coast of County Cork, which passed it to the Canadian Pacific office in Liverpool, which passed it to Scotland Yard, which dispatched Chief-Inspector Dew the next morning by the White Star *Laurentic* from Liverpool as "Mr Dewhurst" on "Operation Handcuffs", unbeknown even to his wife.

The life of a secret with a fortune in its pocket is short among the brigands of Fleet Street. Monday morning's papers announced that Dew had left. He was aboard the Allen Line's *Sardinia* to New York from Le Havre. Crippen had fled, disguised as a cleric with an effeminate son. By Tuesday the Liverpool Courier laid hands on Kendall's message. Crippen was *trapped by wireless!*

The *Montrose* carried the marvellous instrument, which a member of Parliament had tried a fortnight earlier to make compulsory on all ships, but was defeated on the argument of expense. Crippen was under restraint. Miss Le Neve had confessed. No, he was not, and she had not. The only sure news was their sailing westwards unaware of Dew overhauling them in a liner three knots faster. It caught public imagination like a race to the moon.

The front pages had Atlantic maps, the two ships' positions marked daily. The world first learned of Father Point, near the New Brunswick port of Rimouski. "'Dr' Crippen will arrive home in ample time for the adjourned inquest on August 15," observed *The Times* cosily. CRIPPEN'S LIFE AT SEA DESCRIBED BY "WIRELESS", said a special edition of the *Weekly Dispatch*, above photographs of Crippen with his round glasses and moustache, Belle Elmore, Inspector Dew, Captain Kendall in oak-leaved cap, Ethel looking soulful, and even Charlotte the first Mrs Crippen, short-haired and pudding-faced, who had died in fits at Salt Lake City. Mr Eddie Marr, backer of Aural Remedies, appeared at its Kingsway Office and scraped Crippen's name from the glass front door.

The world held its breath – the *Laurentic* was slowed by fog in the mouth of the St Lawrence. Perhaps the pursuit of Dr Crippen might reach the ears of the only couple in civilization still ignorant about it? Perhaps they would jump over the side, and ruin the fun? The *Laurentic* reached Quebec on Friday night. Inspector Dew was cheered from the dockside. At 8.30 on Sunday morning, in a white hat and blue suit disguised as a pilot, a lifeboat rowed by sailors took him to the newly anchored *Montrose* off Father Point quarantine station.

The two men met on the boat deck, abaft the funnel. "Good morning, Dr Crippen." Ethel was in her cabin, reading Georgie Sheldon's *Audrey's Recompense*. She was arrested, screamed and fainted in Dew's arms.

"Murder and mutilation – oh God!" said Crippen. He was searched. He had 10 dollars, and two diamond rings sewn into his undervest. He carried visiting-cards printed, *E Robinson & Co. Detroit, Mich. Presented by Mr John Robinson.* One had written on the back, *I can't stand the horror I go through every night any longer, and as I see nothing bright ahead and money had come to an end, I have made up my mind to jump overboard tonight. I know I have spoiled your life, but I hope one day you can learn to forgive me. With last words of love, your H.*

Ethel had a sachet of white powder. "Doubtless poison," reported *The Times*, though it was a headache cure. The stewardess lent her a blouse, skirt and petticoat. The *Montrose* blew her whistle. The press poured aboard from their pilot boat, overrunning the ship, interviewing every passenger, even if few spoke English. Ten days later, some reporters were struck by measles, which was rampant in the steerage.

"How can the man possibly have a fair trial after this cinematograph chase?" Eliot demanded furiously. "It was completely unnecessary. Captain Kendall could have got him arrested in Quebec. The Canadian police are surely equipped with handcuffs and an extradition treaty?"

It was the Monday morning of August 19. All the newspapers printed a photograph of the gale-swept dockside at Liverpool. Crippen's plea against extradition from Quebec as an American citizen had been brushed aside. The Canadians excitedly discovered that he had lived fourteen years before in Toronto with a plump, fashionable woman, presumably now recovered from the Hilldrop Crescent cellar floor. In prison, Ethel had a dressmaker to provide a costume from the $60 found on her. Crippen so disgusted the other prisoners, he had to exercise alone. The Bishop of London sent him a book, but he never read it. Inspector Dew took a holiday at Niagara.

On the suddenly lowered baggage gangway of the *Megantic* at Liverpool, bowler-hatted, raincoated Dew clutched the handcuffed Crippen wearing his captor's ulster, collar up to hide his face from the booing crowd. As Strachey was writing of General Gordon, Dew had left England already famous and would soon be glorious. The Liverpool police saw no point in shading from his radiance. Their chief took a tender to the Mersey Bar and his officers swarmed aboard in port like bumboat women at Suez.

The homecomers had been reinforced by Crippen's other luncheon guest at the Holborn Restaurant, Sergeant Mitchell, dispatched in the *Lake Manitoba* with wardresses Foster and Martin from Holloway Jail. Dew sailed home as Silas P Doyle, Crippen as Cyrus Field, Ethel as J Byrne, Mitchell as M F G Johnston, but the wardresses remained themselves.

Ethel used the passenger gangway. On the 2.23 to London, the pair had separate compartments with blinds drawn in the reserved coach next to the engine, first class. At 7 o'clock, Inspector Kane was waiting to welcome them at Euston. Groaning and hissing, straining against the wooden barriers, the crowd glimpsed three motorcabs taking them to Bow Street police station.

" 'The most exciting episode in the history of police work,' they call it." Eliot tossed the paper with the Liverpool photograph disgustedly across the breakfast table. "Instead of two lives splintered on the anvil of public ghoulishness." For a month, he had complained angrily about the crowds with their cameras in Hilldrop Crescent. "The organs they dug up might be anyone's."

Nancy sighed. "Eliot, dear, a suspicious mind is unattractive, but even the Archangel Gabriel would purse his lips over that cellar."

"I know more about those famous remains than people on the newspapers, who can have no possible idea what they really look like, or smell like. Remember I went to the Society of Medicine on Saturday?" Nancy nodded. "I met one of the pathologists who's working on them at St Mary's. Bernard Spilsbury, thought a pretty sharp fellow, about my own age. I knew him at St Bartholomew's. Do you know, there's no head? No bones? And they were buried in *slaked* lime, which does nothing to encourage decomposition. A doctor like Crippen would have known that quicklime was a different chemical."

"You always said what a rotten doctor he was."

"There weren't even any sex organs. The body may not be a woman's at all. Belle could still be alive and laughing. The publicity would put her top of the bill for life."

"Miss Le Neve wouldn't do badly either. I saw she was offered $1000 a week to appear in vaudeville in New York."

"She'd do better in London. This country has an unhealthy preoccupation with transvestism. Look at Vesta Tilley – made a fortune on the music halls, dressing as a man and singing 'Burlington Bertie.' Look at pantomime. As much an English institution as Christmas, and the principal boy's always a girl in tights. But Ethel will end up on the scaffold, not the stage," he ended gloomily.

"Perhaps she'll strike a bargain? Get her charge reduced from murder, by telling the police all she knows?"

"Turn King's evidence? Slip the noose round her lover's neck with her own hands? Women don't do that sort of thing." Eliot stared speculatively through the lace curtains of their downstairs dining-room. He ejected Crippen from his mind. "Can you be back at the surgery by midday, Nancy? I'm lunching with my father, remember."

"Are you going to tell him about us?"

"If you like," he said casually.

"What about us?"

"Whatever you like."

"He'll be dreadfully shocked we're not married."

"Less than your father would. In ducal circles, fornication is thought an occupation as healthily natural as hunting. Only the middle class disapprove. I suppose because of their everlasting suspicion of paying full price for slightly shop-soiled goods."

Major Beckett was waiting on the broad marble chessboard of the Imperial Club's hall floor. Eliot found his hand seized with startling enthusiasm. The major usually greeted his son far more casually than his friends.

"You know him. You've met him," the major exclaimed. "By jove! Living just round the corner from Hilldrop Crescent. What's he like? A fish-eyed monster, as the servants say? A smooth-tongued Bluebeard?" He stopped two clubmen. "May I introduce my son, Dr Eliot Beckett? He is a neighbour of the Crippens, on intimate terms with Belle Elmore and Ethel Le Neve."

The pair instantly afforded Eliot an interest never given the son of a duke's man of business.

"It's so shockingly unfair," Eliot repeated as they sat down to lunch. "Crippen and Miss Le Neve have only this morning been faced with, and had the right to reply to, the charges which have already entered our folk-lore."

"Yes, I saw they were due in the police court," said the major absently, ordering the club's famous *hors-d'oeuvre*, which included relishes from India, China, Malay and Borneo.

At quarter-to-eleven, Ethel and Crippen had shared the well-shone wooden bench within the unassuming black cast-iron railings of the Bow Street dock. He appeared from the cells below first, politely standing aside for her, whispering something. He was in frock-coat with wide lapels of grey silk, a high starched collar and striped shirt with a bright print tie. She wore a navy coat and skirt and a large blue hat with a motoring veil, which she raised to face Sir Albert de Rutzen, the magistrate. She kept twisting her black gloves.

Crippen was charged with murder, Ethel with being an accessory after the fact. The booing crowd still filled the street outside. A man from Madame Tussaud's waxworks took their photograph with a camera hidden in his bowler. In court was Sir William Gilbert, librettist of *Trial By Jury*.

"Meanwhile, the inquest on Belle Elmore stands adjourned in the Holloway Central Library," Eliot continued. "With PC Gooch lugubriously telling Coroner Shroeder of five hours' hard digging in the cellar, as though it was his potato bed. The inquest will certainly return a verdict of wilful murder against Crippen. That's enough to commit him for trial at the Old Bailey, if the Bow Street magistrate hasn't obliged already. For a man to be effectively twice on trial for his life, in the same London postal district simultaneously, is something overlooked in Magna Carta."

"Come, Eliot," his father said impatiently. "It's all open and shut, as if Inspector Dew had burst upon the wretch with the bloodstained chopper in his hand."

"May I disagree, sir? Why, some tramp may have intruded into the house while Crippen was out at work."

"Cutting up a man's wife is a procedure demanding more forethought than stealing his gold watch."

"I cannot believe that one as mild, agreeable and loving as Crippen could live six months with Ethel Le Neve while the wife he had killed – or about half of her – was a foot under his boots every time he went to replenish the kitchen fire," Eliot said firmly. "And I think I know as much of the human mind as anyone. Crippen's only peculiarity was a taste for younger women – Belle 13 years his junior, Ethel 24. That's a failing he shares with a few men in this room, I daresay. I'm sorry for Crippen, I'm determined to help him as best I can."

"You'll make yourself dreadfully unpopular."

"Among whom? Not the people who matter to me, the working men, the labourers, the poor."

"Listen to some advice which has stuck in my mind. 'Remember, never to make yourself the busybody of the lower classes, for they are cowardly, selfish and ungrateful. The least trifle will intimidate them, and him whom they have exalted one moment as their demagogue, the next they will not scruple to exalt upon the gallows'."

Eliot smiled. "Who said that? It's shrewd enough for either Charles I or Cromwell."

"A sailor called Parker, just before he was hanged after the Nore mutiny of 1797."

"As innocence is useless without a good lawyer," Eliot resumed, "I'm trying to get Marshall Hall for Crippen. I expect he'll take the brief cheap. The advertisement's worth a thousand times as much."

"No. Get F E Smith."

"Who's he?"

"The cleverest man in the Kingdom," his father told him.

Eliot shrugged. "Did you see about me in the *Daily Mail*?"

"I do not read the yellow press."

"It gave me quite a reputation as a medical missionary. Where one's most needed. Here in London."

"How much longer are you going to throw your talents at the poor? You're like some *nouveau riche* speculator courting popularity by tossing shillings to his tenants," his father reprimanded him. He continued more pleadingly, "Settle down. Make yourself a proper living. The Duke will still help you, I'm sure of that. His concern for myself has increased, as the father of a son with such peculiarities."

"As a matter of fact, sir, I am thinking of chucking the free surgery," Eliot confessed. "The trade unions have stopped supporting me. I suppose they feel their money is buying glory for myself, rather than their officials. So has the Church. It finds that relieving humanity of its pains in the next world is less expensive than in this one. Perhaps I'll go back to Switzerland and open my own sanatorium? Though that's like running a luxurious hotel, in which closest attention to the welfare of your guests cannot prevent your regularly losing a good many customers for ever."

"That would be the end of your political ambitions." His father sounded hopeful.

"I did badly in the last election, I might do worse in the next. What if I became a Labour MP? I'd have to be as respectable as a family solicitor. Look at our dashing, brilliant Victor Grayson. In the House of Commons at my own age, too independent a spirit for the burnt-out firebrands running the Labour Party. He's taken to the bottle in frustration. I'm chucking politics into the bargain. Medicine is far too important a human activity to be complicated by idealism. This club claret is excellent, sir."

His father asked slyly, "May I suppose there is a woman behind this welcome change of heart?"

"Yes. I'm living out of wedlock with an American lady."

"Well, it's among a young man's amusements, *faire la bête a deux dos*. Is she respectable?"

"Entirely."

"No money, I suppose?"

"Oh, yes. About five million dollars."

The colonel dropped his knife and fork. "Good God, Eliot. And I was beginning to think you a bit of a fool."

"How's mother?"

"She has discovered a new sort of climbing rose."

# 18

"So he filleted her?" suggested Eliot.

Dr Bernard Spilsbury nodded. He was tall, straight-backed, handsome, his thick dark hair brilliantined, a red carnation in the lapel of his grey suit. Eliot thought him solemn, aloof and self-opinionated. He thought Eliot cynical and flippant. Both were young doctors of exceptional intelligence with energy as limitless as their ambition.

"If the remains *are* Belle Elmore's," Eliot said.

"Oh, I'm sure of that." Spilsbury was always precise, brief and confident. Eliot had a lingering feeling that he treated his acquaintances as interesting subjects on which he was performing the post-mortem.

It was mid-September. The trial at the Old Bailey was fixed for the eighteenth of the following month. Spilsbury unlocked a cupboard on the wall of his small laboratory at St Mary's Hospital, near Paddington Station. It contained five large glass jars, covered like homemade pickles by glazed white paper tied with tape. Spilsbury's finger indicated the blue-edged labels which might have read "Onions" or "Tomato Chutney".

"That's the stomach, with one kidney and the heart – fatty, obviously of a plump person – and part of the liver. The next contains a pair of female woollen combinations, found under the cellar floor with a female undervest. The next, small gut, more liver and some hair. The last more gut, some muscle and two lungs. When you savoured the Crippens' hospitality you may have observed this garment airing on a clothes-horse."

Spilsbury untied the cover of the last bottle, removing with forceps a long strip of green and white flannel. "The most damning specimen of the case. A piece of pyjamas, found with the organs. Note the curious arrangement of green lines. Exactly like those we know Mrs Crippen bought from the admirable Jones Brothers of Holloway, on January 5, 1909, for seventeen-and-ninepence, cash on delivery by the firm's cart." His forceps reached for a metal clip with a six-inch tuft. "A Hinde's curler, as used by Mrs Crippen."

Eliot nodded. "I recognize the hair."

"Luckily, hair is one of the last anatomical structures to decompose." He dropped it back. "If you remain unconvinced, Beckett, I can show you a strip of lower abdominal skin, with a longitudinal midline scar from umbilicus to pubis. The ovarotomy operation Mrs Crippen underwent at New York in 1893. Doubtless, the defence will try passing it off as a fold in the skin. But it's a scar, right enough, pure fibrous tissue without the sebaceous glands one would find in skin. I have examined it under the microscope, which I shall bring with me to the Old Bailey and invite the jury to see for themselves."

"Isn't that rather *coup de théâtre?*" murmured Eliot, feeling that the pathologist fitted the crime.

"Not at all. I am responsible for my own opinion, which has been formed on my own scientific knowledge. I can demonstrate to the jury exactly how I formed it." He retied the jar. Eliot supposed that Spilsbury's professional attention to Crippen would make his reputation, like Bernard Dawson's to King Edward VII in his own inevitably final days.

"You believe that the hyoscine which killed Belle Elmore was administered inadvertently?" Spilsbury locked the cupboard.

"With good reason. Crippen confided in me that he was giving her hyoscine in homoeopathic doses to dampen her sexual demands."

"The half grain I found in the body was hardly a homoeopathic dose," Spilsbury said mockingly. "It would slay a prize-fighter. Crippen was lying to you, as to everyone else. You know they slept in separate rooms?"

"So do our kings and queens, but we never lack heirs to the throne."

"I don't think you can compare the arrangements in Buckingham Palace with those in Hilldrop Crescent. Well, if you feel strongly he's innocent, you'd better pass your notions on to Tobin."

Eliot nodded. A A Tobin was the King's Counsel briefed to defend Crippen, a barrister on the northern circuit whose oratory customarily mingled with the sea fogs of Newcastle. "I wanted to interest Marshall Hall, but he's abroad on holiday. Anyway, I couldn't get further than Crippen's solicitor. Is Arthur Newton good? I heard he organized the defence of Oscar Wilde."

"He seems to specialize in that sort of thing. He defended Lord Arthur Somerset over the male brothel in Cleveland Street, and got six weeks himself for spiriting away the three telegraph boys involved. I hear he's up to his ears in racing debts, and I suppose wants to boost his reputation. Horatio Bottomley – you know, he edits the despicable *John Bull* – is putting up the cash for Crippen's defence. As an advertising stunt, of course."

"Who's on the other side?"

"Richard Muir will be leading for the Crown. A red-faced Scot, with the forensic subtlety of a whirring claymore. The judge is Lord Alverstone."

"Who's he?"

Spilsbury looked shocked. "The Lord Chief Justice."

"Murderers are remembered, their judges never."

Spilsbury was moving towards the laboratory door. "Perhaps you're right, Beckett, and Crippen never did mean to kill his wife with hyoscine." Eliot looked surprised at the admission. "He intended to shoot her. Dew found a revolver and 45 rounds of ammunition in the breakfast room next to the cellar. But perhaps Crippen was concerned over the noise disturbing the neighbours. Everyone says he was such a considerate man."

"Hasn't it occurred to you that she could have swallowed the hyoscine entirely by accident?" Eliot was becoming irritated with Spilsbury's sarcasm.

"The henbane plant which contains hyoscine is sometimes eaten in mistake for parsnips," he replied authoritatively. "Which in January are not in season."

Eliot wrote three times to Mr A A Tobin, KC at his chambers in the Middle Temple. He had no reply. He supposed despondently that every post brought a hundred letters of lunatic notions for freeing his client. The week before the trial he marched in himself, but the barrister's clerk's peevishness withstood even Eliot's determination. He strode back to the Strand disappointed and angry, though reflecting that a man's lawyers, like his surgeons, required to operate without assistance from interested passers-by.

Crippen was to stand trial alone. Eliot attended the fourth day in Court No 1 at the Old Bailey. It was Friday, October 21, and Spilsbury had usefully provided a ticket. He watched the show in the company of two theatrical knights – Tree the tragedian and Hare the comedian – and Miss Phyllis Dare, the Belle of Mayfair, who was gallantly invited by His Lordship the judge to sit beside him on the bench.

The court had oak panelling and atrocious acoustics. Below the Royal Arms and Sword of Justice sat also the Lord Mayor of London, the Lord Mayor-elect of London, the Recorder of London, two London Aldermen, the Sheriff of London and his undersheriffs. Mrs Martinetti was in a row below with other flashily feathered vultures from the Music Hall Ladies' Guild. Eliot felt a shock at seeing Crippen suddenly appear five yards away, in the witness-box beside the jury. He looked more cheerful than six months previously, when dressed in mourning for his wife. Eliot decided against some small, encouraging gesture towards the prisoner, lest Lord Alverstone ordered his own removal instantly to the cells.

Wigged and gowned, red-faced and square-jawed, eyebrows like iron filings, Mr Muir was cross-examining.

"On the early morning of February 1, you were left alone in your house with your wife?"

"Yes."

"She was alive?"

"She was."

"Do you know of any person in the world who has seen her alive since?"

"I do not."

"Do you know of any person in the world who has ever had a letter from her since?"

"I do not."

"Do you know any person in the world who can prove any fact showing that she ever left that house alive?"

"Absolutely not."

Had Crippen asked at the York Road cabstand whether lady and luggage had left while he was at business? Had he asked the neighbours? The tradesmen? At the shipping offices? Anywhere at all? Advertised in American papers? Eliot stared disbelievingly while Crippen agreed in his mild, vague way of doing no such things, as though in a railway lost property office describing the mislaying of his umbrella.

Why did he flee in July? Because of suspicion, Crippen explained. Suspicion of what? Suspicion of being concerned with his wife's disappearance. On what charge? He apologized for knowing nothing of the law, but he was a reader of romances to a great extent, and had an idea that he might be arrested and held on suspicion until she was found.

"You stayed with Le Neve disguised as your son in a hotel in Antwerp?"

"Yes."

"You stayed indoors all day?"

"Oh, no. We went to the Zoological Gardens."

The man's behaving as though charged with riding a bicycle without a lamp or having no dog licence, Eliot thought irritably and dejectedly. His quaint *Gemütlichkeit* had worsened. Now it was pathological euphoria. Or perhaps he was colour-blind to the myriad hues between right and wrong? Did he risk his neck as a pure moralist, who saw sin and virtue only as black and white? The skin with the scar was being shown him, on an enamel plate from which people ate their dinners. Crippen gave it a mild look through his gold-rimmed glasses. He did not recognise it as Belle's. The court adjourned for lunch.

Eliot decided against returning. The trial was bear-baiting a donkey, fox-hunting a lap-dog. Thick crowds crammed round the brand new granite court, Justice without her blindfold atop its copper dome, stones from Dickens' Newgate prison in its foundations. The police had been on duty since seven in the morning. There had been five thousand applications to the Sheriff for seats.

Eliot pushed into the *Magpie and Stump* public house opposite. The landlord would remember him as a student at St Bartholomew's up the road. A pink-faced young man with a fringe of ginger beard, in shiny blue suit and bowler, asked cheerfully, "Dr Beckett, isn't it? A chum on the *Mail* pointed you out. I'm at the *Bugle*. I hear that you're acquainted with Crippen?"

"Slightly. I had dinner at his house."

"At Hilldrop Crescent?" The reporter looked as though Eliot had supped with the Devil in Hell. "Go on! What was it like?"

"I refuse to discuss my personal affairs."

"The public would like to know."

"Then the public is a prying nuisance, and deserves disappointment."

"Any views on the trial?" he persisted.

"Yes, I have," Eliot said forcefully. "It should be held in the Drury Lane Theatre. It's perfectly disgusting, men and women who wear the airs of leaders in our society, hastening to gloat over another poor human in his agony. I'm equally repulsed by the mass of ordinary British people, who assume this man guilty as unthinkingly as that the sun will rise and the public houses open every morning. They would like him hanged from Nelson's Column in Trafalgar Square, on a Saturday afternoon so they could take a picnic and enjoy it."

"That's coming a bit strong, doctor," the reporter complained amiably. "From one who stood as a Labour candidate."

"Truth is a distant relative of politics and newspapers, I fear. Every man Jack of you on Fleet Street knows your proud columns about this trial 'showing British justice at its best' are humbug, for which the public has an insatiable appetite. Look how they've made a hero of plodding Inspector Dew, who let the pair slip from under his nose and gain a fortnight's lead on him, then spent three days searching at Hilldrop Crescent before showing enough intelligence to dig up the loose bricks of the cellar floor. Look at the ridiculously melodramatic Captain Kendall, with his amazing discovery that a boy with wide hips and large breasts might be a girl. By the wits of their pursuers, Dr Crippen and Miss Le Neve deserve to be living peacefully in California by now. Yet the fuddled British public sees the voyage to Father Point as the most spectacular stroke of revenge since Birnam Wood came to Dunsinane."

"What wood was that, doctor?"

"Birnam. No 'h'."

The reporter nodded, busy with his notebook. "But wouldn't you agree with everyone, doctor, the Crippen case has shown how the law has new weapons?"

"Wireless simply caught the imagination of the feckless public like a new show at the fairground."

"Against Marconi, are you, doctor?" asked the reporter encouragingly.

"I'm against no one except – if I may be frank – your editors and proprietors, who hope to see fortunes and titles sprout from fields so assiduously spread with manure."

"How about a photo?" He indicated a cloth-capped youth beside him with a glass of gin-and-water and a camera.

"As you like," Eliot agreed off-handedly.

Eliot learned in the *Magpie and Stump* a principle which twenty years later assisted him to worldly success – never address the most insignificant representative of the press without care, caution and cunning. He sent Laura the parlourmaid for a copy of the *Bugle* before breakfast. She returned with eyes sparkling excitedly. "You're all over the front page, sir, photograph and everything."

Eliot stood before the freshly lit fire in the dining-room. CRIPPEN'S FRIEND, said the headline. "THE STUPID BRITISH PUBLIC," he was quoted below.

*The most amazing statement of Crippen Week was made outside the Old Bailey by Dr Eliot Beckett, self-appointed 'People's Doctor' of Holloway*, it began.

Eliot ran his eye through the column. From his censure of Inspector Dew, he might have attacked Wellington the morning after Waterloo. From his acquaintance with Crippen, he might have played surgical assistant disembowelling Belle and second gravedigger in the cellar.

*Dr Beckett, who pretends to be the people's friend, gives free treatment in a greengrocer's shop round the corner from Hilldrop Crescent*, Eliot read. *Very strange treatment! Mouldy bread!! The* Bugle *asked the King's physician, Dr Bernard Dawson of the London Hospital, if mouldy bread ever did anyone any good. "None whatever," said the King's doctor. "It seems a cranky notion to me."*

*Perhaps Dr Beckett is obliging the neighbours, by getting rid of their old loaves?*

*Dr Beckett stood for Parliament in the election as Labour candidate for Holloway — at which he dismally failed — while despising those he urged to vote for him. Perhaps he wants a seat in Parliament at all costs? The doctor is moons away from the working man he claims to represent. He does not lack money. He enjoys with a wealthy American lady the same relationship our readers will have read about elsewhere in Holloway.*

Eliot handed the paper silently to Nancy, who came downstairs in her nurse's uniform. She read it calmly. "Is it libellous?"

"Only infuriating, I'm afraid. Robert Knox had to tolerate the same sort of thing at Edinburgh in the 1820s. He taught anatomy, and after the Burke and Hare murders the newspapers whipped up feeling against him. He was as upright as I am, and traded with body-snatchers only for the sake of his students, just like any other surgeon."

"You're taking it very calmly."

"How else can I? If I wrote complaining, they'd make me look a bigger fool than ever."

"How do they find all this about us?"

"The patients. Perhaps our servants. In Holloway, you can learn a lot about a man for sixpence."

Laura threw open the door without knocking. "Oh, sir — " She looked frightened. "The baker's boy's just said that something terrible's happening down at the surgery, sir. They're breaking the windows, sir."

Eliot jumped up. He told Nancy to stay in the house, seized his hat and muffler, and strode in the bright autumn morning to the corner of Brecknock Road. He stopped. A crowd of men and women were shouting and gesticulating in the street outside the surgery. Two policemen separated them from the smashed-in shop front, urging everyone to move along. Heads stuck from windows. The pavements were choked with those who preferred to be spectators rather than perpetrators, and some fifty excited children.

Eliot strode on angrily. The mob outside were the same who had sat inside, the slaughtermen, market porters and their families. They had come from the pubs, Eliot knew, and in a mood of mindless bellicosity. He wondered how many were literate enough to spell out the front page of the *Bugle*. He supposed its story had run round the neighbourhood, gaining strength as it passed from mouth to mouth, like the germs men were continually breathing over each other.

"I'm Dr Beckett." A third policeman was regarding the affray from the corner. "That's my premises they're damaging."

The policeman held out an arm. "Shouldn't go down there, if I were you, sir."

"I'm not frightened of people who attack nothing more dangerous than plate-glass."

A grey-haired woman in a shawl pointed at Eliot from the edge of the crowd. "There 'e is! That's the doctor. That's 'im. Friend o' Crippen."

Eliot found himself suddenly the centre of a jeering, jostling circle. "Mouldy bread!" they shouted at him. "Murderer!" screamed another woman. "Crippen! Crippen!" yelled the rest. It was the fashionable malediction. Eliot remembered Belle on the stage at the Metropolitan.

"None 'o that," the policeman directed, adding urgently, "Run along, sir, while the going's good."

"I refuse to be intimidated by a mob."

"Go on, sir! Crippen's a strong word."

Eliot felt a flick against his cheek. He raised his fingertips. Someone had spat at him. "Contempt is impossible from the contemptible," he snapped. He turned and strode away, pursued by boos.

He had sat almost quarter of an hour glaring into the fire, legs stretched, arms folded, unspeaking, Nancy on the arm of his chair.

"I'm never going back to the surgery," he announced.

She said in her practical way, "Then you'd better get the window boarded up, or you'll have the place looted."

"They can help themselves to as much mouldy bread as they please." He added despondently, "It doesn't work, anyway. The *Bugle* was right."

There was a timid tap, Laura reappeared, looking more frightened than ever. A policeman was at the door. Eliot found an inspector, in cape and shako. He warned gravely that the inflamed people of Holloway would find Eliot's address, fill the street outside, break his own windows. The inspector advised him to lie low somewhere. There was the safety of the American lady to consider. He's been reading the *Bugle* too, Eliot thought.

"Lie low? For how long?" Eliot asked.

"Just till they've hanged Crippen," the inspector assured him blandly.
Eliot returned to the dining-room. "We're moving this morning."

"Where to?"

"The Savoy."

"But we can't!" Nancy objected.

"Why not?"

"We're not married," she pointed out.

"Oh, very well! We'll get married. We'll use a registry office. They're quite fashionable."

She put her arms around him. "Oh, Eliot! You *are* so romantic."

He smiled. "I suppose your father would have loved a show in New York?"

"He's reconciled that his daughter's an oddity. He bears me no rancour. I'm just a business bid which failed, I guess." She kissed him. "You're really as romantic as Romeo, aren't you, dearest? But you always want to seem absolutely different from everyone else."

"From now on, I'm going to be absolutely the same as everyone else. But I'm going to be better at it."

Eliot took a Savoy suite with two bedrooms. Guests, however wealthy, were not permitted by the management to sleep there with ladies other than their wives, or who allowed themselves to be passed as such. At 2.15 the following afternoon, the Old Bailey jury retired. Twenty-seven minutes later, they returned. Barely a minute afterwards, everyone stood except the judge. His elderly clerk, in his best morning coat, laid on his Lordship's wig a square of black silk. The judge reminded the prisoner that he had cruelly poisoned his wife, concealed his crime, mutilated her body, disposed piecemeal of her remains, possessed himself of her property and fled from justice. On the ghastly and wicked nature of the crime, the judge would not dwell. He assured its convicted perpetrator that he had no hope of escaping its consequences and recommended making peace with Almighty God.

"I have now to pass upon you the sentence of the Court," continued Lord Alverstone. "Which is that you be taken from hence to a lawful prison," he spelt out with the law's ghoulish relish, "from thence to a place of execution, and that you be there hanged by the neck until you are dead, and that your body be buried in the precincts of the prison where you shall have last been confined after your conviction." Implying that his judicial exhortation extended further, he ended his grisly catalogue, "And may the Lord have mercy on your soul."

*The prisoner was removed in the charge of the warders,* Eliot read in his *Times* on Monday morning. Crippen's amen, he thought.

# 19

Exactly a week after her lover was first brought into the same court-room, Ethel Le Neve faced the old gang reunited – Lord Alverstone, Mr Muir and Mr Travers Humphreys, his junior. Humphreys was winning double fame. At Fareham in Hampshire, he was simultaneously prosecuting Lieutenant Siegfried Helm from the 21st Battalion of the German Emperor's Nassau Regiment, for imperilling the State by sketching the forts at Portsmouth. The lieutenant was young and good-looking, the court crowded, mostly by ladies.

There was one newcomer. F E Smith, Member of Parliament, aged 38, who had been the youngest ever King's Counsel and was to be the youngest ever Lord Chancellor.

Ethel had avoided the debt-ridden solicitor Arthur Newton. She instructed the staid firm of Hopwood and Sons. Eliot wrote to them, passing on his father's suggestion. He never knew whether this was the cause of its implementation. F E Smith was tall, handsome, with thick eyebrows, a mouth turning down arrogantly, a pearl tiepin the size of a Muscat grape and a liking for long cigars. He and Ethel's case suited as man and wife.

He defended her with one speech and one argument. How could a simple typist, in her twenties, live blithely with Crippen on the run, had she the slightest suspicion he had recently dismembered his wife and buried most of her in the cellar? The prosecution had no stomach for the fight. Perhaps they were exhausted by their sustained indignation the previous week. Perhaps they saw their depiction of Crippen as too fiendish for another member of the human race to receive, comfort and maintain him, as Ethel was accused. She was freed in a day. F E Smith called no witnesses, not even his client. The judge later criticised him for it. "I knew what she would say," F E told him, "you did not." All day, the new Home Secretary sat in court, Winston Churchill.

As a drowning man gives a final shout, Crippen took his case to the Court of Appeal. In a few minutes, Mr Justice Darling threw it out. It was Guy Fawkes' Day. A fortnight later, on Saturday, November 19, Eliot and Nancy were married at Holloway Registry Office.

Nancy had a scheme for them to separate, and meet at the altar like any decent couple. Eliot objected that he was an atheist. Nancy consoled herself that his love was rooted in the soul he affected not to possess. Nancy's father neither crossed the ocean to see his younger daughter die nor to see his elder one wed. The Duke gave them a Lanchester motorcar. Eliot wondered desperately how the devil one worked it.

There was no honeymoon. The week after Crippen's conviction at the Old Bailey, Eliot had received a letter from the King's physician, forwarded in his father's hand from the ducal castle.

"Bernard Dawson apologizes for his mouldy bread remarks in the *Bugle*. He never knew the particular witch-doctor was me. A paper with their morals wouldn't hasten to enlighten him. He's atoning for making me the second most unpopular man in England."

He tossed the letter to Nancy across their sitting-room, overlooking the Thames at the Savoy.

"He ran into Dr Pasquier, of all people," Eliot continued. "He's over from Champette for a meeting at the Brompton Chest Hospital about phthisis. Dawson's offering me a job in a free sanatorium for the poor, which he's opened on money raised in the City. At Bognor. The south coast, you know. Sea breezes. I suspect phthisis would kill me with boredom, but a step by Dawson can mean a leap to higher things. What do you think?"

"Take it."

"I'm sure that's right. Oh, I'll have my plate up in Harley Street in no time," he asserted. "The rich shall provide my living and the hospital poor my reputation, just like everyone else. How much more sensible to use the familiar machine, rather than trying to dismantle it and make a different one from the worn parts."

Eliot called on Dawson the following week at his home, No 32 Wimpole Street. He found himself obliged to be vetted by the London Hospital board of governors on the Monday morning after his wedding. He returned to the Savoy after the interview to find his bride with a telephone message from the medical officer at Pentonville jail. Would Eliot call that afternoon? He was puzzled. Crippen was in a condemned cell, to be hanged there two mornings later on Wednesday, November 23.

The prison was only half a mile from Hilldrop Crescent, across the Cattle Market. It was a wheel of radiating blocks, on which the spirits of 1000 prisoners were painstakingly broken by solitude and silence. Eliot left his cab at the *Balmoral Castle* public house, on the corner of Brewery Road, opposite the facade of untidy classical columns rising among terraces of small, neat, law-abiding houses. A dozen plane trees fronted the high wall, behind it rose the grey, barred, slate-roofed blocks, in the middle poked a fat square chimney. The visitors' entrance was to the right of the vast oak Gothic door.

Eliot gave his name to the warder in high-necked tunic and shako, key-chain dangling against his thigh. He signed a ledger on the counter inside the gate-house, which had a good fire and a singing kettle, two other warders brewing their tea in a brown metal pot. Eliot was led across the courtyard, to a block with stylish columns between the windows of the first floor. A stone corridor with gates at each end, which his cicerone unlocked and locked behind them, led to the prison hospital.

There had been little room for Crippen in Eliot's head. He thought of him as the 26 sailors in the French submersible *Pluvoise*, hit by a cross-Channel paddle-steamer earlier that year, her bows above the surface but her crew doomed to die under the eyes of the world. He was shown into a small, green-painted gas-lit office, with a desk opposite the fire. On a horsehair sofa sat a woman in a serge suit, who rose as the warder left. It was Ethel.

"Dr Beckett!" She was as surprised as himself. Her large velour hat was shrouded in a motoring-veil. She looked pale. A smile flickered on her lips.

Later, Eliot saw kings and queens stark naked, but never again felt as awkward.

"How is he?"

"Bearing up. Sometimes, he seems his usual self. Others, he cries."

"I'm here to see the prison doctor. I don't know the reason."

"He's ever so kind to Peter. So's Major Mytton-Davies. He's the governor. He's quite convinced that Peter's innocent, you know. That a man like Peter could *never* commit a murder, not in all his born days. And he's not the only one – just think, *fifteen thousand* people signed the petition to spare Peter's life. The prison doctor's with Peter now. That's why I'm waiting."

"Give him my – " Eliot stopped. What greeting could anyone send a man due to hang in 40 hours' time? "Assurance that he is ever in my thoughts."

"He's written me some lovely letters."

She felt in her large handbag. Eliot wondered if she had the inexpressible, almost unthinkable, pride of a woman who drives a man to terrible deeds which drive himself to destruction. Delilah behind a typewriter.

"Would you like to see one?"

As she seemed eager, Eliot took the lined buff sheet, stamped with the Royal Arms and *H M Prison, Pentonville*. It was a pathetic mixture, protestations of innocence, references to a God so bafflingly reluctant to establish it, directions to Ethel about his own past business affairs and her future ones, impregnated with sentiment towards "my own wifie dear".

*I see ourselves in those days of courtship, having our dinner together after our day of work together was done, or sitting sometimes in our favourite corner of Frascati's by the stairway, all the evening listening to the music. I sometimes thought that a little corner of Heaven on earth.*

*And now my prison dinner is just waiting, and I must eat it while it is hot. Have just had a nice dinner – roast mutton, vegetables, soup, and fruit – and now back to my wifie again.*

Eliot handed the letter back. A man who could write of roast mutton in the condemned cell would feel *gemütlich* in the grave.

"How are you?" he asked kindly.

"Always so tired. Life's difficult in silly little ways. I have to go about in a closed cab. If people saw me in the street there'd be a riot. Mrs Jackson was very good – my old landlady, you know." Eliot nodded. "Of course! You met her at the house that Sunday afternoon, just after the old King died."

Ethel stopped suddenly. Eliot had a vision of Belle's clothes. Ethel said quietly, "But I don't want to see any of the old crowd, none of them. Never again."

"How will you manage after – " He hesitated. "In the future?"

"I can't stay here, can I? I'm going to America. I'm booked on the *Majestic* from Southampton on Wednesday, under the name of Miss Allen."

The most loving relatives of patients *in extremis* at Champette, Eliot reflected, had to plan beyond their release from the sick room.

"Then I shall go to Toronto. Peter talked so much about it on the boat. I'll start a new life."

"I wish you all the luck in the world, Miss Le Neve." Her interview with a new employer for the position of his lady typist was a scene beyond Eliot's imagination.

"Thank you." She ran her tongue over her full lips. "There's something – " She stopped.

"Yes?"

"There's something no one knows. It never came out at the trials, Peter's or mine. I can't bear keeping it locked in me, it wakes me at night. It's worse than any memory I've had of these awful four months."

"Keeping secrets is as much second nature to a doctor as staunching blood."

"I know that. I'd always trust you, Dr Beckett. Peter did, more than anyone he knew. The hatbox...you remember I told you that same Sunday afternoon, the doctor's hatbox was stolen on the boat? On our way across to fetch little Valentine from Boulogne – "

To Eliot's annoyance, the door was opened by a pink-faced man with grey hair cut like a brush and a grey stubby moustache, wearing a blue serge suit. After him came a warder.

"It wasn't stolen," Ethel finished breathlessly. "It was dropped over the ship's rail."

She turned, nodded at the intruder, and followed the warder.

"Dr Beckett? I'm Dr Campion," said the grey-haired man. "Most kind of you to come. I hope that didn't embarrass you? I'd no idea Miss Le Neve was here."

"Not at all. I've been acquainted with Miss Le Neve for a whole year." Eliot sat facing the doctor across the desk. Ex-medical officer in the army or navy, he supposed. A good job for a man expended of ambition. He wondered what it was paid — £500 a year, he speculated, two-thirds the governor's salary.

"You were almost a neighbour at Hilldrop Crescent, I believe?" Campion continued in a friendly way. "The prisoner talks sometimes as though you were close colleagues."

"Why did you want to see me?" Eliot demanded. His thoughts were still on the hatbox. So she *did* know Belle was dismembered and beheaded. Before they ran away.

The doctor stared at the ceiling, rubbed his large red hands, and returned his eyes to Eliot.

"I face an awkward choice, Dr Beckett. Crippen himself is a model prisoner. Indeed, everyone has grown very fond of him. Not only the guards who must watch him day and night, but the chaplain and certainly the governor. Though he *did* attempt suicide," he revealed. "Strangely enough, I've never seen that before in condemned men."

"I suppose they grasp at hope to the end? Like the sick the miraculous fingertips of Jesus."

"Last night he managed to break off the steel side of his glasses. The warder noticed it, and searched him. He'd slipped it up the seam of his trouser-leg. He must have intended to divide his radial artery with it, under cover of his blanket."

"He wouldn't be the first medical man. Horace Wells — the American who discovered anaesthesia — killed himself by severing a femoral artery with his razor, in the Toombs Prison one January night of 1848. He'd been run in for throwing vitriol in prostitutes' faces."

Dr Campion paid little heed. Eliot reflected that the occupation of prison doctor gave little encouragement to the intellectual embellishment of the profession.

"My choice is between defying the Home Secretary, and possibly losing my position, or honouring my professional principles and keeping my good name. Mr Winston Churchill is a busybody. He suddenly wants to know about the smallest items for which he nominally carries responsibility. His personal secretary sent a stiff note to Major Mytton-Davies about the procedure for executions. Everything's in Home Office Regulations, of course, but Mr Churchill demanded a simple description of a single sheet of paper the same day. He particularly wished to know if the man had anything to help him face the ordeal, more substantial than the ministration of the chaplain. He gets half a mug of rum, of course. Some refuse it. They say they want to meet their God with a clean breath. That's usually the drunkards. Mr Churchill is always straining to bring in something new – so we hear from the Home Office. I suppose he wants to appear a progressive young politician. Now he's demanding that some drug be administered, so that the prisoner may be hanged in a merciful state of coma."

"Who's going to prescribe it?" Eliot asked immediately.

"Exactly. For any doctor, that would be contributing to the extinction of life, and against our principles."

"And against the law."

Dr Campion nodded. "There is a difference in assisting a man to die on the end of a rope and in bed. We can perhaps allow ourselves sometimes to be part of the natural process, but never of the unnatural one. Otherwise, we should become executioners ourselves. But Mr Churchill is most wilful. He cannot understand these ethical niceties are so important to us. He imagines that we are being pig-headed."

"You asked me here to sign the prescription?"

"You have saved me a deal of unhappy explanation, Dr Beckett. Crippen was known to you, as to no other medical man – "

"Give me the sheet of paper," said Eliot at once.

"You realize, Dr Beckett, that the General Medical Council could be sticky about this? Should some enemy in the profession learn of your action – "

"I'd be struck off?" Eliot added thoughtfully, "I'll risk that, for Crippen."

"What drug will you give?"

"There's only one powerful enough. Hyoscine."

Dusk comes early to London in mid-November, but the night is short for the man who knows he will not see the end of another day. The condemned cell was fifteen feet square, with a high-up barred arched window. Crippen wore a rough grey jacket and trousers, and a white calico shirt. He had no tie, and tapes instead of buttons, lest he swallowed them and forestalled his execution, or awkwardly deferred it with an operation for obstruction of the intestines. Several others had worn the same outfit, but the authorities fumigated it in between, as though they had died undramatically from smallpox.

The clocks untidily struck away the hours with terrible unconcern. At midnight, Major Mytton-Davies brought his last word from Ethel, an opened telegram just delivered by a boy on a scarlet bicycle. At seven, the governor was back. There were two hours to go. Crippen was hunched on the black-painted bedstead like a prison hospital cot. Two warders sat with practised stolidity under the gas, at the two-foot square table where he wrote his daily letters to Ethel, the blotches on its greasy surface as fixed in his mind's eye as a map to a treasure-hunter. The warders enjoyed three days' special leave from that morning. They had played cribbage and snakes-and-ladders with Crippen, to divert his mind. It was in the regulations.

The governor had the dose in a mug of cocoa. "Something to buck you up," he explained. Crippen drank it, grimacing at the bitterness. The governor wondered if the doctor knew he was poisoned near to death.

At his customary three minutes to the hour, hangman Ellis entered the cell. He wore a blue suit, a high starched white collar and a black tie. Folded in his jacket pocket was an Order to Hang, half-a-dozen lines penned in clerk's copperplate and signed by Charles Johnston, Sheriff of London, which spared Ellis being as black a murderer as his victim. Behind came assistant hangman Willis.

The two warders had already been joined by the chaplain, robed for a funeral, lost at ministering to a prisoner comatose beyond confession or repentance. Crippen lay on the grey blanket, breath faint, cheeks dusky. With his gold-rimmed glasses on the table was the half-mug of brandy, inexorably provided by the regulations. The warders eyed it, having agreed to share.

Though Crippen was nearer corpse than man, rules required following. Ellis carried a foot-wide buckled black-leather bodybelt with four pairs of straps across the front. He slid it round Crippen's waist, securing it at the back, strapping wrists and elbows across his midriff. He took from Willis a short black strap which he loosely secured below Crippen's knees, and a conical linen cap to stick on his head like a dunce.

"*I am the resurrection and the life, saith the Lord,*" began the chaplain. Had Belle had Crippen converted, he would have got it in Latin.

A hanging was a singular legal-ecclesiastic ceremony. Outside the cell, a procession had assembled. The chief warder led, followed by the chaplain, who had reached, "*Man that is born of woman hath but a short time to live, and is full of misery,*" by skipping. Next came Crippen, limp between two warders. Then Ellis and Willis, Major Mytton-Davies, under-sheriff Rupert Smythe in frock-coat and black cravat, Dr Campion and the deputy chief warder for the rear.

The way was short. The execution shed stood open beyond the facing oaken doors of half-a-dozen condemned cells. A stout beam ran from one whitewashed wall to another, with three shiny hooks like a butcher's. From one hook, a brand new rope two inches thick hung by a brass eyelet. Attached to its end by a clip, like dog-collar to lead, was a yard of soft rolled leather, tapering to a small brass eyelet which created the noose. This hung precisely over the trap, a thread drawing a loop of rope towards the cross-beam. The scaffold was well-tried, designed for the Home Office in 1885 by Lieut-Col Alten Beamish of the Royal Engineers. The thread was Ellis' own idea, of which he was proud. Hanging does not invite much innovation.

The sides of the trap always under-ran two planks. The public imagined the objects of its retribution standing a few remorseful seconds awaiting the drop, but a man can seldom support the weight of a body from which life will be shortly squeezed. Two warders held every prisoner by the armpits, as they were obliged with Crippen. The obligatory onlookers made the shed crowded. Willis pulled cap over face, Ellis applied the noose by snapping the cotton, securing it with a stiff leather washer behind the right ear. He pulled the iron lever, shifting an unseen pair of well greased steel bolts under the twin trap-doors of three-inch thick oak, which crashed into their hooks on the whitewashed brick walls of the pit below. Crippen disappeared.

A faint slap came from the stone floor of the pit, as one of his slippers fell off. "*Forasmuch as it hath pleased Almighty God in his great mercy to take unto himself the soul of our dear brother here departed,*" said the chaplain. The violently twisting rope slowed. The body needed stay an hour, before delivery to Mr Shroeder, the coroner who had "sat on" Belle half a mile away. By noon, Crippen would end in quicklime, and they were letting him have Ethel's letters dropped in. Ellis got £5, Willis £2. 10s. On October 10, five miles to the north, they had buried in Finchley Cemetery all they had left of Belle.

The black-framed notice on the prison gate was signed by the governor, the under-sheriff and the chaplain. The customary bell was not tolled, from official tenderness towards three other men inside shortly to undergo the same procedure.

It was uncharacteristic of Eliot to take a cab from the Savoy that misty morning. He had always shunned the carnivals of the people, especially the macabre ones. He felt impelled to see the end of the drama he had watched before it began. And he was anyway the executioner's assistant, as last intended with the German Emperor.

The crowd at nine o'clock was thinner than Eliot expected. Perhaps the public was growing either tired of Crippen or ashamed over him. As he strode away afterwards, a touch came to his elbow.

"Mouldy bread!" Bill Edmonton stood grinning. It had become a Holloway catch-phrase.

"Hello, Bill! How's your boils?"

"Gorn, doctor. I changed me job." But not your habits, Eliot thought, catching the reek of beer. "I'm on the railway nah."

Eliot found half-a-crown in his pocket.

"Thank you, doctor. Always said you was a proper gen'man." Bill pointed his short clay pipe towards the prison across the Caledonian Road. "Remember when I met 'im? In the free medicine shop." Eliot nodded. "I got ter know 'im pretty well," Bill continued proudly. "Used ter come to the cattle market regular, in the mornin's, on 'is way ter work. 'E'd bring scraps, bones, wot Mrs Crippen 'ad left over, or cadged orf of the other ladies rahnd 'illdrop Crescent. Mind, 'e stopped coming' abaht the middle o' last February. Then o' course he 'adn't a wife no more to do 'is shoppin', 'ad 'e?"

"What did you do with these bones?" Eliot asked, horrified.

"They all went in the boiler," Bill told him amiably.

" 'Poupart's Piccadilly Potted Meat'," observed Nancy, when Eliot hurried back to the Savoy. " 'Londoners Love It'."

"Well, Belle always wanted them to, didn't she?" Eliot pointed out.

# 20

On Tuesday, February 5, 1952, the ailing King George VI went shooting at Sandringham, and the next morning was found by his valet dead in bed from a coronary thrombosis. His daughter learned that she had become Queen Elizabeth II, at the Outspan Hotel near Nyeri, on the outer slopes of Mount Kenya. "In his last months, the King walked with death as an acquaintance whom he did not fear, in the end death came as a friend," said Winston Churchill.

The Coronation was Tuesday, June 2, 1953. Eliot and Nancy were driven home from Westminster Abbey in their post-war Rolls-Royce.

"I told you we did this sort of thing rather well," said Eliot.

"Darling, after 45 years I am still amazed by the British flair for ceremony and understatement."

"Did you notice the beautifully dressed old gentleman with the duty of holding a pole of the canopy? He was a patient, when I still practised. Urinary incompetence. Dreadfully embarrassing at a party, not to mention a Coronation. He telephoned last week for advice. Down his velvet breeches was an invaluable rubber device called a Why-Be-Wet."

They wore scarlet robes, Eliot's ermine caped, Nancy's ermine trimmed. She had a close-fitting dress of silver lamé, the bodice embroidered with rhinestones and sequins. Eliot's coronet was in a leather box at his feet. Nancy preferred a cap of state. Eliot was 71. Too old to rejoin the army, he had run London's medical services from the start of the blitz. Nancy was an American citizen who had become the best-known Englishwoman. She had organized the wartime evacuation of children from city to country. She shared the cover of *Life* with Wendell Willkie, when he wore a tin hat in London air-raid shelters trying to stop Roosevelt's third term in 1940.

After 1941, Nancy turned her energy to keeping American forces and the British on the best terms possible – the relationships between allies in any war being only slightly worse than with the enemy. "If by hazard the venom of Herr Hitler strikes me down," Churchill had told a House of Commons in smiling mood shortly before D-Day, "I am tempted to think that we can continue to go forward with the war organized by Lady Beckett."

"We don't see much of Winnie since he became prime minister," Eliot observed, as they drove home among the Coronation crowds.

"Or became so wonky."

"Or so gaga. Charles Moran told me last week that Winnie's already had three strokes. The first was in Monte Carlo in 1949, the last under a year ago."

"I suppose he'll soon hand over to Anthony?"

"If the British will accept a divorced prime minister. Any news of Margaret's romance, by the way?"

"I heard nothing at the Mountbattens."

"Who's coming tonight?"

"Beaverbrook and the Lunts – did I tell you they were across for the Coronation? I hope to get Willie Maugham, but Evelyn Waugh definitely not. Perhaps that's good. Actors always seem to get on well together, writers never."

"Actors make their living by submerging their feelings, writers by exposing them."

It was a cold rainy day. Eliot stared for some time at the people on the pavements. "How lucky they are!" he exclaimed. A Coronation concentrates memories. "Do they know it? The germs which prowled for most of my professional life as dangerously as hungry tigers have been killed by Domagk, Fleming and Florey. Now Waksman's won the Nobel for streptomycin, and tuberculosis – what we used to call phthisis – has followed its victims to the grave. Did you hear, the Swiss sanitoria are changing themselves into hotels? They'll go bust otherwise. I actually saw a brochure from the Clinique Laënnec, renamed the Hotel Sporting de

Champette. It advertises the spacious sunny balconies. I wonder if the guests realize how many people died on them?"

"I'd like to see the clinic again. It would be like walking over the Somme. A violent old battlefield, turned impotent with the passage of time."

"Like us," said Eliot.

Their town house was among the embassies in Belgrave Square. Eliot's secretary was at the door. "Lord Beckett, we had a telephone call from Mrs Stanley Smith — "

"Urgent?"

"The doctor in Addiscombe says she's in heart failure. And she particularly wants you to see her."

"Tell Chevons to keep the car. Though I must divest myself of these glad rags. They might raise an eyebrow in suburban Parkview Road."

"Surely you're not going, Eliot?" Nancy scolded him. "You'll need a good rest before dinner."

"I have retained few patients. Mrs Stanley Smith is the most important."

"Really, Eliot. I can't understand why you're still obsessed with the Crippen case."

"Because I still don't think he did it. But I suppose any doctor who prescribes the wrong dose deserves hanging."

"*I* think he killed her in cold blood."

Did he?

Or didn't he?

# 21

Mrs Stanley Smith, who was Miss Ethel Le Neve, died aged 84 of cardiac failure on August 8, 1967, at Dulwich Hospital in South London. In 1955, Eliot suffered a fatal coronary thrombosis in the lobby of the Waldorf Astoria in New York, when on his way to give a lecture at the Massachusetts General Hospital in Boston. While this book was being written, Nancy was still living, at Shiplake Castle in Kent.

# RICHARD GORDON

## DOCTOR IN THE HOUSE

Richard Gordon's acceptance into St Swithin's medical school came as no surprise to anyone, least of all him – after all, he had been to public school, played first XV rugby, and his father was, let's face it, 'a St Swithin's man'. Surely he was set for life. It was rather a shock then to discover that, once there, he would actually have to work, and quite hard. Fortunately for Richard Gordon, life proved not to be all dissection and textbooks after all... This hilarious hospital comedy is perfect reading for anyone who's ever wondered exactly what medical students get up to in their training. Just don't read it on your way to the doctor's!

'Uproarious, extremely iconoclastic' – *Evening News*
'A delightful book' – *Sunday Times*

## DOCTOR AT SEA

Richard Gordon's life was moving rapidly towards middle-aged lethargy – or so he felt. Employed as an assistant in general practice – the medical equivalent of a poor curate – and having been 'persuaded' that marriage is as much an obligation for a young doctor as celibacy for a priest, Richard sees the rest of his life stretching before him. Losing his nerve, and desperately in need of an antidote, he instead signs on with the Fathom Steamboat Company. What follows is a hilarious tale of nautical diseases and assorted misadventures at sea. Yet he also becomes embroiled in a mystery – what is in the Captain's stomach remedy? And more to the point, what on earth happened to the previous doctor?

'Sheer unadulterated fun' – *Star*

# Richard Gordon

## Doctor at Large

Dr Richard Gordon's first job after qualifying takes him to St Swithin's where he is enrolled as Junior Casualty House Surgeon. However, some rather unfortunate incidents with Mr Justice Hopwood, as well as one of his patients inexplicably coughing up nuts and bolts, mean that promotion passes him by – and goes instead to Bingham, his odious rival. After a series of disastrous interviews, Gordon cuts his losses and visits a medical employment agency. To his disappointment, all the best jobs have already been snapped up, but he could always turn to general practice...

## Doctor Gordon's Casebook

'Well, I see no reason why anyone should expect a doctor to be on call seven days a week, twenty-four hours a day. Considering the sort of risky life your average GP leads, it's not only inhuman but simple-minded to think that a doctor could stay sober that long...'

As Dr Richard Gordon joins the ranks of such world-famous diarists as Samuel Pepys and Fanny Burney, his most intimate thoughts and confessions reveal the life of a GP to be not quite as we might expect... Hilarious, riotous and just a bit too truthful, this is Richard Gordon at his best.

# RICHARD GORDON

## GREAT MEDICAL DISASTERS

Man's activities have been tainted by disaster ever since the serpent first approached Eve in the garden. And the world of medicine is no exception. In this outrageous and strangely informative book, Richard Gordon explores some of history's more bizarre medical disasters. He creates a catalogue of mishaps including anthrax bombs on Gruinard Island, destroying mosquitoes in Panama, and Mary the cook who, in 1904, inadvertently spread Typhoid across New York State. As the Bible so rightly says, 'He that sinneth before his maker, let him fall into the hands of the physician.'

## THE PRIVATE LIFE OF JACK THE RIPPER

In this remarkably shrewd and witty novel, Victorian London is brought to life with a compelling authority. Richard Gordon wonderfully conveys the boisterous, often lusty panorama of life for the very poor – hard, menial work; violence; prostitution; disease. *The Private Life of Jack The Ripper* is a masterly evocation of the practice of medicine in 1888 – the year of Jack the Ripper. It is also a dark and disturbing medical mystery. Why were his victims so silent? And why was there so little blood?

'...horribly entertaining...excitement and suspense buttressed with authentic period atmosphere' – *The Daily Telegraph*

## TITLES BY RICHARD GORDON AVAILABLE DIRECT
## FROM HOUSE OF STRATUS

| Quantity | | £ | $(US) | $(CAN) | € |
|---|---|---|---|---|---|
| ☐ | THE CAPTAIN'S TABLE | 6.99 | 11.50 | 15.99 | 11.50 |
| ☐ | DOCTOR AND SON | 6.99 | 11.50 | 15.99 | 11.50 |
| ☐ | DOCTOR AT LARGE | 6.99 | 11.50 | 15.99 | 11.50 |
| ☐ | DOCTOR AT SEA | 6.99 | 11.50 | 15.99 | 11.50 |
| ☐ | DOCTOR IN CLOVER | 6.99 | 11.50 | 15.99 | 11.50 |
| ☐ | DOCTOR IN LOVE | 6.99 | 11.50 | 15.99 | 11.50 |
| ☐ | DOCTOR IN THE HOUSE | 6.99 | 11.50 | 15.99 | 11.50 |
| ☐ | DOCTOR IN THE NEST | 6.99 | 11.50 | 15.99 | 11.50 |
| ☐ | DOCTOR IN THE NUDE | 6.99 | 11.50 | 15.99 | 11.50 |
| ☐ | DOCTOR IN THE SOUP | 6.99 | 11.50 | 15.99 | 11.50 |
| ☐ | DOCTOR IN THE SWIM | 6.99 | 11.50 | 15.99 | 11.50 |
| ☐ | DOCTOR ON THE BALL | 6.99 | 11.50 | 15.99 | 11.50 |
| ☐ | DOCTOR ON THE BOIL | 6.99 | 11.50 | 15.99 | 11.50 |
| ☐ | DOCTOR ON THE BRAIN | 6.99 | 11.50 | 15.99 | 11.50 |
| ☐ | DOCTOR ON THE JOB | 6.99 | 11.50 | 15.99 | 11.50 |
| ☐ | DOCTOR ON TOAST | 6.99 | 11.50 | 15.99 | 11.50 |
| ☐ | DOCTOR'S DAUGHTERS | 6.99 | 11.50 | 15.99 | 11.50 |
| ☐ | DR GORDON'S CASEBOOK | 6.99 | 11.50 | 15.99 | 11.50 |
| ☐ | THE FACEMAKER | 6.99 | 11.50 | 15.99 | 11.50 |
| ☐ | GOOD NEIGHBOURS | 6.99 | 11.50 | 15.99 | 11.50 |

ALL HOUSE OF STRATUS BOOKS ARE AVAILABLE FROM GOOD BOOKSHOPS OR
DIRECT FROM THE PUBLISHER:

Internet: www.houseofstratus.com including author interviews, reviews, features.

Email: sales@houseofstratus.com please quote author, title and credit card details.

## TITLES BY RICHARD GORDON AVAILABLE DIRECT
## FROM HOUSE OF STRATUS

| Quantity | £ | $(US) | $(CAN) | € |
|---|---|---|---|---|
| GREAT MEDICAL DISASTERS | 6.99 | 11.50 | 15.99 | 11.50 |
| GREAT MEDICAL MYSTERIES | 6.99 | 11.50 | 15.99 | 11.50 |
| HAPPY FAMILIES | 6.99 | 11.50 | 15.99 | 11.50 |
| INVISIBLE VICTORY | 6.99 | 11.50 | 15.99 | 11.50 |
| LOVE AND SIR LANCELOT | 6.99 | 11.50 | 15.99 | 11.50 |
| NUTS IN MAY | 6.99 | 11.50 | 15.99 | 11.50 |
| THE SUMMER OF SIR LANCELOT | 6.99 | 11.50 | 15.99 | 11.50 |
| SURGEON AT ARMS | 6.99 | 11.50 | 15.99 | 11.50 |
| THE PRIVATE LIFE OF FLORENCE NIGHTINGALE | 6.99 | 11.50 | 15.99 | 11.50 |
| THE PRIVATE LIFE OF JACK THE RIPPER | 6.99 | 11.50 | 15.99 | 11.50 |

ALL HOUSE OF STRATUS BOOKS ARE AVAILABLE FROM GOOD BOOKSHOPS OR
DIRECT FROM THE PUBLISHER:

**Hotline:** UK ONLY: **0800 169 1780**, please quote author, title and credit card details.
INTERNATIONAL: **+44 (0) 20 7494 6400**, please quote author, title and
credit card details.

**Send to:** **House of Stratus Sales Department**
**24c Old Burlington Street**
**London**
**W1X 1RL**
**UK**

Please allow for postage costs charged per order plus an amount per book as set out in the tables below:

|  | £(Sterling) | $(US) | $(CAN) | €(Euros) |
|---|---|---|---|---|
| **Cost per order** | | | | |
| UK | 2.00 | 3.00 | 4.50 | 3.30 |
| Europe | 3.00 | 4.50 | 6.75 | 5.00 |
| North America | 3.00 | 4.50 | 6.75 | 5.00 |
| Rest of World | 3.00 | 4.50 | 6.75 | 5.00 |
| **Additional cost per book** | | | | |
| UK | 0.50 | 0.75 | 1.15 | 0.85 |
| Europe | 1.00 | 1.50 | 2.30 | 1.70 |
| North America | 2.00 | 3.00 | 4.60 | 3.40 |
| Rest of World | 2.50 | 3.75 | 5.75 | 4.25 |

PLEASE SEND CHEQUE, POSTAL ORDER (STERLING ONLY), EUROCHEQUE, OR INTERNATIONAL MONEY ORDER (PLEASE CIRCLE METHOD OF PAYMENT YOU WISH TO USE)
MAKE PAYABLE TO: STRATUS HOLDINGS plc

Cost of book(s): —————————— Example: 3 x books at £6.99 each: £20.97

Cost of order: —————————— Example: £2.00 (Delivery to UK address)

Additional cost per book: —————————— Example: 3 x £0.50: £1.50

Order total including postage: —————————— Example: £24.47

Please tick currency you wish to use and add total amount of order:

☐  £ (Sterling)     ☐  $ (US)     ☐  $ (CAN)     ☐  € (EUROS)

VISA, MASTERCARD, SWITCH, AMEX, SOLO, JCB:

☐ ☐ ☐ ☐ ☐ ☐ ☐ ☐ ☐ ☐ ☐ ☐ ☐ ☐ ☐ ☐ ☐ ☐

Issue number (Switch only):

☐ ☐ ☐

Start Date:                          Expiry Date:

☐ ☐ / ☐ ☐                       ☐ ☐ / ☐ ☐

Signature: ————————————————

NAME: ———————————————————————

ADDRESS: ———————————————————————

———————————————————————

POSTCODE: ——————————

Please allow 28 days for delivery.

Prices subject to change without notice.
Please tick box if you do not wish to receive any additional information. ☐

House of Stratus publishes many other titles in this genre; please check our website (**www.houseofstratus.com**) for more details.